A Shot Of Gin

Phoebe Wagner

For the partner, Andrew.

*I wrote this book while settling on the unceded land of the
Indigenous people of the Great Basin, including the Wa She Shu
(Washoe), Numu (Northern Paiute), Newe (Western Shoshone),
and Nuwu (Southern Paiute). I also worked on this novel while
a settler on the unceded land of the Susquehannock people. I
also acknowledge the people of the Haudenosaunee Confederacy
—the Mohawks, Oneidas, Onondagas, Cayugas, and Senecas—as
well as the other people seeking refuge in this area as the
traditional custodians of the land I occupy. I pay respect to their
elders past, present, and emerging.*

So many books, so little time.

— Frank Zappa

Part One
High Stakes

"Nevada's senior senator and other state leaders say they were given no notice of the unapproved nuclear waste delivery, which only came to light because the Energy Department decided to declassify it in court documents filed before a federal judge in Reno. That disclosure sparked a protracted court battle and an ongoing war of words between Nevada leaders and agency officials." –*Reno Gazette-Journal*, July 10, 2019

1

Trouble came from the south. It loomed like a storm hung up in the Sierras. I kept looking over my shoulder while taking a walkthrough of the Saints Casino. The knowledge of bad times coming had been growing for months—nightmares, anxiety, an itch when faced southward—but I hadn't sensed it was a *thing* until tonight.

My boss Colton called these developments "growing pains," what I get for being half-human and half who-knows-what. I needed to tell him about this itch, but with Halloween in two weeks, he was preoccupied with wrangling the logistics for the arrival of his fellow vampires.

I rolled my shoulders, straining against my denim jacket. The instinct wound tighter. Usually, the Saints' familiarity calmed me down, but tonight, I inspected every new face for hidden fangs or looked for bite marks on necks and wrists. Not that spotting vampires was part of my job. Like any business trip, the vampire council meeting featured a little work but mostly play—I just watched for lines being crossed. Anyway, many of them wouldn't arrive until next week.

For one a.m. on a Wednesday, the casino floor looked busier than usual—a large group of Australian tourists, a sorority party, plus the locals. I checked in with one of the long-time waitresses, Greta, but she said there hadn't been any trouble. A few vampires playing slots and eyeing necks, but they'd followed the rules.

"Colton came through looking for you, though," she said. "Told me he'd be at the Haunted House if you came by."

My mouth went dry. I sighed. "Did he say what's up?"

She shook her head, then squeezed my shoulder before weaving into the web of noise, lights, and drunkenness.

Colton looking for me anytime in October made me jumpy. Usually, when working, he'd just text. I considered excusing myself by claiming to break up a bar fight, but he'd probably be pissy already from dealing with all the stuck-up vampires coming for the council. I cut across the slots floor to the nearest elevator bank and slapped HH for Haunted House. Back in the day, this floor had been one of the Saints' gimmicks, a haunted house open year-round. Over the past decade, Colton had transformed it into an international attraction that was truly scream-worthy.

He observed from a deck designed to look like a spider's nest. His black Stetson shadowed his eyes, but he wore a gray T-shirt and worn jeans, what I thought of as behind-the-scenes Colton, not the mythic Cowboy of the Casino buying rounds for the regulars. He braced against the railing, his arms wide, almost brooding over the simulated open grassland with triggers that made the grass rustle as if a monster were hunting.

I copied his pose. "You could have texted—"

"Scheduling change. You're working Halloween."

When I accepted his offer to work and live at the Saints, I'd made one hard and fast demand: Halloween, I had off. That night two years ago had screwed me up enough that I preferred to stay in my room with the door triple-locked. "You promised—"

"And you're coming to the council meeting."

I took a breath. Colton usually kept me out of politics, and I learned the happenings of Reno's Darkside from Franklin Pérez, his right-hand man. Even he didn't attend the council meeting.

"Why?"

He slid closer. "You were requested." He lowered his voice, and his arm brushed mine. "I said no but was overruled."

Requested only two years after Colton discovered me, just long enough to get a handle on my abilities—not good. Which meant something bad was about to happen again.

"All right, I'll come in for the meeting."

He shook his head. "I want you working the masquerade."

I grit my teeth. "I made it clear I don't work Halloween."

"You do when I need you." He flashed a showman grin that didn't reach his eyes. "And this time, I need you." He stalked out.

My head fell back. "Fuck!"

My pulse spiked so fast that my chest tightened with that old fear of what monsters lived in the dark. I placed a hand over my heart and took a few calming breaths. Working the masquerade didn't mean I had to participate, and I definitely wouldn't. I just had to keep it together until after the council meeting. Then things could go back to normal. Well, the new normal. And I'd tell Colton about the weird ache in my head.

My hands shook, and I slapped the railing, leaving a dent where my palm met cold steel. I hated when he ordered me around like that.

I stomped to the elevators, but instead of taking up my position at the blood vaults where Colton had scheduled me to keep out any inquisitive visiting vamps, I hit the ground floor. I needed air.

The Saints always looked her best this time of year. Reno's casino skyline flashed neon, a garish reassurance of fun, fun, fun—until the money ran out. Colton's buildings alternated between orange and purple, lighting up one word, then another: *All—Saints—All Saints.* The casino had always been the Saints, but, as the story goes, he kept the title when he took over in the fifties. Saints Casino was oxymoronic enough; now add a vampire owner. It still cracked him up.

I hustled across the manicured cement strewn with jack-o-lanterns, broken or otherwise. Lasers projected Halloween scenes between the golden windows framing the buffet dining room and the flickering slot floor. I sniffed and rubbed my nose. During my first weeks living here, I'd wallowed in the luxury. Now, the rich smells made my stomach hurt. Humans and those disguised as humans stuffed themselves while unhoused folks froze and nonhumans struggled in a desert-turned-boomtown.

The southern instinct buzzed in the back of my head, and I rubbed my neck. A dull hunger stemming from other growing pains—my jumping ability had nearly turned Superman-esque the past few months—made me duck into the buffet. I loaded up a plate and hurried out, even as the Head of House, Leonard the half-elf, glared. He always claimed my shabbiness broke the ambiance, but this was Reno—I am the ambiance.

I circled the casino, down East 6th to North Center, until I hit the Walgreens. A few folks huddled on city benches, sharing a pack of cigarettes: Jackie B, Carlos, and a new kid who introduced himself as Ramen. I passed them my plate and took a cigarette. They asked for my latest wild casino story, and I'd just sat down when the warning instinct pickaxed the back of my head. I clasped the base of my skull with a grunt.

Simultaneously, my phone went off. Iron Maiden's "Hallowed Be Thy Name" signaled trouble at the Nightmare Club.

When I shook off the white-hot pain, I sprinted two blocks around the corner.

The club's entrance line stretched the block, full of half-naked humans and other nonhumans ready to take advantage. Bloody zombies, Captain Americas, corseted witches, apocalypse nurses, fake punks, retro waitresses, and werewolf masks, all in various stages of inebriation. God, I hated Halloween.

Instinct pushed me past the line, and I hopped the rope before the bouncer, Johnnie, could drop it. He yelled after me, asking what was wrong, but I just shoved into the sweaty crowd.

With a blink, I snapped my sight to night vision, perfect for watching gloomy club corners, but tonight, the lasers and strobes immediately disoriented me.

Colton's training drummed in my ears. *Stop and think. Use your instincts. You're not a foolish human anymore.*

A figure in an ill-fitting suit crawled onto the DJ platform, dragging a bloodied woman by the throat. Fortunately—or unfortunately, depending on the circumstances—the Nightmare had a reputation for whacked-out shit like this. Usually, shit was real, but the human patrons rarely recognized that. So the DJ kept playing, and only the nonhumans wove toward the door.

Which left five hundred drunk and horny people between me and whatever *that* was.

I jammed a path to the bar, swung onto the bartop, and launched myself to a catwalk fifteen feet overhead. My shoulders screamed as I kicked onto the grating, and the metal cut open my hands. I sprinted toward the platform where the woman shrieked and beat at the nonhuman mauling her leg.

Closer now, recognition crashed into me—Kia. That monster had Kia!

The wolfish thing lifted its maw, stretching red flesh from bone. I slammed against the rails, hands slippery with my blood. I wanted to lunge over the catwalk and rip the head off the thing hurting my friend. Rage gripped me so hard my hearing fuzzed out until Kia's scream split my skull.

Colton's training beat with my pulse: *Study the scene. Don't rush.* I grit my teeth but focus. Thirty seconds, then I would jump regardless of what I could suss out. Kia didn't have more time than that.

Beneath the suit, the nonhuman's body seemed broken. A zombie or zombie makeup, maybe? But Colton said zombies were extinct. A blood-mad werewolf? Then why wasn't he going into a frenzy on the crowd rather than making a show of a single victim? It was most likely not of fey blood since any of the fey I had passed in line would have taken care of this guy before he could even hit the dance floor.

Thirty seconds up—I bet on werewolf. Now, to get him off Kia.

I dropped, the landing jarring my bones. Colton's voice snarled in my head: *Roll with it, Gin. Break a bone, and you're a meal.*

My werewolf guess was only part right. He raised his head and hissed, showing a mangled canine jaw but also the splotched, veiny skin of a zombie. But a werewolf-zombie was impossible—

He leapt, and I dodged right. Audio cables tangled around my boots as I whirled to face the creature. He slid on all fours, gouging the platform, then bounded toward me. I lunged to meet him, but the cords caught at my boots, and I sprawled on my back. The cold meat slab of him crushed my chest. The rotting smell was overpowering, making me gag.

The DJ finally stopped playing, and the house lights flickered on. My vision readjusted in time to block a bite, and the werewolf-zombie sank fangs into my forearm rather than my neck.

My blood splattered across his muzzle and jaw, and the skin melted away, fizzling as if my blood were acid. He howled and jerked backward, but his face sloughed off, clean to the bone.

I crawled after him and straddled his back so he couldn't reach Kia again. I looped a cable around his neck and pulled, but the tissue dissolved, giving no resistance as the cable passed through to the bone, dislodging his head with a *pop*. His fleshless skull rolled off the platform, and the headless body bucked twice and then stilled.

I collapsed to the side, panting. Now *that* hadn't happened before.

Screaming replaced my momentary relief.

"Kia!" I pulled myself toward her, my arm trailing blood. Not weird blood, though. It didn't sizzle or smoke on the floor, but even now, the droplets ate holes through the zombie's body, and my bloody hands had left charred marks.

She'd scrambled into the shadows, leaving a swipe of red across the wooden stage. The monster's claws had raked apart her thigh, and she'd stripped off her shirt, holding it, already sopping, to her leg.

I levered to my feet, clutching my arm against my stomach, and stumbled over. I dropped to my knees with a grunt.

"Kia, it's all right, I promise, I promise. It's all right." My mouth kept yammering as I yanked off my denim jacket and wrapped it tightly around the wound. She whimpered and clutched at my hands, her skin sticky.

Police and EMTs shoved past the fleeing patrons. Four of the officers and both EMTs were on Colton's payroll and vampires, so I didn't have to worry about containment right this second. Chuck and Max hauled their gear onto the stage, and I scooted back.

"Her leg—it's bad."

Max peeled off my jacket. "Jesus!" He glanced at me as his hands automatically opened his bag as if to say, *How did you let this happen?*

I struggled upright and backed off. If I'd been at my station at the vaults downstairs, could I have sensed that thing? Maybe. Instead, it'd taken out my friend, who'd probably come to the club for a half-priced drink on her night off. Hell, she might have texted me to join her. All because I was mad at Colton— who would rip me a new one as soon as he heard the news.

I waited for Colton at the bar of the now-empty club. The lost earnings alone would count against me, not to mention a mauled employee. His right-hand man sat beside me, sipping an Old Fashioned. Franklin was pure human and seventy years old, a rarity among vampire assistants. He didn't really consider himself a familiar, though. To him, the Saints was just a job that he loved. He'd taken over the books a decade ago, and even though Colton made jokes about Franklin dying without putting in two weeks' notice, the Saints would implode without him.

Franklin had seen the whole thing and had been the one to trigger the alert system. His book, a creased John le Carré novel, draped over his crossed legs. He traced his silver mustache with his thumb, lost in his considerations, as I bandaged my arm.

I tore the gauze with my teeth. "You don't have to wait," I said, eyeing his drink. If I had a sip, Colton would accuse me of drinking on the job—give me shit about all the addiction recovery he paid for.

"I believe Colton will be too hard on you otherwise, Juniper."

I sighed at my name. Colton had given me the nickname Gin, which stuck, but Franklin refused it.

"I can wrangle Colton. Been doing it for two years."

"Tonight, he has more on his mind. Don't take it personally."

"Never do. I assume he's told you about the council wanting to see me?"

Franklin nodded and sipped his Old Fashioned.

I managed to tie off the gauze after three tries. "Does this mean I fucked up?"

"On the contrary. Unfortunately, you're an asset. Reno is growing, which means so is Colton. You are a question mark in his operation."

I thumped my forehead against the bar. "I didn't sign up for vampire politics."

"GIN!"

I flinched upright, and my arm throbbed. Guys yelling always made me nervous—too many memories of Dad and Mom fighting. A man with power added to the nerves, and Colton held my future in his hands—even if we were work partners...or maybe colleagues? I'd lived at the Saints for the past two years. It was my home and the only job worth having with no college degree and too much knowledge of what lurked in the shadows.

Franklin patted my knee and slid off the stool, tucking his book under his arm. "Over here, Colton."

He shuffled to intercept as The Cowboy flowed into the Nightmare. Colton hated that nickname, grumbling that he was *a* Black cowboy, not the only Black person driving cattle—a comment always followed by a "Myth of the American West" lecture. Tonight, he looked singular in his straight-brimmed hat, black trench, silver-etched boots, and silver-rimmed sunglasses, a change from his street clothes a few hours before. He wore this signature outfit when schmoozing with vampire visitors, so my screw-up must have interrupted an event, making him look bad.

He tried to side-step Franklin, his fangs bared, but Franklin caught his sleeve and shoulder-checked him, murmuring in his ear.

I pretended to tighten the bandage. Without asking, I knew I was being groomed to take over as Colton's right hand whenever Franklin didn't show up to work some night. Facing down an angry vampire so easily seemed impossible. I could barely laugh with him when he was in a playful mood, though I pretended otherwise. But I wanted it. Four years in Reno, half the time living in the dark, had made it home. I didn't want to leave—or, more precisely, for Colton to kick me out—and even if I could, half a college degree in Reno guaranteed me a spot in the trailer park beside my mom.

I let my sight soften and tried to heighten my hearing like Colton taught me. Franklin's smoker's rasp came clearer, but only the cadence, not the words.

Colton's voice rang loud, though, "She should be scared. She fucked up."

All right, then. I pushed off the stool and stalked over. The angry vampire shoved past Franklin and stepped into me, toe-to-toe. Staring down a six-foot-three cowboy with fangs was much scarier than whatever monster my blood had decapitated tonight.

I crossed my arms, and Colton smirked. *You're showing your fear*, he would have said.

He bared his fangs. "And?"

"I came as soon as I received the alert—"

"Don't lie to me, Gin."

Franklin touched his arm. "She was here in seconds."

He bent over me. "You were posted at the blood vault, but something like that came into the building without you knowing?"

Franklin raised an eyebrow and shifted, facing me and on Colton's side in more ways than one now.

I leaned closer, baring my human teeth as I snarled, "You broke my one rule about working on Halloween, so yeah, I fucking abandoned my post." This twisted a smile out of him. He preferred it when I shoved back. "Look, it was just an itch. I didn't know what it meant, but it got worse this week—"

"You felt that thing coming for a week? Why didn't you say something?"

"Because you were busy preparing for the council meeting!"

"Then interrupt me!"

Franklin sighed and ran a hand down his face. "Save the quarreling for your quarters, will you?"

Heat washed up my neck. I'd never told Franklin about the crush on Colton that I couldn't stomp out, but sometimes it seemed like Franklin guessed, anyway. If Kia were here instead of in the emergency room, she'd giggle.

"I had this itch that something was coming from the south. I didn't know what. It got worse tonight, but I was upset about Halloween and went for a walk. When Franklin triggered the alert, the itch got really bad."

Colton took off his sunglasses and hung them from his open shirt collar. His eyes sparked brown and golden, contrasting with the silver in his outfit. "You were sloppy, as seen clearly on the video spreading all over the dark web. A woman—your friend and one of my best employees—nearly died because you were mad at your work schedule." He turned on his heel, his coat fanning behind him. "You're back on security until you learn to follow the schedule."

My fists clenched, and the shakes traveled up my hands, through my arms, and into my shoulders. The anger was split between me and him. He was right; maybe if I had been in the building, I'd have sensed the supposedly-extinct zombie, and Kia wouldn't be wondering if she'd walk again. I'd let her down.

Franklin hooked an arm through mine, patting my hand as he guided me out of the empty club. "I'll talk to him, Juniper. I'll talk to him."

He walked me back to my room on the Saints' top floor, next to his. On the way, Franklin steadily talked about the latest kitchen gossip, the trouble one of the bartenders had last night with a Jeremy Renner look alike, and that one of our regulars had a new grandkid named Linda, which Franklin thought was too old-fashioned. The patter helped lower my heart rate, and I thanked him as he stood outside my door.

I closed the door, flipped the bolt, and let out a long sigh. The night shift had just started, and I was two fights deep, already sapped by adrenaline. I still had to report to the security team before sunrise.

I walked to the large window overlooking Reno's neon skyline and leaned against the cold glass. Top floor is a perk of working for a casino vampire boss, I guess.

The downside—all the guests can sniff you out.

2

I'd stepped into the shower and settled into replaying the conversation with Colton, trying to figure out how to sound tougher for next time, when Clarisse slid open the shower door.

I yelped and crashed into the corner, knocking down my old shampoo bottles.

She lounged against the tile, one bra strap sliding free, the black lace barely containing anything, while the matching panties cut patterns over her white skin. "Want some company, Gin?"

I slammed the shower door so hard the glass spiderwebbed. Not for the first time, either. "Get out!"

Of course, "get out" only meant "of the bathroom" for Clarisse. She retreated as far as my bed, where she lounged in a purely PornHub-ready pose.

I stalked into the room, feeling silly wearing a Saints-branded crimson bathrobe, but I'd left my clothes on my bed. "I meant get out of my room, and you know it."

She rolled onto her stomach, her chin propped on her fists and feet in the air. "Gin, sweetheart, don't be that way."

I rubbed my eyes. "What do you want?"

Clarisse was part of the trio that discovered vampires couldn't drink my blood when I'd stumbled into a vampire party. A LARP sounded like a good homework break sophomore year. I hadn't read the fine print when I signed a waiver and, like my friends, ended up drunk with a vampire sucking on my neck. The difference being that my blood wasn't consumable. Didn't make them sick, exactly, but they did have to spit it out. Since that night, Clarisse has tried to get in my pants whenever she comes to town. Colton claimed she wanted information. As the blood daughter of the clan ruling most of Vegas, Clarisse had to want something.

Seeing her after dealing with an angry Colton did not improve the night, but I swallowed down the memories and the tightness in my throat.

She wiggled off the bed and sauntered behind me. "You look stressed. I can help with that."

As she ran her hand along my shoulders, I whirled around and stepped into her, teeth bared, just like Colton had done to me.

Her jaw cracked as she flashed her fangs.

"Sure, bite me. We know how that turned out last time."

She sighed and raised her hands. "All right, all right."

I stepped aside, and she stalked to the mini-fridge. "Look, my mom thinks I've been fucking you for the past two years. Can I just chill here for a while so her little spies don't get any idea I've been lying?"

My jaw went slack. Six or seven times, Clarisse had shown up in my room, flirted with me, and this was why? "You—you could have said something."

She groaned, rummaging through the drinks. "Ha, Colton must think you like vamps." She pulled out an old blood-twisted cider that had probably been in there since I arrived.

"Hold on, hold on. You've been harassing me—"

She thumbed off the cap, showing off her vampire strength. "You started it, though I think you were pretty drunk."

I tightened the bathrobe. Memories of Clarisse in this same lingerie were hazy at best. I'd experienced a pretty serious breakdown when I discovered vampires—along with everything else imaginable—were real, quit college, and moved into the casino. Free alcohol did not help.

She took a long sip, and her eyes brightened, the blue more saturated and other-worldly. "Wanna try it sober?"

"Why does your mom want us to—to be involved?"

"To fuck?" She flipped on the TV and scrolled through the channels. I wasn't sure I'd ever turned the thing on. Maybe cable was still interesting if you were a hundred years old. "Information, I guess."

I walked to the fridge and took my time choosing a soda, reminding myself that she's not a spoiled twenty-something, even if she looked it. "I'm helping you out, so I need something in return."

She grinned, still focused on the TV, a *Survivor* rerun. "You get better at this every time. Did Colton tell you there's one piece of official business on the council agenda?"

I popped open an orange Jarritos and took a long sip. "Let me guess—me?"

She turned toward me and clapped twice. "Look who's learning."

I huffed. "Tell me something I don't know. Colton has already warned me your mom wants to buy this place—is that how she will use me at the meeting tomorrow?" For the thousandth time in the past two years, I felt like a child playing pretend in a suit. I couldn't even stand up to Colton, but was supposed to bluff an ancient vampire on some secret council? Sure.

Clarisse downed her cider in two long swallows and let out a satisfied sigh. A redness tinged her dead lips. "More like jealousy. Colton got a pretty toy when none of them wanted to bother with you." She patted my shoulder. "We're all very petty, Gin. You know where to find me if you want more information." She winked as she sauntered out the door. Still only wearing lingerie. Just walking around mostly naked. Very vampiric.

I sank onto the bed and exhaled heavily. Nights like these, I hated being twenty-two among the eternal—always one step behind.

3

Sick of vampires and my growing guilt over Kia, I bagged up my gore-stiff clothes for housekeeping and changed into leggings and an oversized Hot August Nights hoodie. I decided on The Hideout since I could drink there all night and distract myself with the end of a show. Of course, around Halloween in Reno meant I'd run into who knew what, but at least I wasn't responsible for any of it.

On casino grounds, I never truly lived off the clock. Franklin said I should get an apartment. Truth was, I felt too afraid. Knowing what goes bump in the night has its downsides. Sure, the normies know it too. Everyone has a friend of a friend who's seen a UFO or a jackalope, but folks shrug it off. They ignore it, just like the latest Nazi posters or Amazon buying up everything. Because if they don't ignore it, the world cracks just a little more, and they teeter even closer to the edge. I'd already fallen through the crack. I'm not much of a monster slayer, more like a deterrent. Vamps can't drink me, *weres* can't turn me, fey can't fool me, witches can't curse me. It's not something special I can turn off and on; it's just how I am. But my powers wouldn't stop a serial killer from hacking me apart.

Makes me a good casino ornament, though.

The Hideout featured the regular lot of metal heads and late-night PBR hipsters. I'd missed the headliner, but the post-show was raising money for Washoe County's "Food Not Bombs," which meant Winston would be around. His brother's band warmed up with an acoustic version of Sabbath's *Iron Man*, a weird choice considering their fey blood, but hey.

I found Winston smoking at the bar, and he caught me up in his signature hug, lanky arms crushing me close and lifting me off the ground. His blond hair was wrapped in a black handkerchief, offset by purple eyeliner and lipstick. He yelled over the shrieking guitar and bass, asking how I was holding up. I motioned him outside—there were way too many human ears around, even with the band riffing.

We stepped onto the small patio just as a few smokers went inside. I leaned against the railing, inhaling the trailing smoke and fumes from busy Midtown.

Winston hip-checked me. "You smell stressed."

Winston was a pureblood human, but he'd been swapped with his fey brother playing inside. A childhood in fey-land had given him some advantages over regular humanity. Winston argued it hadn't really, other than aging him more slowly. He adamantly maintained that humans just needed to recalibrate and not think about the next iPhone.

He was also an anarchist and made it pretty obvious.

"I'm sure you've seen my night on the darknet."

"At the Saints? Well, yeah, but I was gonna let you tell it."

I swigged off his Miller, then passed it back. "That bad?"

He scrunched his face. "Colton's got hackers scrubbing it off, so yeah. Heard anything about Kia?"

I shook my head, made a show of picking up a cigarette butt and throwing it away.

He touched the bandage under my jean jacket. "You should get that looked at."

I crossed my arms. "I have been bitten by numerous things under Colton's pay, and nothing has knocked me out yet."

He kissed the top of my head. "Doesn't mean something might not try."

I shifted away from him. "Careful, might have some blood on me. Don't want to burn a hole through your face." Thing was, I only half-joked. My blood had never burned like acid before, but maybe I'd discovered a new ability, a particularly sucky one.

He pressed the beer into my hand. "I've seen you in too many scraps, and nobody's skin melted off. It had to be something about the zombie thing."

"You hear about anything like this over in fey-land?"

"Nah." He retied the black handkerchief. "Somebody would know if a necromancer came to town, and wild zombies aren't really a thing anymore. Maybe it was just bad luck."

I downed the lukewarm beer and crushed the can. I wanted to tell him about being summoned to the council meeting, but if Colton found out I'd spilled vamp secrets, he'd have my ass for the second time. Still, it all seemed too coincidental for comfort.

Even worse, the danger-from-the-south instinct still tickled the back of my neck.

～

Around two a.m.—Colton's afternoon—he texted to remind me I'd been demoted to joining the security team again, and I had a six a.m. meeting I better not miss. I'd learned pretty early that whatever flowed through my veins let me skip sleep, at least for longer than the average twenty-two-year-old, so I stayed at The Hideout until gray dawn silhouetted the hills. I joined the guys at the six a.m. shift change. I knew them all, of course, and had gotten bloodied up with nearly all of them except for the head of the night squad, Crispin, who wore the latest expensive suit. The story was he could because he'd never gotten a drop of blood on one—except for the one time I broke his nose.

When Colton brought me into the casino, I never quite jived with the team, and he had taken over my training after a few months. The guys didn't say anything, exactly, but a twenty-year-old with a shaky grasp of the Darkside asking too many questions and unable to tell the difference between a weredog and kitsune just slowed them down. I'd learned later some were jealous that I'd shown up out of nowhere and been the boss's project after they'd been protecting the casino for years. Which was fair but not my fault.

I hurried to a seat, trying to act casual with my hands in my pockets. The rolling chair almost slipped out from under me, but the guy next to me steadied it.

"Happened to me, too." He smiled, showing a missing tooth, then ducked his head. He wore a Nevada Boxing hoodie, so I guessed he was the new guy I'd heard about—a fighter who'd joined up three weeks ago. He probably knew the Saints's crew from the tournaments the neighboring Sierra Nevada Casino sponsored in their basement. Scabs covered his knuckles, and his white hands were chapped.

"Nash, right?"

"Yep, Nash Neverman."

Head of security Caleb Isaac (or Isaac Caleb, nobody was sure) clapped his hands. "Name like that, and he fits right in. If you haven't heard, bossman sent Gin back to us to learn to follow orders, so nobody let her off the hook."

I rolled my eyes. "Yeah, yeah, you say jump, I say how high. I get it."

He pointed at me. "It's no joke, not with Halloween in two weeks. Two noobs on my team, and Colton wants to double the masquerade attendance. I tell ya." He shook his head as he passed around a calendar. Most of the team snapped a photo on their smartphones. "Now, there's half a dozen Halloween parties happening among the casinos, and the first one's tonight at the Circus Circus, which means we'll get spillover. Anybody in a zombie costume, triple-check that *they are human*, or else you're taking puke duty from the cleaning staff. Got it?"

Nods all around the table.

"Day squad, you'll be running man-to-man in your zone since the Vegas vamps already sent in a delegation. Fucking two weeks early, I tell ya."

I raised my hand, which made Caleb Isaac rub the spot between his eyebrows. "Yes, Gin?"

"Just wanted to say Clarisse is definitely snooping around. She broke into my rooms yesterday, so—"

Jaxson, one of the younger guys, snickered, but before I decided whether not to power-whip a pencil at him, Caleb Isaac kicked his chair.

"I don't want to hear it from you after the thousands bossman lost because you couldn't keep your eyes on two vampires at once. Gin's information is correct—the night squad lost Clarisse because we didn't have enough staff, so that's my other news of the day. We're running doubles every other night until after Halloween." He raised his hands as the groans rolled in. "The night squad will be doing the tough stuff, tailing the vampires, so we will just be doing zone security. Don't fuck up, and bossman promised some handy holiday bonuses. All right?"

He passed out zone assignments to the two-man crews. "I

know we aren't usually on high alert this long before Halloween, but after the zombie fuck up last night"—he glared at me—"we cannot afford another mark. Assume every scuffle is a distraction." He stopped behind Nash and me, so we turned our chairs around as the others filed out of the room. "You two are on door duty." He pointed at me. "Teach him how to spot nonhumans." He pointed at Nash. "Teach her everything you've learned in the past three weeks."

"Yes, sir," Nash said, standing as if at attention.

I slouched further. "Door duty, really? Colton has been training me for two years."

He bent over me. "Yeah, and you tied yourself up in audio cables last night while a zombie ate Kia's leg!"

I stood and crossed my arms. "I get it."

"Good. Keep getting it." He stomped off.

I huffed and lowered my arms. I could throw the man across the room if I wanted to, but no, that didn't matter. Fucking door duty.

Nash looked after Isaac Caleb and then at me. "I can't tell if he really likes you or wants to beat the shit out of you."

"Pretty sure it's the second."

We walked to the supply closet and took the last set of earpieces and radios.

"They only put me on door duty," Nash said. "Everyone just looks human to me, so hopefully, you can help. You gotta be the best at spotting OTHs."

I stabbed the elevator button. "OTHs?"

"Other-than-humans."

I smiled at the shorthand, and we stepped aside as some of the relieved night crew came out. Half of them were vampires, usually paired up with a nonvampire.

Crispin's second in command, a vampire named Justin,

who was turned as a teenager, shoulder-checked me. "Nice job last night, Gin."

My lips twitched. Some days, I wished I had fangs.

We entered the empty elevator. Halfway to the casino floor, I turned to Nash, my fists clenched. "Just so you know, I won't let anything happen to you." Well, that wasn't exactly what I wanted to say. "I mean, I know you're good at what you do, or you wouldn't be here, but I'm not going to put you in danger. I promise."

The elevator door dinged open. Nash grinned, bearing his missing tooth. "Didn't think you would." He sauntered onto the casino floor with a confidence that I had to playact. He must've looked good entering the ring.

On my lunch, Colton called me to one of the big cold storage units where he'd frozen the zombie. Franklin and Caleb Isaac also joined us, shivering despite their parkas while the cold slid off me and Colton.

Frozen viscera stuck the wolfish head to the table. Without animation, the shriveled body twisted in on itself, the emaciated arms wrapped around the headless stump with the knees drawn up to the sunken chest. My first guess had been werewolf, and looking at the still body, it was clear why: human and canine parts were mashed together. The human head had been scalped and furred with what could be coyote ears. A fox tail dangled from the hips like a war-torn flag. The hands had been overlaid with some type of paw, the claws overgrown. Yellow pustules and burn marks collected around the seams where rotting human skin transitioned to carrion. In some places, skin draped over bones like wet paper, and in others, tumor-like bumps rose from chunky flesh.

Caleb Isaac rubbed his nose. "What is this?"

Colton bent over the head, examining the seam along the scalp. "Nothing I have ever seen."

Franklin pulled out a penknife and started cutting around one of the tumors, but Colton stopped him. "Let me. We don't know if this could be contagious." He cut off a sliver of the tumor and placed it in a plastic baggie before handing it to Franklin. "Have one of our UNR people examine this."

Franklin wrapped the baggie in a handkerchief and pocketed it. "I have a feeling what they will discover. We lived through the Cold War, Colton. You know what this is."

Colton braced against the table, his head bent.

I glanced at Caleb Isaac, who shrugged. "So, what is it?"

"Acute Radiation Syndrome." He gritted his teeth, his fangs pressing against his lower lip. "What the poor creatures in Chernobyl suffered."

Caleb Isaac asked, "So how did a Russian zombie get all the way to Nevada?"

"It didn't," Franklin said. "We did our own nuclear testing here. The government didn't care about miners or Mormons."

Colton still gripped the table, his fingers making impressions in the stainless steel. But why was one zombie flipping him out? It'd probably wandered from some ghost town in the desert. Maybe it'd been trapped in an old building or mine that was finally weathered down to nothing. Big deal.

His hand shot out and snatched my wrist, yanking my arm over the body. Instinct attempted to jerk my hand free, and I banged my hip against the table.

"Hey!" I hated when he just manhandled me. Couldn't he at least ask?

"Hold still." He pulled a knife off his belt. He slit the back of my hand, blood dripping onto the zombie.

Each drop hissed. A small hole opened where my blood pattered onto the frozen shoulder meat.

Caleb wiped a hand down his face. "Jesus."

Franklin twisted his mustache. He ducked under the table. "The blood isn't dissolving the steel."

Colton swiped his thumb over the cut before releasing my hand. He sucked his thumb clean, then spat. "I wouldn't think so. She tastes the same."

I pressed the hem of my black T-shirt over the cut. Dude hadn't even asked before he just licked up my blood. Right in front of Caleb Isaac, too. Now, all the guys would think he regularly checked my blood like I was some party favor. "Is this why vampires can't drink my blood?"

He wiped his hand on his jeans. "Who can say. Do you sense the zombie now that it's not animated?"

I shook my head. "There's still a faint buzz that something is coming from the south, but it's not like last night. It's just there—like wildfire smoke."

Colton muttered something about smoke signals, and I raised an eyebrow at Franklin, who looked away. Seemed like Franklin knew something above my paygrade. Maybe Colton had learned something about my freaky blood, and that was why the masquerade was stressing him out. He wasn't *this* distracted at the last vampire masquerade. Or maybe I hadn't noticed—I'd still been drinking heavily, trying to adjust to living life in the dark.

Colton straightened and squared his shoulders. "Caleb, make sure the security teams know what they are looking for. Show them the body if you think it will help. Also, I want you to prepare a briefing on what to look for to all staff." He faced me. "Gin, I want you to find anything available on zombies returning from extinction. Ask around, check in with the locals."

"Uh, aren't local connections your thing?"

"You have contacts here—the changeling boy, Leia Jones—use them."

"But—"

"It's your blood, Gin. Figure it out."

Anger tightened my chest, but I tamped it down. I'd just learned about all this shit two years ago, and he expected me to figure out secrets he didn't understand? But I also knew I'd been disappointing him since week one. It wasn't just that I didn't catch on quick enough or the fuck up with Kia. I could be studying more, training more, learning more—that would be his comeback.

I shoved my fists into my pockets. "Yeah, yeah."

Colton's lips twitched as if I'd pushed him far enough that he wanted to show fangs. "Your lunch is over. Don't you have door duty?"

Caleb Isaac made a shooing motion, so I left them staring at the zombie as if they'd just found it on the side of the road. Zombies were supposed to be extinct, sure, but extinct creatures were found again sometimes. The Saints was full of mysteries, and a new one stumbled in weekly. It had been that way since I moved in. For some reason, this one had Colton white-knuckling. Since I'd come to the Saints, he had an answer to every question I asked—except what I was. Now, he expected me to find the answers.

That evening, Colton asked me to his office. I took a deep breath when I knocked on his door. He called me in, though the growling edge from last night was gone. Either he'd cooled off, or things were worse than I thought.

He lounged in his desk chair, his boots propped on the glossy antique desk. A brass floor lamp left the room in perpetual shadow, but a tablet in Colton's lap cast a blue glow over his face. Rather than a casino owner, his windowless office made him look like a professor. Ornate bookcases lined the walls, packed with everything from well-read James Baldwin to UFO conspiracy theories. More books piled on two rickety cane chairs. On top of a squat bookshelf, a record player whined Johnny Cash's "Hurt."

Another stack of books waited on the winged-back chair where I usually sat. He nodded at them. "We've delayed readings about zombies since they are relatively extinct in North America. Perhaps that is changing. Also, blood magic. Read those first."

I shifted the stack to the floor and perched on the seat's edge.

He tossed the tablet onto the desk and nodded at it. "We've been growing lax, it seems. Steady stream of sightings reported from the south."

I picked up the tablet and thumbed through the blurry photos. Zombie-looking deer, jackalopes, coyotes, even a tree. "How do we kill them?"

"Burn the bodies." He steepled his fingers and looked from under his hat. "But no mention of the creatures reacting so severely to blood."

I shrugged. "Unique circumstance?"

He drummed his fingers together. "Maybe. But, Gin..." He leaned forward and gave a soft smile that hid his fangs. "I acted too harshly. Yes, you were sloppy, but boxing with a zombie is a dangerous thing, even though you're immune. If these creatures are coming this direction, you need better tools of the trade."

I narrowed my eyes. A Colton apology was about as rare as a jackpot. "Okay."

He led me out of the office into the tunneled recesses built under the casino, an addition he kept expanding: a variety of vaults, living quarters, storage spaces, and a large training room where the rest of the security team and I practiced sparring. Colton had been turned while working in a cramped silver mine, so he had an uneasy relationship with tunnels, which had become a necessary part of his vampire lifestyle under the casino. Tonight, he took me into a vault next door. Spotlights illuminated weapon displays and turned the room into more of a museum exhibit than an armory.

He leaned by the door and hooked his thumbs on his belt. "See what calls to you. Until we know what flows in your veins, no weapon may be an exact fit, but it's time I armed you."

I tried to copy Colton's disinterested face while the teenage video gamer inside me went wild. Though, when I glanced back, he was grinning, his fangs dimpling his lower lip.

My breathing hitched as my eyes landed on his mouth, and I quickly turned to focus on reading the panel beneath an old sword until the flush burned away.

He sauntered over. "Any growing pains giving you guidance?"

I shook my head as I wove between the displays, trying to stay a step ahead of him. He'd warned me that vampires sensed emotions much more clearly than humans. The last thing I needed was Colton taking advantage of my irritating crush.

He caught my arm. "Slow down. Take a breath. We've talked about how you probably didn't notice your abilities earlier because you didn't take the time."

I sighed and closed my eyes. His body was a cold wall at my back. His hand rested between my shoulder blades, reinforcing his words. "You're safe here. Listen. Feel."

When Colton said things like that, my eyes welled. He was right. Thanks to him, I had safety in so many ways: physical, financial, job security, a home, and knowledge. Growing up in a central Nevada trailer park, those things had seemed so far away. As much as I grumbled about living at the Saints, I knew everyone who worked here—had gotten embarrassingly drunk with most of them—and the old-timers who recognized what the Saints *really* was trusted me to keep them safe.

Instinct ticked at the base of my skull, but as I let the room's quiet sink into my skin, so far below the Saints' glitz and buzz, a warm glow seemed to press against my head. Not coming from Colton, but around me, the quiet comfort of weapons forged for a purpose beyond mass-produced killing. Not necessarily for a more noble reason, though.

Colton's hand remained between my shoulders as I felt a path toward that warm glow. It narrowed to a cone before my eyes until it felt like a match flare.

My feet bumped into a pedestal, and he let out a low hum.

I opened my eyes. A long brand rested on a swathe of velvet. No plaque told its history.

I stepped beyond Colton's reach. "Great, my instincts take me to the only non-weapon in the place." Rust flaked the handle, which curved into a wicked thorn. A cracked leather strap threaded a hole at the end. Faded geometric designs indented the shaft while the brand head twisted in a complicated pattern I couldn't picture, though a pair of horns grew from it.

"I wouldn't say that." He nodded. "Pick it up. See what happens."

My palms sweat. "But it's not—"

He growled. "Gin."

I wrenched it off the stand. "Happy now?"

The brand flashed molten orange.

I dropped it, and it clattered, cold, on the cement. "Holy shit!"

Colton flicked it into the air with his boot and snatched it.

The brand remained dead. "Interesting." He set it on the pedestal. "Take it again."

"Not until you tell me what it is."

"An artifact from Los Alamos, when the scientists were stationed there to create the atom bomb."

I hovered my fingers over the handle. Nothing happened. "So, it was just there? Like in someone's house."

"Yes."

I motioned to the pistols, rifles, swords, bows, knives, and other weapons surrounding us. "Why is it here?"

"A hunch that it had absorbed some of the deadly energy on that mountain."

With a wince, I slowly picked it up. The brand glowed, heat wavering off the cherry-red metal. I twisted it, hefting the weight. It felt good, actually. Not too heavy but still satisfying to swing. "Seems about right for me. The oddball monster hunter should have an oddball weapon."

"I imagine it would be rather effective against many creatures, human included. In your hands, who knows what it might do."

I tried swinging it like I used to with fake swords as a kid. The hot end sizzled through the air. I couldn't help but grin.

Especially when Colton retreated. "Add it to your daily schedule. See what you can unlock with it." He whisked toward the door.

"Hey, wait." I took a carabiner off my keychain and hooked the leather strap to my belt, but the brand banged against my calf with each step. At least it didn't light my jeans on fire. I'd have to rig a strap across my back. Even cooler.

I jogged after him. "What does this mean, though? All of those weapons, and I chose this? After we got some radiation zombie in the club? It's a sign, right? About where my powers come from?"

Colton shrugged one shoulder. "Perhaps."

"But then, why couldn't I get a cool weapon?"

He sighed like an overwhelmed parent as he climbed the stairs to his office. "Gin, what you learn to do with this brand will mean more than the choice itself."

Cracking the secret door to his office, he went still in that eerie, dead-person way, then shut the door again.

"Something wrong?"

He picked at his fangs with his tongue. "Not particularly. Would you mind leaving through the garage?"

I rolled my eyes. "Don't want me to be seen by your vampire pals?"

He sighed. "It's more complicated than that."

"Oh, you don't want them to think we're screwing." I hoped the tunnels were dark enough to hide my blush. "I'm your head of security—sort of. It's natural we would be alone in the tunnels under your casino."

He twisted a ring on his finger that signified his council position. "That is usually not what vampires do with humans in the dark."

"I'm just saying there are lots of options."

He pulled his hat lower. "Please use the garage entrance."

I unhooked the brand, and the tip glowed, underlighting Colton's face. "Fine, fine. Have fun with your fellow vampires." I meandered down the dark tunnel, swinging the brand like a torch.

He sighed into the darkness, and I smirked. Score.

5

In return for the brand, I started on Colton's research the next day. After lunch, I went to the Black Cat Path, a library and shop for those living in the dark, hoping Leia Jones would be in class or researching or whatever graduate students in secret magic programs do. My timing was terrible. She sat at the glass counter, books and loose paper spread over the top while she scrolled on her phone. Two years ago, we'd shared the same floor at the UNR dorms and become friends, two shy weirdos who weren't that interested in partying or hooking up.

Leia didn't look up when the bell tinkled. "What are you doing here?"

"Colton sent me."

She sighed. "Not an answer to the question, Juniper."

I twitched at my legal name. It just seemed so—innocent. The name of some naïve kid ripped by her roots from the high desert. "I'm here to buy information or pay for access to your library. I'm looking for information on zombies."

Leia nodded at a sigiled doorway partially blocked by the counter. "Knock yourself out. Colton's paid his yearly dues."

She slipped her phone inside her jacket and bent over her papers.

I stuffed my fists in my pockets and shuffled by. I'd hung out in the Black Cat before, back when Leia and I were still trying to make our friendship work. At first, Leia was excited to help me learn what it meant that vampires, fey, werewolves, magic—all of it—were real. And I was excited to learn, but I let the glitz and glamor of working for a vampire at a casino go to my head. I blew off meet-ups, showed up drunk a few times, and started contradicting her with "Colton said" this and "Well, Colton told me" that.

I acted like a total jerk but was also mad at her for not telling me in the first place. She'd let me go to the vampire party on Halloween two years ago—watched me walk out of the dorm room with all the other clueless girls. If we'd really been friends, she'd have stopped me somehow, even if it meant telling me it was all real.

I stepped into the small library and stared blankly at one of the shelves as I relived my anger. Someone cleared their throat, and I turned around. A Latine person in psychedelic leggings whispered, "You mind taking your negativity outside? There's a bathroom around the corner where you can cool off."

I ducked my head. "Sorry." I hurried back into the hallway and meandered until I found the bathroom. I splashed cold water on my face and dried off with a lavender-scented towel. Leia had chosen her secret coven over me. I couldn't blame her; I'd chosen Colton over a lot of things at this point, including trying to pick up the pieces of our college friendship.

After a few deep breaths, I returned to the library. The Black Cat Path was built out of an old house, with the library spilling from the dining room into the sitting room. Inset book-shelves insulated the walls, stuffed to overflowing with books on witchcraft, history, and the magical world in general. More than half of the books were readily available, not secret, but the Black Cat collected them in one easily accessible place. Plus, margin notes were encouraged. Some books had sticky notes of continuing conversations among the readers pasted right inside.

A large communal table split the first room, but more private desks were set into the corners to allow for personal study and use of a private Book of Shadows. The desks were all filled, so I joined the Latine practitioner at the large table with most of the shelf on "raising the undead" in my stack, which made my tablemate raise an eyebrow. I hunched over a book called *Haitian Vodou* by Mambo Chita Tann, though I doubted whatever came crawling from the desert had Vodou origins.

I'd finished skimming the introduction when Leia plucked the book from my hand. "That's got nothing to do with the zombie, and you know it."

"Uh, it's what was on the shelf."

"Last thing we need is another white girl reading about Vodou." Leia sorted my books and set them all on the reshelving cart. "You're thinking like a cop show instead of a half-human. Don't focus on the zombie or any closed practice that might connect to the undead. The other night wasn't some ritual gone wrong."

"I mean, it could have been. Some kids shitbrained on mushrooms in Black Rock or something."

She gave me a withering look. "You think it's that easy? Really. It came for the Saints. If it wanted a casino, the Circus Circus was closer, meaining it was on a mission. Now, rumor has it the video shows it reacting weirdly to your blood, so was it coming for you or the Saints?"

"Uh, I'm not sure." Except it must have been going for the Saints because I wasn't in the building at the time. If it was coming for me, was tracking me, then it should have detoured, right? "The Saints—it was the Saints."

She pulled a warped paperback missing its cover. "Which means it was probably after Colton." She handed the book to me, a vampire hunter manual.

I grimaced. "That thing couldn't have killed him."

"No, but it might have been trying to draw him or the other vamps out." Still staring at the stacks, she held out two more thick hardbacks. I paged through them, a two-volume self-published set on vampire politics.

"Sabotage for the council meeting," I said.

Leia scanned the index of a chunky paperback, then reshelved it. "Could be. Trying to make him look weak—like his security isn't up to hosting such an important event."

"You know, that could be it. One of the vampires from the Vegas coven was here early."

"You mean Clarisse."

I swung around in my chair toward Leia. "How the hell do you know Clarisse?"

Leia dropped three more books about gambling magic on the table. "We have a sister Path in Vegas that keeps good relations with Clarisse's coven."

"Oh, okay." Leia made it all sound about as normal as the local baseball rivalry.

The front doorbell chimed, and Leia stepped into the hall, then poked her head around the doorframe. "And Juniper, I don't think we should rule out the zombie coming for you. Your presence is so mixed up with the Saints and Colton that a monster with such simple programming might not be able to distinguish one from the other." She hurried toward the front shop, her combat boots thumping the worn floorboards.

I tilted back in my chair. A dozen books spread over the table, ranging from histories of the mass deaths of miners to self-published gambling rituals. Well, time to start connecting some dots.

6

Two nights later, Colton texted me at ten p.m. to come train—he wanted to try something. Vague, and since he texted like a Boomer with no exclamation points and too many ellipses, I wasn't sure if I was going to my death or if he wanted to teach me a new anti-fang chokehold.

Walking into the padded room to find Colton barefoot and in leggings, baggy basketball shorts, and a frayed undershirt always made me double-take. He felt stripped down without his coat or boots. Maybe he thought the same thing about me in running shorts, sports bra, and shredded *Red Jumpsuit Apparatus* T-shirt, showing too much skin that was slowly becoming the same shade as a wedge of brie cheese. I needed to get out more, as in during the sunlight hours.

Colton stepped beside me and angled his tablet so I could see the screen. Security footage looped, showing my less-than-spectacular zombie takedown. I winced as a replay of my flailing in a pile of cables flashed across the screen.

He frisbeed the tablet onto a sagging couch. "Now, what did you do wrong?"

"What? Not going to delegate me to Crispin so he can beat me up twenty times and call it 'teaching?'"

He dragged a tangle of jump ropes onto the mats. "You broke Crispin's nose last time, so he refused to train with you."

"He's a vampire—he heals."

"You fought dirty in a training bout. You know how he is about honor." Fair. Crispin had lectured me, blood pouring down his chin, about how I needed to respect the mat.

Colton stepped across from ropes, pacing out the approximate distance between the zombie and audio cables that had tripped me. "Now, what did you do wrong?"

I tied my hair into a jagged tail. "I didn't pay attention to my surroundings."

"Why not?"

I crossed my arms. "Because a zombie was eating my friend, and I got distracted."

"Or you were careless."

I glanced at my loose laces. "Yeah, that too." I crouched and retied them. Carelessness had turned into a habit as bad as my early drinking. Even if I could heal just as fast as a vampire, Kia couldn't. She wouldn't leave the hospital until tomorrow.

"Good. Where should you have landed?"

I took a few steps to the left to have the same angle on the scene as last night. If not for the audio cables, I still liked the spot. Just out of reach of the zombie, but I could close the distance fast enough to help Kia. Any closer, and I risked the zombie catching me as I landed. "I should have jumped on the zombie. It's gonna hurt, but it's the fastest way to take it out, which is the primary goal since it was a packed club."

Colton rolled his shoulders. "If you had control of your strength and could make a precision landing, then you have all the space in the back half of the stage."

"I could get tangled in the backdrop."

"Not if you had precision. Besides, you would launch forward as soon as you touched ground."

I raised my hands. "Okay, okay! I'll practice my jumps."

He motioned to begin, and I waffled between arguing or acquiescing. An eight-hour security shift had left me braindead and achy, even if chatting with Nash made it go a little faster. Then again, if I could convince Colton I was serious, he might let me drop off the security team after Halloween.

I settled into a downward dog, stretching my calves.

Colton sunk into the couch, his arms spread along the back and his head tilted as if taking a nap. Didn't he have better things to be doing?

The training room stretched a basketball court in length. Gear for weapons practice lined the walls, and a few slacklines offered balance courses overhead.

On a good day, a running start could get me halfway across the room, but I usually faceplanted. So, I started warming up by jumping a quarter of the room, doing a ten rep, but only counting the ones I actually stuck.

Walking back from my sixth rep, my ears fuzzed. I shook my head, immediately making myself sway like I'd been drinking. I lowered into a crouch. The troubling itch pointing south didn't grow stronger or weaker, so hopefully, this wasn't preparation for another zombie attack.

Bass music washed over me, but I shouldn't be able to hear it all the way down here. I raised my head, but the training room had been replaced by one of the Saints' private rooms, drenched in purple and maroon.

The scene glitched out as quickly as it had started, and I fell backward onto my butt. The training room returned, cool and quiet.

I scrambled to my feet, whipping around, searching for anything to explain how I'd shifted between rooms or memories or something. The room was empty except for Colton, still relaxed on the couch, his eyes closed.

Shit. I rubbed the heel of my palm between my eyes. *Keep it together, Gin.*

The last thing I needed was Colton thinking I was losing it. My legs shook as I walked to the water fountain, stealing a few seconds to regroup.

The training room blinked out again, and I was suddenly sitting on a plush chair. Something sticky and hot ran down my neck. Colton stood over me, his arm extended to keep another figure away. Clarisse. Her lips glistened red, covered in blood— my blood. This was Halloween two years ago. Had to be.

But how? Was I hallucinating?

The vampire I now knew so well crouched in front of me. His traditional cowboy outfit clashed with his bared fangs, and I tried to stand, get away, scream...but just like that night, I sat there, happily numb.

A muffled voice that I couldn't quite place cut through my memory. "Gin! Can you hear me? Is it you?"

Let me go!

The training room snapped back into place. I was face-first on the mat. Blood streamed from a split in my eyebrow—I must have hit my head on the fountain.

I rolled onto my back and scrambled to my feet. My head spun, and I braced against the water fountain. Blood smeared the corner.

Colton jerked off the couch and ran a hand over his hair. "Well then."

I pressed my palm against the throbbing scrape along my forehead. *Well then?* That was it? "What did you do?"

His smile straightened. "You're bleeding." He hurried over, but I backed into the wall.

"Stay the fuck back."

He took off his shirt and tossed it to me. "I didn't notice you by the fountain. I should have been more careful."

I wiped the blood off my face. My hands shook, and I couldn't tell if it was from the head injury, fight, flight, or rage. "What did you do to me? I was—it was two years ago."

"I know."

"And? What's going on?" His shirt slipped from my hands, and I crouched to pick it up, fumbling it again. My breath hitched. How could I have been back there?

He motioned to the couch. "Will you come sit with me?"

I slid down the wall, my legs losing the last of their strength. "No."

He sighed but sat cross-legged well out of reach. "Only Franklin knows this, so I'm trusting you."

I gritted my teeth. I trusted him to not make me relive that night. We didn't talk about it, the staff didn't talk about it, and I did not work Halloween. Except one by one, he was going back on those promises. Yet, here I was, in a few nights' time, working the one night a year I requested off and now getting my memories messed with somehow. My wrist ached at the scarred spot where Colton had bitten me that night. I cradled my arm against my chest.

"You know that vampires grow stronger as we age. When vampires reach a certain age, new traits develop. We call them century powers. Mine have started to show, and I need people I can trust to help me develop them."

I threw his shirt back at him. It fell short. "I'm not your fucking guinea pig."

He stood, picked up the shirt, and sat against the wall next to me. I would have scooted away, but I was too busy glaring at my shoes to make sure no tears slipped out. Maybe Bobbi and Kia were right that I needed more therapy. I couldn't break down just remembering that night. Except it wasn't a memory —I was there *again*. Colton was taking advantage of me again.

"I should have said something. I only made contact with Franklin after hours of work and two dozen tries. I didn't expect to reach you so quickly."

I drew up my knees and hugged them. "Is that all I am to you? An experiment? I don't even deserve a heads up."

"No." His voice deepened. "You matter to me and the Saints. That's why I'm telling you this. I shouldn't have been so careless." He placed his hand on the mat between us but didn't try to touch me.

I pressed my face to my forearms to squeeze back the tears. I always let him get away with an apology because I wanted to believe him so badly. With a deep breath, I raised my head. "So, what are your powers?"

"I'm becoming a dreamwalker. When I'm fully in control, I'll be able to communicate with people while they are awake and see their dreams while they sleep."

"Let me guess, you need a powerful memory in order to—to activate it or whatever."

"Close enough."

I flexed my legs. I felt strong enough, so I stood. "Don't ever use that memory. And fucking ask me before you pull a stunt like that again."

He rose, fluid as a shadow. "It's our strongest moment together." Which meant there would be a next time, whether I liked it or not.

I looked up at him. "I don't care. I never want to relive that."

He dipped his head. "As you wish."

Then he hugged me. I flinched—he wasn't a hugger, and I really just wanted to punch him—but he squeezed me closer. His cold, dry skin felt surprisingly good, and he still smelled like the leather he almost always wore. I let my body relax into his, my head settling on his chest.

7

After my day shift, I had a few hours until I worked a rotating double with the night crew. I thumbed through the schedules on my phone to see Bobbi had taken one of Kia's shifts since she was off until after Halloween at the very earliest. Bobbi was managing one of the pop-up Halloween stores in the corridor between the Saints and the Sierra, so I picked up a cold brew for them and a black coffee for me.

With working so much, I hadn't noticed masquerade prep had gone into full swing. I passed maintenance in Corridor A off the main floor, swapping the usual black and white photographs of Tahoe and the Sierras for graveyard-themed paintings. They also switched every other bulb in the sconces with an orange bulb while more staff added fake cobwebs to the plastic ferns. The head of maintenance, a buzzcut woman named Terry, lowered an Ansel Adams reprint to the ground. "That for me, Gin?"

I raised my coffee cup in a salute. "No can do. Got another shift in a few hours—unless you want to trade me?"

She made a face. "Not around Halloween."

"That's what I thought."

I turned right into Corridor B, which connected to the Sierra. The pop-up shop filled the small atrium where the casinos met. One of the burner stores downtown had sponsored it, so the costume pieces looked like they'd been excavated from a *Mad Max* movie set: goggles, leather straps, studded belts, bloody bandannas along the more typical hemp hippie bags and hats.

Kia's laugh stopped me, the coffee sloshing over my hands. I hissed.

She swung around the cashier's counter in a wheelchair, her mangled leg supported on an extended leg rest. "Gin! Finally!"

I hurried over, trying not to spill. I slid the coffee onto the counter where Bobbie leaned over a sketchbook. They snagged the cold brew. "You're a lifesaver."

I hugged Kia, mentally whispering *I'm sorry, I'm sorry* as I squeezed her as hard as I dared. She still smelled antiseptic. "When did you get out?"

She held onto me long enough I felt my guilt ease a little. "Last night. They finally figured out I wasn't going to turn into an undead cannibal, so I split."

"Sorry I didn't see you in the hospital." I'd wanted to go, but she'd been quarantined for a while, and then...the thought of seeing her all strapped up to an IV or sensors or whatever freaked me out. I tried to make up for it by texting her.

She wheeled back and forth. "Forget it. I looked like shit, and visitors always showed up when I had to pee."

I hitched my thumb toward the casino. "Shouldn't you be on, like, bedrest and not here?"

"Do you know how boring hospitals are?"

"Fair." I leaned against the counter and offered her my coffee, but she waved me off.

"Then I'll have to pee, and that is a whole other thing."

I craned my neck to see Bobbi's sketchbook, but they tilted it away.

"It's a surprise," they said. "Kia isn't missing Halloween just because of a zombie bite."

I swallowed my comment about the dangers of Halloween with a big sip of coffee. "You're still coming?" Only Kia would want to risk partying with monsters on one good leg.

"Hell yeah. Wouldn't miss it. Even if I'm just wingman." She swung in a circle. "And this year, you'll be there!"

Bobbi nudged me. "Can't overlook that, miss badass."

"Right, like that will change anything."

Kia snatched a steampunk top hat off the rack. "We haven't partied in for-ev-er." She cocked the brim over her eyes, even as dust puffed from the fabric. "I told Franklin this was bad place-ment and needed to be in Corridor F. Wannabe burners don't stay at the Sierra. They stay at the Circus Circus—or an Airbnb. Gross."

I leaned my elbows on the counter. Kia had given the same rant at least five times; to be fair, Franklin should have trusted her. She went to more clubs than he did—at least, I was pretty sure she did. "You can say I told you so on November first."

She nodded at my side. "Your arm all healed up?"

I rolled up my sleeve to show the white scratch. "I was fine by Monday."

She whistled. "Think you can bottle that up for me?"

"Yeah, you and every other human in the Saints. Have either of you heard anything from the regulars about that night?"

Bobbi closed their sketchbook. "It's just another local legend for the Saints casino like Franklin and Colton wanted."

"So, none of the truckers or reserve guys seen anything down toward Vegas?"

Kia stole Bobbi's cold brew and took a long sip. "I can ask around." She slapped the side of her chair. "One thing I can do is sit and talk."

"Franklin hasn't put a moratorium on that?"

She waved me off. "It doesn't matter. Colton got you doing research, or have you finally gotten curious about your powers?"

"Uh, Colton."

Bobbi groaned. "You literally have superpowers and don't care where they came from."

I took a long sip of the too-hot coffee. Kia was my friend since day one at the Saints, and Bobbi came along not long after, but they both wanted more than anything to not be just another human. There were plenty of ways for humans to walk in the dark, but they came down to two categories: business and craft. Kia claimed she had no head for memorizing spells or using tarot cards, so she went business. Bobbi hadn't chosen a path other than sticking close to the Saints, whether that meant selling their blood for vampires or picking up kitchen shifts.

Kia dusted off the steampunk hat and returned it to the rack. "The zombie has to have something to do with your heritage, right?"

"We all saw the video," Bobbi said. "Your blood melted that thing."

I shrugged. "Coincidence, maybe."

Kia massaged her thigh, and I felt a little sick to my stomach. "Have you talked to Leia about it?"

I popped the lid off my coffee, blew on it, then sipped. "Yeah. I had to use her coven's library."

"She's known you longer than even Colton—and she's a great witch. She doesn't have any ideas?"

"We don't talk about that kind of stuff." *Not anymore.*

We fell into silence, sipping. One of our regulars, Chris, hurried past, only giving a quick wave.

"Must be three o'clock," Bobbi said. "Says his luck has been changing at three, so he has to change casinos."

When I first came to the Saints, the way people were addicted made me talk about quitting. Some of them were gamblers, some needed a community, even one they had to pay to talk to them. Some were workers who practically lived in the building and barely left. As a kid, enough of my neighbors burned up their paychecks on slots, cigarettes, and booze that I swore never to try any of them. I made good on one out of three.

At first, I could barely talk to the regulars. One night when I'd been pissed about something else, I'd gone off on Colton about how he was just making a haven for addicts, how that was a shitty thing to do, blah blah blah. He had this amused look on his face, the one he gave me when I was being a short-sighted human kid. He'd shut me up with one question: *Do you know any of their names?*

Bobbi tapped their pencil on the sketchbook. "Hey, there was something. Our UPS guy said he'd taken a trip to Vegas last weekend, and there was a weird amount of roadkill. And it was all spread out. He thought it was big coyotes or something, but maybe it was your zombie. They eat dead things, right?"

Kia huffed. "I'd say they prefer the living."

I tossed out my coffee. "They're supposed to be extinct, so who knows."

~

That night, seeing the line of Halloween costumes gave me the shakes. Last year, I'd worked day shifts to avoid the worst of it and binged *Parks and Recreation* at night to blot out the partying. With security stretched thin and my inhuman ability to work doubles, I'd been on shift for sixteen hours, the last three at the Nightmare.

My guess was Colton wanted me to get out all the anxiety before Halloween night. Or he just didn't care. Usually, he was the caring kind of boss who listened to the sob story about needing daycare for the toddler, so how about a raise? When I saw Caleb Isaac had scheduled me for shifts at the Nightmare the whole week, I almost went to Colton, but then I'd have to admit how that night still fucked me up and . . . I didn't want to look that weak, not after I was a mess during his so-called training session on top of my screw-up with the zombie.

So, I shoved my fists deep into my denim jacket pockets and slid on a pair of shades. Nash worked every other night with me, and this Friday, we stood on either side of the entrance with the door person on Nash's side. I made Nash take pat-down duty since I would not be able to deal with the comments from drunk white guys without punching someone. The line curved around the block by ten, just like last week when the zombie attacked. Tonight, the dull instinct that had alerted me to the zombie remained an itch at the base of my skull, so I told Nash not to worry. The regular Reno nightlife represented more of a threat than another zombie.

Tonight, the patrons in line seemed to be mostly human. My senses registered a few shape-shifters intent on being human for the night, one fey with two guys on his arm, and our vampire regulars. I made sure to introduce them to Nash so he knew who not to worry about: Jersey, a former baseball major leaguer; Lev, a buddy of Colton's from WWII; Reese, an ancient card shark that had been kicked out of Vegas a few too many times; and Christy, a Hollywood actress before the talkies. Colton didn't lead a coven or clan, but vampires usually kept tabs on each other. I'd asked Franklin if Colton intended to start a group from his vampire friends, but Franklin insinuated he wouldn't until he was ready to truly challenge the Vegas vamps. Otherwise, it's better to play it cool and look small, even if he really ran the Darkside of Reno.

I scanned the end of the line as Nash patted down the fey and his two enamored humans. A female figure slid out of line and sauntered toward the entrance. Clarisse.

"Ah, shit."

Nash motioned the fey through. "What is it? What am I missing?"

"A vampire."

He squinted. "The guy in the Hulk Hogan costume."

"What?" I looked at him and couldn't help but chuckle. "No, even if it's dated enough to be a vampire's costume."

"Wait, I see her. The steampunk white rabbit gal."

She cut the line as a drunk frat guy in a Captain America T-shirt hollered. We ignored him. She leaned close enough that I smelled the blood on her breath. "Want to follow me to Wonderland?"

I edged back until I pressed against the wall. I placed my foot against the brick, trying to look casual. "That's your best line?"

She half-smiled, bearing a fang. "Worked on your puppy." She brushed past Nash, who tried to follow her.

I snagged the hood of his sweatshirt and whirled him around, crushing him against the wall. "Get it together, dude."

He shoved off the wall, rocking me on my heels. His head angled after Clarisse, but I leaned into my strength and shook him. "Nash?"

He took a deep breath. "Holy shit. You weren't kidding about glamour."

I let him go and stepped back. The frat boy in line stared at us with his mouth slack. I motioned him through as Nash leaned against the wall, rubbing his eyes.

"Technically, she's not supposed to do that," I said. "Sorry, she was messing with me."

He shook his head and stepped up to do his job. "How do I stop it?"

I handed him my aviator shades. "These help. Don't make eye contact. That's why we always work in pairs." I slapped him on the shoulder as I stuck my head into the club. Clarisse parted a wave of admirers, some following her like pilot fish.

I radioed Crispin. "Clarisse is in the club, and she's glamouring people."

His sigh crackled over the radio. "I'll take care of her. Damn it."

I returned to my post, but my phone buzzed.

Colton texted: *Heard your chatter... see what she wants ... Crispin will cover your spot.*

God, I hated his ellipses. I shoved my fists in my pockets. "Order from Colton. Crispin is coming to cover for me."

Nash paled. "But Crispin hates me."

I shouldered past a slutty nurse and her apocalypse boyfriend. "Just keep working."

Humans and some nonhumans packed the club. The nonhumans blended into different areas for their various desires: a few fey on the dance floor, werewolves packing a booth, vampires "hunting" along the two bars—Colton paid plenty of "juicers" willing to play along. Clarisse perched on a stool close to the door. Her vamp-ness and at least one glamoured admirer had drawn around some unsuspecting humans like flies sipping at a sore.

I tapped hard on her protruding shoulder blade. "Tone it down, Clarisse. You know the rules."

She raised her arms like a drunken sorority girl about to hug me. "You did follow me!"

I squinted at her. "Colton wants to know what you're doing here."

She shrugged off the human mannerism. "Partying. The Saints has the best-looking juicers, so figured I'd enjoy my privileges."

I squeezed into the bar, shouldering in front of a guy wearing a fedora—probably not part of his costume. "C'mon, I let you hang in my room long enough to fool your coven. Give me something to tell Colton."

She stirred her too-red drink. "That one cute friend of yours still juicing? Bobbi, wasn't it? They around?"

My jaw twitched. I gripped the edge of the bar. "People like you convinced them there were better jobs than juicing."

She sipped her drink. The syrupy liquid trickled from the corner of her smile. "Shame. They were good at it. Takes a certain flare to feign the surprise and fear, as if we hadn't all signed a contract."

A shiver made me flinch. My heartbeat spiked, but I took a deep breath and counted it out, just like my nonhuman therapist had advised last year. The DJ mixed some creepy industrial house with "Thriller."

Clarisse's fingers brushed the back of my hand. "I thought you didn't work much around Halloween."

I twitched away, and she smiled wide enough to show her fangs.

"Relax, Gin." She rested her chin on her fists. "I was hoping another zombie might show up so you'd put on a show. If the zombies come from the south, my coven would like to know." She drained her drink and waved for another.

I straightened. The south? How'd she know that? "You see them on your way from Vegas?"

"See who?"

"A zombie. You said they were coming from the south. That's your territory."

"Did I?" She took her second drink like a shot and sauntered away from the bar.

"Hey!" I snatched at her wrist, but she flinched aside with those vampire reflexes. She hurried onto the edge of the dance floor, but I backed up to the bar. No way was I following her into that crush of people, even if she knew something about the zombies. Or she was just baiting me. She'd been there two years ago and knew this time of year wasn't my best.

Goddamn, I had to toughen up. I couldn't let her take advantage of me like this, or else I'd be a weak spot in Colton's security every year.

I took a deep breath through my nose and stomped my steel-toed boots across the dance floor. She'd already collected two humans, but I hip-checked one guy aside. He eyed my security jacket, then raised his hands and wandered off.

Clarisse rested her forearms on my shoulders and linked her hands behind my head. I didn't flinch this time. "You going to ruin my fun all night?"

I shouted over the bass. "You said the south. Why? What have you seen?"

She leaned closer. "Relax, Gin. We all have our little spies. I haven't seen anything, just heard what you know."

"Why are you telling me this?"

She swayed closer. "Maybe I want to win you over."

I shrugged her off. "Nice try." She probably wasn't wrong. The Vegas vamps had made me an offer before, but not a very serious one. They didn't match what Colton was paying me to stick around, but it didn't mean that wasn't Clarisse's job. Made sense why she kept trying to get into my room. Maybe they'd finally realize the prospect of free sex wasn't working.

She wiggled her fingers in a wave. "Tell Nash I say hello." She stepped back into the crowd and melded among the bodies. I shook my head, but she'd disappeared into the crowd.

Tell Nash—I hadn't said his name, had I? Maybe she'd overheard us talking or—fuck, he was the spy. He had all the information, attended all the briefings, and was the newest hire —right before Halloween.

Anger shot adrenaline through me. No wonder he'd connived to get on door duty with me. Nobody could really be that bad about telling the difference between humans and nonhumans, and I'd fucking fallen for it. Hell, maybe Clarisse had come as a distraction. Nash could have let a weapon into the club, no problem. Crispin would be watching for nonhumans or magic, not a gun.

Colton would flip shit if I messed up again. Goddamn it.

I sprinted toward the door. I shoved among a drunk bachelorette party and slammed past a Superman and a Spider-Man, my frustration rising. As I crashed out the door, Nash turned, sliding into a fighting stance, but my inhuman speed guaranteed I cracked his jaw.

Crispin snarled and angled between me and the line of observers. "Gin!"

Nash slumped against the wall. He shook his head. "What's going—"

I shook him by the front of his shirt. "You're working for her, you asshole!"

"Who?"

Crispin hauled me off by the back of my jacket. "Calm your shit, Gin. We're being watched."

"Good." I spat between Nash's shoes. "This fucker has been working for Vegas."

Nash raised his hands. "I swear, Crispin, I work for Colton, no one else."

"I know, Nash. I know." He shoved me back and pointed inside toward the coat check.

I stomped inside even as my adrenaline burned away. Crispin would to say Clarisse was playing me, and—she probably was. But I needed Colton to see me trying to do my job. If I was right and Nash had let something into the club, someone could die or give Clarisse an opening to more dangerous information.

Crispin followed me to the back corner, where a few chairs were set up behind the coat racks. He rubbed the back of his head. "Nash's good. Colton's sure of it."

I crossed my arms and leaned against the wall. "Well, I'm not."

"No, you let Clarisse get under your skin." He shook his head, a few stray curls falling in front of his eyes. "He needs you to work out whatever's got you scared. And he needed it worked out yesterday."

I stared at my shoes. "I know. I'm trying."

Crispin took off his suit jacket and adjusted his shirt, half untucked from pulling me off Nash. "Listen, you know I won't let anything happen to Colton. I keep a clean house. Clarisse is right; there're a few spies, but I know who they are and keep them where I need them. Nash is clean. Just trust me." He finished tucking his shirt and slung his jacket over his shoulder. "Look, just take the rest of the night off. Don't need you freaking out the guests just because you're frayed."

I started. "Uh, really?" The night crew claimed Crispin was a hardass compared to Caleb Isaac.

He motioned toward the front. "I don't know all that happened to you two years ago, but I don't need a traumatized superhuman out tonight. Just relax and be sharp tomorrow, got it?"

I nodded. "I will, I promise."

He slapped me on the back as he passed. "Goodnight, kid."

I turned away as he joined Nash at the entrance. I'd take the backdoor. Tomorrow, I'd figure out the best way to apologize to Nash.

8

A week before Halloween, Caleb Isaac took Nash and me off door duty. He said some of the guys wanted an extra shift, so we headed downstairs to train with Crispin. I'd trained daily with Crispin for six months when I first arrived, but Nash only had a few lessons, which seemed a bit unfair to him. Taking on a vampire was an entirely new experience, MMA fighter or not. A human fighter's primary weapon wasn't their teeth.

Crispin was shirtless, showing off his death-sculpted body. Colton had turned him over fifty years ago, so his body had lost its human impurities and left him tinged with the etherealness that cloaked most vampires. Shirtless also meant we would be bloody by the end of training. At least, I would be. I rarely landed a touch on him. There was a reason he and Caleb Isaac ran security.

He pointed at me, then at the mat. "Take off whatever you don't want blood on."

I kicked off my shoes, peeled off my socks, and then

stripped to my sports bra. My jeans already had holes along the inner thighs, so they were good as goners anyway.

"I'm coming hard for you so Mr. Neverman can see how capable vampires fight."

"I've watched the training videos," Nash said.

Crispin huffed. I took my stance and mentally braced for the pain. At least it never stuck around long. He and I had learned pretty early in those training sessions that superficial cuts, bruises, and whatnot healed up in a few hours. Broken bones took longer, but not long enough to dissuade him from breaking my arm upon occasion.

Crispin bared his fangs, and I rolled right just as his hand snatched the air where my throat had been. His reflexes were faster than any vampire I'd faced. Colton had once explained that vampire traits were passed through lineage, so I'd come to assume he also must be an excellent fighter when the need arose. I'd yet to see it.

I feinted right again but shoved forward. Crispin either hadn't taken the feint or read my intentions, so my tackle attempt barely clipped his side. His fist shot out and cracked a rib as easily as snapping a twig.

I rolled into the momentum even as the sharp pain speared my side with each breath. I scrambled to my feet and swung around just in time to duck another swipe at my throat. One finger nicked my ear and sliced me open. I went for the tackle again. Close range with a vampire wasn't the usual human's first choice since that meant the fangs got involved, but since my blood made them vomit, it could be used as a weapon. Crispin wouldn't suck any blood during training—those were the rules—but he'd be happy to see me trying the moves he'd suggested to Colton.

I managed to get my arms around his waist and throw him, even as he clawed a line up my back. As we fell, he snapped two jabs into my broken rib. I screamed as pain seized up my body.

Crispin flipped me, straddled my waist, and had his teeth at my neck.

"Game over."

"Damn it!"

Crispin stood and hauled me upright. Blood from my back and ear smeared the mat.

Nash blinked, then pointed at me. "But she has powers. And you beat her in, like, ten seconds."

Crispin adjusted his headband, keeping his curls pinned back. "Correct."

I let Nash stammer as I limped to the mop bucket, an arm pinned against my side. I'd found a video of Nash knocking out an opponent on the first swing so he could end a fight in ten seconds or less, but at least he had the smarts to recognize his own humanity.

"Let's try that again." Colton stood in the shadow of the doorway. He tossed me the brand, which made me drop the mop. Damn it, he must have taken the brand from my rooms. Shithead didn't need to see how far behind I was on laundry. "I think we've been unnecessarily limiting Gin."

Crispin turned toward the weapons rack, then nodded at the brand. "What's that?"

"Literally a piece of metal." Except as I adjusted my grip on the hilt, the end turned cherry red.

Nash backed up. "Oh shit."

Colton motioned to the wet spot on the floor. "Dry that up for them, Nash. Let's see Gin get to work."

Nash hurried to get a towel as I took a few swings with the brand, whistling it through the air. My rib should have hurt like hell, but holding the brand seemed to dull it. I could push the pain aside.

I took a kenjutsu stance that my body still remembered from Crispin's training with the bokken. To be fair, we'd tried weapons before, and other than being a decent shot with any sort of gun, other weapons tangled me up. I didn't even bother to carry a knife when on duty.

Colton motioned Nash to sit with him on one of the couches along the wall. Crispin tilted his head, then slowly circled me. I turned with him.

With a burst of uncanny speed, he swiped for my side. Instinct instructed that I take the blow and strike while he extended past my guard. He ducked under the whistling brand and scored a bloody scratch down my thigh. I grunted as I spun away, trying to build momentum into my next swing. I went for his hip, but he scooted back just in time—the brand's jackalope horns almost scorching his brown skin.

I took a step forward and whipped the brand up for a downward arc. Crispin side-stepped, and I pressed on, advancing as he retreated out of my range. He flashed under my guard just as I drew the brand upward.

The killing blow materialized. All I had to do was stab him with the butt as he tried to claw my waist again.

My elbows drew close as I let the brand slide between my palms, gripping it midway and slamming—

A strong grip pulled me back. I smacked against Colton's chest as he wrapped his arms around me, trapping the brand against me, except it didn't burn.

I squirmed and tried to step on his foot. "Let me go!"

"Take a breath, Gin. You had him. I saw it."

I breathed in his leather and copper smell and blinked away the haze. "Sorry—I was, I wasn't being careful."

Colton reached around and took the cold brand from my hand. "All this means is your instincts were right when you chose this weapon. Might not look like much, but it's your killing machine." He released me, and I bent over. My head pounded, and my hands shook with fight energy. I wanted to go to town on a punching bag or run it off.

Crispin picked blackened skin off the back of his neck. I'd been close enough to scorch him. I wouldn't have been able to stop myself.

I walked over, hand outstretched. "Hey, I'm really sorry. I should have been—"

He knocked aside my hand and pounded me on the back instead. "You actually went for it. Been training you for a year and a half, and you finally went for it."

I grimaced as he touched the long scratches. "I guess, yeah."

"Six days until Halloween," Colton said. "You have time to train her, Crispin?"

"I'll make the time."

"That's what I like to hear." Colton headed for the exit, giving my shoulder a squeeze as he passed. "Now, whip that one into shape"—he pointed back at Nash—"and we'll actually have a team."

9

Saturday morning, I joined Winston and the Food Not Bombs crew in distributing food at Idlewild Park. Vegan breakfast sandwiches, five big pots of chili, and lots of peanut butter sandwiches made up the menu, and I slathered peanut butter as Winston ladled out chili. He'd started bringing me out to volunteer, no matter how hungover or panicky I felt, a few weeks after I went full-time at the casino. He said I needed the sun and human contact.

He wasn't wrong. I recognized many folks from their spots near the casinos or further along Sierra Street. Colton let anyone take a rest outside the casino and even had a special bathroom built just inside the rear entrance for anyone who needed to use it. He wouldn't let the blue-shirt Reno ambassadors harass anyone, either. That earned me plenty of goodwill when volunteering with Winston, even if I had nothing to do with it. My guess from a few hints dropped by Franklin was that the unhoused community represented part of Colton's network, and they informed on everything from cop patrols to what strangers might have come to town.

Winston traded out his empty chili pot for the next full one kept warm on a camp stove. "Things calm down over at the Saints?"

"Other than the general Halloween prep, yeah," I said. Christie and her lab mix, Sandlot, came up, and I handed her two sandwiches, one for her and one for Sandlot. "You need any dog food, Christie? We have a few bags."

She pointed to the cart attached to her bicycle. "Already got one. Thanks for coming out today, Gin. Feel like I haven't seen you in a while." She handed me a folded-up piece of paper—her way of saying thank you. She took thrown-out paperbacks and made eraser poetry.

I smiled as I unfolded it. "I'll hang it on my wall with the others." Judging from the words highlighted against the black pencil, it must've been a romance paperback: *Strong arms ... curl ... a cave ... inside pressed ... the warmth of a winter fire.*

Nobody else waited in line, so I used up the last of the bread to make to-go sandwiches. "Colton wants me to ask around about the zombies. I know you said the other night at The Hideout that this seemed like a one-off, but any chance it wasn't?"

He puffed out his cheeks. "I didn't hear anything about it when I was living in fey-land, but it's not like I'm an authority. In my circles, nobody's worried except for some of the old timers cracking jokes about the Wild Hunt."

"Wait, that's real?"

"Uh, just don't worry about it."

"Great," I muttered. Another addition to the list of bad things that could happen to me.

Winston kept giving me side-eye, so I faced him and crossed my arms.

He winced. "There may be a small—shall we call it a bet? On whether or not you'll drop down dead soon."

"Because?"

"Well, if it was some sort of sign of the Wild Hunt, then you are probably going to die soon."

I groaned and let my head fall back. Winston raised his hands as if I'd pulled a knife on him. "Relax, relax. It could be metaphysical, like the death of your ego or something, and it's not like zombies are *usually* associated with the Wild Hunt. They just *could* be."

I smooshed a sandwich into a plastic bag only to discover a hole in the bottom. "I'd rather not experience any kind of death, thanks."

"The Wild Hunt is a myth, mostly. I wouldn't worry about it. If I thought it was trying to steal your soul, I wouldn't let you out of my sight, okay?" He gave me a side hug as I worked on the next sandwich.

"Yeah, yeah, my big fey protector. Now, if you could just convince Colton I shouldn't work Halloween, I'd be golden."

10

The night before Halloween, Colton held the employee and friends party for all those who walked in the dark (the employee party for the normies happened the week before). Usually, he scheduled it the day after—on All Saints Day, appropriately—but Franklin said something or other about a wedding reception. As usual, we locked down most of the casino that night to finish decorations, cleaning, and catering and let in the nonhuman crews who added the *magical* touches.

As much as I disliked the Halloween fever that reminded me daily how I fell into this world, even I had to admit the Saints looked her best in October. Part of the reason was that time of year, the crispy browns and burnt oranges set against dark trims and copper fixtures felt in the right place. The thick, fake-gilded frames holding prints of artists like Goya, Dali, and Caravaggio mixed in with local weird and surrealist artists added a level of spectacle the other casinos didn't bother with for the season.

A new energy came to the old building as if she enjoyed the preening—sensed her purpose.

Since the fey decorators were still in the Nightmare handling the decorations for the Masquerade, Colton held the party in the private ballroom on the third floor. A wall of windows overlooked the hollow center of the casino, the Haunted House animatronics making the view. Real pumpkins on long vines spread along the walls and stacked in the corners. Dead sunflower bouquets mixed with large pots of mums decorated the tables. Haybales delineated the dance floor. This year's theme was apple picking in both the cute date night way and Eve plucking the fruit, Hera's golden apples, the apples of Idunn, and so on.

Colton caught my eye when I slouched in, hands in my pockets. He tipped his black hat while continuing his conversation with two of the newer employees, Ada and Chris. They'd been shepherded into the Saints' Darkside crew from the hotel hostess crew after walking in on a noise complaint that turned out to be a bloody orgy. It happened sometimes.

I nodded at him, then scanned the crowd, pretending to be looking for someone. Nights like this, I'd prefer to be working security. At least then, I belonged there. Parties hadn't been my thing in college—except for the one time I ended up at the wrong one, also here. Leia and a few other young witches had dressed as a biker gang in leather jackets or vests, helmets, and chaps. I smiled and waved before I could wonder if that was the right response. I'd only seen her at the casino one other time when her mother had a meeting with Colton soon after I officially accepted his offer. Of course, maybe Leia and the coven always came to the Halloween party. I sighed and headed for the bar.

To give all the bartenders a break, everything was self-serve. Half the two hundred people here had probably filled in as a barback at some point, anyway. I pulled out a milk crate and stepped up to reach a third-shelf whiskey. I chose the one with the prettiest label featuring an elk. Usually, I stuck to sneaking well drinks, but if Colton was going to make me come, I was drinking the good stuff whether he liked it or not.

When I turned around, Nash leaned against the bar. "I thought you drank gin and tonic."

I poured two fingers, then offered him the bottle. "I get that a lot."

He nodded, so I poured him a shot. "Then where'd you get the nickname?"

"My real name's Juniper." I raised my glass, then slugged it. Well, good whiskey still burned like lousy whiskey.

He looked at me blankly.

"You know, gin is made with juniper berries, so Colton just started calling me Gin."

"Oh, oh, right." He downed his whiskey. "Makes sense." His face reddened, and I hoped it was the booze, not from embarrassment.

"I had to ask Franklin to explain it when I first started working here," I said. "I wasn't even twenty-one yet, so I wasn't drinking a lot of gin." I left out that the drinking came later.

I circled the bar to lean beside him. "Feeling ready for your first Halloween?"

He reached behind the bar and snagged the tequila. "Crispin still isn't thrilled with me."

I huffed. "He's not happy with any of us unless we are actively saving somebody or stopping a crime."

He poured us each a shot. "I guess you're right. How's it going with your brand weapon—thing."

I added limes to the rims. "Good—well, better than good. I'm an okay fighter, not anything like you, of course. But, like, when I take hold of that brand, it's like I can see the fight better."

He took his shot and sucked on the lime. "I get it. Some moves just feel good. And damn, watching you with Crispin the other night. I knew you were fast, but that was some next-level shit."

"You miss fighting?"

He rolled his neck. "Uh, not really. I feel like I fight a lot here, but it's different. There's a purpose to it other than making rent, you know?"

"That's why most of us stick around. It's weird, it's exciting, and we're making Reno a better place." I tipped back my tequila. "That's what we tell ourselves, anyway."

Someone called Nash's name, and I followed his gaze to a group of the security guys. They yelled for him to bring a round of shots. He lined up a row of glasses. "Wanna join us?"

"I'll swing by later. Waiting for a friend."

Nash ducked his head. "Sure, see ya." He managed to hold the six glasses steady as he passed through the crowd.

I sighed and let my head fall back. Could have made that sound better, even if I was waiting for Kia and Bobbi. That easy way some girls were with guys—I didn't have it unless it was all business and bloody knuckles. There was a reason the Saints suited me better than being a normie at a frat party. If I just hung alone around the bar, I'd look like a drunk, so I meandered toward the ever-present gambling tables to bum with spectators until Kia or Bobbi texted they'd arrived.

Franklin was playing Texas Hold'Em, so I edged in beside the second-floor janitor, a werewolf named Lincoln. We nodded to each other. One of our regulars was dealer, and as he flipped the river, Franklin's last opponent folded.

Franklin smirked as he scooped the pot toward him—a stack of chips Colton handed out as Halloween bonuses. Smart folks cashed them in immediately, but plenty tried their luck against the house tonight.

Franklin stacked his winnings. "Enough for me, friends. I just want to play a friendly game with Miss Juniper."

"Too steep for me, anyway," said the last player to fold, Sarah. "Always learn something when I play with you, Franklin."

A few spectators hung around as I turned my chair and straddled it, my chin resting on the backrest. "You know I suck at poker."

He shuffled. "Then how else will you get better if you don't play?"

"I don't have any chips on me."

He slid me a stack of pink, red, and blue chips. "A friendly game, Juniper."

He flicked over my hole cards so they slid just beneath my fingertips. I peeked—two tens. Okay, maybe I'd survive.

He glanced at his cards and dropped his voice below the party ruckus. "What do you think of Nash?"

I tossed in a pink chip. "Uh, I don't really know him."

Franklin slid in a red chip. "Colton and I make decisions on less."

I called. "That's why you get paid the big bucks."

He dealt the flop: two of clubs, ace of spades, and ten of hearts. "Juniper."

I rocked my chair. "All right, all right. He's nice. He wants to please—do a good job." Now, I needed to figure out how to bet. I hated this part. I bet low.

Franklin smiled as he sipped a Corona. "He's a puppy dog." He raised.

I grimaced as I called. "That's insulting."

"Only if you don't want loyalty."

"If you say so." I side-eyed him. "You ever say that about me?"

He dealt the fourth card—two of hearts. "I called you a stubborn mule once."

"I'll take that over puppy." I pretended to waffle over my bet, then went low again. Sitting with a full house felt good. I'd go high on the last bet and see if he'd fold. That was probably a noob strategy, but this was just for fun—at least, I hoped he'd meant that.

He raised me twice until half the chips he loaned me were in the pot. "Jobs like ours, loyalty comes first. Then you find the smart ones, the clever ones, the ones who can move and shake." He flipped the final card, a five of hearts. He met my gaze. "Is Nash one of those?"

I scooted three black chips into the pot. "I've worked with the guy, like, three times."

He went all in. His chips slumped across the table. "If our lovely friend Clarisse"—he nodded toward the door, and I flinched as she wandered through the crowd—"had decided to slit your throat the other night, he would have been your backup."

I stared at my hand. Who'd invited her? It's not like she wouldn't crash anyway. "Friendly game, my ass." Truth was, Clarisse had gotten in my head. Didn't seem like Nash took it personally. He'd done nothing wrong, and I'd doubted him bad enough to involve Crispin. If Franklin wanted him on the team, I'd take Nash as backup if he'd have me—that was the real question after my screw up.

Franklin settled back in his chair. "You're playing with *my* chips. You have nothing to lose while we could lose everything."

Oh. This was about the Saints. I had a decent hand—worth betting on, even if neither of us would fold. I couldn't, now.

Franklin would have some moral to this whole story, but he wanted me to get the point on my own. Besides, it cost me nothing to go big. Cost me nothing to quit, either.

I swept my chips into the pile. "You know I'm all in." I cringed a little. It had sounded cool the second before I said it.

"That's what I like to hear, Juniper. I'll be out of chips before you know it."

Without showing his cards, he left the table and a couple thousand in chips. At least I passed his test, or he would have started moralizing over his Corona. Franklin had dropped hints like these before, but tonight, he'd come right out and said that he and Colton were betting on me. Shit. Hopefully, Franklin didn't have a foot in the grave and wasn't telling anyone.

I brushed back my hair. No reason to ruin the night speculating. Probably, he just wanted me to keep it serious over Halloween—no more screw-ups.

He'd left too many chips for my pockets, and I didn't really need the cash, anyway. Kia and Bobbi hadn't arrived yet, so I snagged a box from behind the bar. A few other groups had broken out into games, but I had to be careful dropping off a few thousand. Some folks resented Colton taking me in so fast, and others wanted to have his ear through me. The extra cash could hurt me or help me.

Ah, perfect. The security guys were just dealing a game. About everyone was there except Crispin and two others from the night crew, who were probably on shift right now. I walked over just as Caleb Isaac texted me to join them—*that's an order*.

I dropped the box in the middle of the table.

Caleb Isaac spoke around his cigar: "Goddamn, you've had a lucky night."

I lounged in a chair beside Nash. "How about you consider it a thank you for putting up with us knuckleheads." I nudged Nash.

"Shit yeah," Jaxson said as he divvied up the chips.

Caleb Isaac narrowed his eyes at me while smiling around his cigar. "All right, kid. Let's see how much of it you win back."

I played hard and fast, choosing to drink rather than win, not that I would have anyway. Most of these guys had grown up around casinos. Other than Jaxson, I was definitely the worst at the table, and he might get better if he wouldn't let the guys bait him. When Kia finally texted she'd arrived, I folded and tucked my last two black chips in my back pocket. The guys joked I was saving face, letting them off easy, better get more chips, but I knew from the laughs I'd definitely won a few points tonight.

Kia waited by the door, already surrounded by well-wishers. She still used a crutch but had spray-painted it black and stuck bats and pumpkins along the metal. Like many other guests, she wore red, a long slinky dress that I guessed would contrast with her outfit for tomorrow night, which usually went full Halloween slutty.

She hugged me. "I'm so glad you're here!"

"Yeah, well, Colton made me."

"C'mon! You're having fun."

Maybe the booze had loosened me up, but I grinned. "Yeah, I guess."

She handed me her crutch and leaned on my arm instead. "To the bar!"

We limped forward, Kia leaning on me harder than I expected. "Wait a sec." I rested her crutch against a table. "Milady." I scooped her up and sauntered toward the bar, snatching her crutch along the way. Kia was as tall as me, so it looked a little ridiculous, but it made Kia laugh and made me feel like less of a failure.

I settled her on a barstool. "What will you have?" I swung

behind the bar, but one of our regulars, an actual bartender from Death and Taxes, elbowed me aside.

"First one's on me, Kia," Peter said. "The usual?"

"Aww, Petey, thanks."

"So, how're you feeling?"

That's all Kia needed to launch into the gory details. I shifted from the bar and settled on a stool behind her as more folks gathered. Most of the staff had heard the story, but the party included a dozen or so of our regulars who knew what the casino was really about. Those folks hadn't seen Kia since she'd been off her regular shifts. Other staff offered to get her food, drinks, and a more comfortable chair—they even carried over one of the craps tables.

All evening, Colton and Franklin made rounds, but both joined Kia's court to toast her.

Franklin handed out shots of top-shelf tequila as Colton raised his glass. "To Kia, the one-and-only survivor of the Saints Zombie Apocalypse—may there never be another one!"

I clinked glasses with Trish, a former employee who now ran her own cleaning business.

Colton caught my eye and gave me a nod. I took it as approval for taking control of my fuckup by helping Kia, which I would have done whether it was my fault or not.

Bobbi and Winston finally strolled in, with Winston hiding something behind his broad back. Bobbi wore a mechanic's coveralls, complete with a tool belt, the loops and pockets filled with beer, liquor, and weed. Winston hadn't dressed up except for his usual bright makeup—orange eye shadow and lipstick.

Bobbi elbowed apart the dozen or so people who'd gathered around Kia. "Sorry we're late, babe. 3D printing always takes longer than I think." They motioned to Winston, who removed a set of crutches from behind his back.

Kia gasped. "Oh my god, I love them!"

The crutches, matte black, curved from leather-padded underarm rests into elegant devil's legs, complete with rubber-bottomed split hooves. Scaley wings rippled from the back of the crutch where the design couldn't hinder Kia. For a second, the wings seemed to flicker with sparks. I blinked and focused past the boozy blur. The silver glow of fey magic outlined the crutches. Winston must have enchanted them or asked one of his fey friends to do the trick.

I checked my phone—one in the morning. I felt the good kind of boozy, where a few tacos would bring me right back down and off to bed. If I stayed at the party, I'd get way too smashed. I used the distraction of Kia's gift to slip away and work the edge of the crowd to the door. Tomorrow would suck in all kinds of ways, but at least I could hold onto this memory. Maybe I should have come last year instead of holing up in my room.

I shouldered through the door right into Clarisse's arms.

"Leaving so soon?"

Her cherry-copper smell sent me into a panic, adrenaline pumping through my body. I slapped aside her touch and side-stepped, fists snapped into place, ready for a fight.

She tilted her head, one fang slipping over her bottom lip. "You didn't even hit the dance floor."

I relaxed my shoulders and lowered my fists to my sides, but I couldn't unclench them or risk showing their trembling. "Because I knew you were there."

She stepped closer, and her right hand brushed my fist. "I terrify you that much."

"No. I *dislike* you that much." I mean, yes, she did terrify me that much. Clarisse embodied everything I feared about vampires—ultra sexy, and they thought every human was a blood bag. Colton didn't keep that kind of vampire around long, but they came clubbing. The thing was, those types of vampires always ignored me once they learned my blood was a no-go. Except Clarisse.

"What do you want tonight?" I asked.

She motioned to the door. "Plus one status. I've already been politely invited to visit other parts of the casino."

I shoulder-checked past her. "Then I'll be doing my duty by saying no."

She caught my collar and jerked me back, shoving me against the wall. Her hips pressed against mine. "I'll make it worth your while." She winked. "Promise."

"Stop it!" I pushed her just as the doors opened.

Colton strode into the hall, his long coat swirling around his cowboy boots. "Clarisse." He snarled her name in a way that didn't entirely sound like a word. He pressed forward, his presence filling the hall as he placed himself between us. He spat out something else in what I guessed was Vampiric, and Clarisse lowered her head, almost submissive. She backed away, then hurried around the corner.

Colton tipped back his hat. "Have to hand it to her; she doesn't quit."

I wondered if that's the type of right-hand person he wanted, willing to break any rule—go to any lengths. I might never be as steady as Clarisse or willing to cross a vampire like Colton. If our roles were reversed, I wouldn't be doing shit in front of the matriarch of the Vegas vampires.

I stuck my hands in my back pockets to hide the shakes. I had to be better than this or risk more friends getting caught in the middle. "What did you say to her?"

"I reminded her I'd already made it clear once tonight that she was not welcome here."

"Well, thanks. She wasn't taking my no for an answer."

"Outlaws usually don't. She's just like her mother, trying to take what she can't have." He gripped my shoulder. "You did good in there, Gin."

I dipped my head but couldn't help smiling. "And I'll show up again tomorrow." I didn't add, *even if that meant puking in the bathroom.*

"I know you will. You've put in the work these past two weeks. The others have said so."

I nodded. "I won't let them down again. I promise."

He chuckled. "Don't get too noble on me, now." He pulled open the doors and stood framed in the party's golden light. "See you at sunset."

11

I came in with the rest of the night staff around seven and checked the schedule posted outside Colton's office. The crack under the door showed no light, so I didn't bother knocking.

He'd assigned me to work the Nightmare. Exactly where I'd been two years ago. Goddamn it.

I branded his door. *Try buffing that out.*

In my hands, it had only felt like a weapon, and I hadn't thought to use the brand as it was originally intended. For the first time, its design became clear: a jackalope, the hare's face in profile with large ears and extra-long antlers that could take someone's eye out easily enough. Maybe I could even poison the tips.

I tucked the brand into a sheath sewn inside my jacket. Sitting iron-rod straight had a new meaning, but it was the only slightly inconspicuous idea I could manage. Hopefully, the brand would be a deterrent. Not that I could threaten Clarisse on a club floor with a molten piece of iron. That's definitely not what Colton intended.

The sun had just set when I joined Franklin at the club entrance. Nonhumans already filtered into the club-turned-ballroom through the fey magic Colton hired to be cast each year. The magic's stale popcorn smell still clung to the air, though braziers dangling from nothing spread pine and woodsmoke scents through the room.

My stomach tightened as the smells and atmosphere stirred up my memories, and I flexed my shoulders, loosening the tightness. The long brand rubbed my spine, reassuring me. Costumes ranged from vintage Victorian to messy playboy. Even so, the fey, elves, weres, and others still honored the vampires tonight with plastic fangs and sunglasses or colored contacts. It was a masquerade LARP, after all.

Most of the humans milling the floor before the doors opened were Colton's employees. My all-too-human friends Bobbi and Kia took shots at the bar, Kia's crutches leaning between them. I ducked away. They loved Halloween for this party, but I couldn't fake my way through their enthusiasm.

I eased between the tall double doors, magically engrained with silver. Franklin stood behind a black podium, coffin-elegant in an ancient tux with tails and a top hat. He wore the costume every year and called it "looking his age."

"Dashing, as always." I picked up the clipboard of waivers for all the humans, knowingly or not, coming to have their blood drained. A shiver ran up my arm, and I looked away. It hadn't changed since I signed it two years ago. Franklin said it was mostly so the casino could threaten legal action if somebody, like I did, experienced something real bad—as if anyone waiting to go party at the notorious Nightmare bothered to read it (and plenty weren't sober enough to understand it).

Franklin eyed me up and down. "Colton had a feeling you might not dress for the festivities." He pulled a large black bag and box from behind the podium and handed them to me. "Before you say no, at least take a look."

I sighed and made a show of stomping to the restroom but cast a grin over my shoulder.

Black tissue paper wrapped a knee-length black coat with silver hooks down the front. White fur lined the collar, a bright shock against the cotton drawing the eyes up the silver hooks to my face. I shrugged off my leather jacket. The coat covered my regular clothes and matched my combat boots in a sort of apocalyptic Western look. I felt bigger inside it, somehow, like I took up more space in the room. A soft leather sheath hung from the waist, and I belted in the brand. A silver-lined handkerchief like Colton often wore around his neck was also in the bag, next to a velvet box.

I popped the lid on the box and grinned. A fedora, the brim decorated with a pair of silver antlers. Underneath, a mask featured a stylized rabbit face that opted for intense rather than cute—a jackalope when paired with the antlers.

I tied it in place and faced the mirror. The effect made me sigh. For once, I didn't look like the half-human who accidentally stumbled into the life of a vampire's bouncer. I looked...*otherly*.

I couldn't help the sway in my hips as I passed the growing line of humans. I tied the handkerchief bandit-style around my neck.

Franklin let out a low whistle and dipped his head. "Señora."

I pressed a hand to the wooden doors and swept my arm toward the growing line. "Shall we?"

Colton relieved me from duty at check-in, wearing his cowboy getup—all black leather, silver-lined, his long coat brushing the tops of his worn but shining boots. He topped off the outfit with a coyote mask, the trickster of the desert, an appropriate facade. The council convened in two hours, but he always made an appearance at the LARP first. When he offered his arm, I wanted to vomit.

"You will be safe with me," he said.

He was right, of course. Nobody would dare mess with me tonight, even if they thought I was just some normie, but his fangs had left that scar on my wrist from our first Halloween encounter when he confirmed my blood was undrinkable. Two years later, I still felt unprepared to face what lived in the dark. Still, I took his arm. Maybe that was the difference—now we were on the same side rather than me being on the menu. Tonight was probably going to suck, but whatever happened, I had Colton's protection, and, walking in together, he was going to make sure everyone knew it. I had made my choice. Time to face it.

He pulled his coyote mask into place, and we entered the party.

While I'd glanced in before the party started, entering now that it was in full swing transformed the scene. As if growing stronger with the night, the magic tasted rich as honey butter. A musky iron scent waited underneath like a fine grit. Nonhumans dripping enticement and enchantment strutted through the humans, who were drunk or high or so thoroughly seduced they might as well be. Colton had named the theme animal fable, so waiters swayed through the crowd dressed as maenads, leopard print barely keeping them decent. The nonhumans glittered in their masks, usually predator animals—eagles, wolves, lions, tigers. I wasn't so sure about my jackalope mask with so many predators about. At least I had horns.

Most recognized Colton in his signature look, but their stares pried at my mask. Colton never introduced me as we worked the crowd, which was fine by me, but he always kept his body wedged between me and his admirers. Steadily, he circled the room toward the dance floor. An elven DJ dropped enchanted bass that had the bodies pretty much screwing while standing. I could not fully imagine Colton grinding on anyone, let alone me, so I assumed we would cut to the bar, but he paused at the stumbling edges of the dance floor, and his mask brushed against my ear.

"Shall we?"

He spread an arm toward the dance floor, and the music shifted to a slow, soft "Moonlight Serenade." A favorite song of his, he played it on the rare rainy days when I'd walk in on him swaying, thumbing through a Pablo Neruda or Langston Hughes collection.

And fear struck me stiff as the brand belted to my side. "I-I can't dance. *You* can't dance with me." That kind of gesture meant something to vampires—not the kind of attention I wanted tonight. And I didn't need anything fanning the flames of my crush at a time like this.

He tilted his head. "I dance with whomever I please. If you'll have me." Beneath the mask, I imagined him smirking, showing one fang.

My phone buzzed in my pocket, three quick texts. Probably from Kia gossiping about whoever Colton was about to dance with—she always teased me about my crush on him. If she knew, she'd be squee-ing for me to do it.

I dipped my head. "All right. I warned you, though—no rhythm."

He took my hand and led me onto the dance floor. I let

him ease me into a slow sway. What had moments ago been a dancefloor mired in sweat and sex became stately. Colton might not be the king of the vampires, but in the Saints, he was.

And we were really, really close. The scent of blood lingered beneath the usual warm note of leather. He must've... eaten before he came down. My wrist twinged, and I swallowed down the nervous nausea.

He dipped his head close, our foreheads almost touching. "It occurs to me—through Franklin, I must admit—that these past two years have been very much about navigating the horrors of living on my side of the night but none of the pleasures."

"Are you offering me a good time?" I almost ran from embarrassment as soon as I said it, but Colton chuckled. "Rather—rather than, uh...bumps and bruises and sweating in the training room?" I cringed and prayed to whatever was in my blood that the handkerchief and mask hid the heat pulsing up my neck.

"Exactly what I meant."

"Don't get all 'milady' on me."

"Would you prefer something more modern?"

He raised a hand and snapped his fingers. The bass spiraled in and crushed the slow lilt of Glenn Miller and his Orchestra.

I pulled back as other bodies shifted closer. Something was up. Colton never acted like this with me or any nonvampire. At other meetings, I'd seen vampires act like they could drink or fuck as much as they liked, but that wasn't Colton, at least not publicly.

Colton stood at the head of the throng, one hand extended, inviting me.

"What is this?" I shook my head, wishing I could see better

through the mask. "You never come to your own clubs, let alone dance. Everyone knows it."

He took my hand, his fingertips brushing over his blood-sucking scar on my wrist. "Everyone? I've been around a long time." He turned away, and the bodies parted before closing back around him as he entered the dance.

I let out a long breath, pushing against the mask. What the hell was that? Instinct said he was down to...do something. My dangerous little crush buzzed around in my chest, ready to sting.

I pulled my hat low and tucked my chin into the handkerchief, weaving toward the bar. Kia and Bobbi were back (or had never left), and Kia must have caught sight of my mask because she whispered to Bobbi while she kept side-eyeing me.

I hurried over, tugging down the mask. "It's me, just me."

Kia clutched her phone to her chest. "*You* were dancing with Colton?"

"Don't want to talk about it."

Bobbi leaned against the bar, boxing me in. They looked dashing in crimson velvet, emphasizing their blue-black hair. They pushed their Manhattan toward me. "Drink up and tell all."

"He just got me this." I waved my hand at my getup. "And he said he wanted to dance." I took a big swallow and closed my eyes as the Manhattan burned my throat. "I can't think about this now. We are meeting with the council later, which you didn't hear from me."

Kia raised her phone and dragged me in for a selfie. "Everyone knows about the council, hon." She plucked at my silver-lined sleeve. "I have a feeling this was his apology. Or he likes his ladies in leather."

I huddled over the drink. "Kia, stop. I don't want to think about it."

Bobbi propped their elbows on the bar. "Look at it this way. You got to dance with a badass vampire while everyone watched." They nudged me. "Not bad for a human girl."

"Half-human," Kia and I said in unison, though it sounded like a curse from me and a wish from her.

Bobbi straightened, their contact-red gaze looking over my shoulder. "I sense an audition."

"Chip a tooth," Kia said as Bobbi sauntered past, joining two vampires at the corner of the bar, though only one had real fangs. The other had an enamel juicer pin—a Bugs-Bunny-style carrot—pinned to her lapel. I let out a short breath. The vampire was most likely going to follow the rules. Bobbi had started as a juicer, but after I told them a few horror stories, they accepted a better job I had weaseled Franklin into offering. College students sell plasma; other college students sell their veins.

I swirled the Manhattan. When I'd first learned about what lived in the dark, Bobbi and Kia gave me the grand tour of the Saints' lifestyle, at least until I mastered the basics. Both had stumbled onto the Saints because too much weird shit happened for it to be the average casino if you paid attention. Bobbi had been working there for five years, straight out of trade school. Kia had known Bobbi from around town, and they got her a convenience store manager position four years ago. They both probably still knew more than me about the Saints, but, of course, Colton's favor had gone to my head. I acted like I knew all the dangers and said they should work at a safe, human-run casino. It about broke our friendship, and I learned to shut it unless I was really high or really drunk. Ultimately, we stopped partying together for the most part. Truth was, they'd accepted the dangers as part of the job while I almost couldn't handle the idea of working Halloween. The danger was worth it to them for the chance to be near the otherworldly while I wished they'd play it safe.

Kia ordered a Stranger Thing, code for cranberry juice and Sprite. "You know, Colton gave you a fun pass for the night. After seeing you on his arm, probably half this room wants to fuck you."

I glanced over my shoulder, and all the stares made my spine crawl. Yet another sensation to add to the distant thrum at the base of my skull. At least the southern itch didn't signal any zombie trouble tonight.

"Too bad it still feels like reliving a nightmare." It didn't help that the normie college students stood out in their Wal-Mart masks and thrift store gowns or suits if they even bothered to dress up. Yeah, the rules stated that vampires and other nonhumans couldn't cause permanent damage, but that didn't mean the normies had any idea they were attending anything other than a Halloween party with high-end decorations. The response always was "getting a little blood drawn never hurt anyone." Bobbi and Kia said they enjoyed even those types of festivities, but it still made me queasy. At least they knew what manner of party they were signing up for.

Kia nodded over her shoulder at the crowd. "C'mon, he's not going to let anything happen to you."

I sighed. "But all this—it's just not for me. Like, who doesn't want to hang around with sexy vampires. Me, apparently." I swung around on my barstool and leaned against the counter.

The party spread like a gothic painting, orange and red lights turning it fiendish. For a second, I thought I glimpsed a familiar face sinking into the crowd: my old college roommate. Except, Leia wouldn't have been caught dead with vampires on Halloween night because she knew better. She was a witch and had tried to convince me to stay in the dorm and study with her two years ago, but I didn't know how to listen.

This was not the life the girl fleeing a trailer on the edge of the desert to major in business and history had planned. This was the life Colton wanted me to want, though why I was wrapped up in his desire was another question. Sure, the Saints felt more like family than what I had growing up, but I still couldn't figure out what made me catch Colton's eye. A two-hundred-year-old vampire didn't need a quarter-life crisis dragging him down. I'd rather be one of the staff than be responsible for making sure they didn't get bit.

Across the bar, an elf bought Kia a drink, and she wandered off, hanging on his arm, her left leg supported by one of the fiendish crutches Winston and Bobbi had crafted. I turned my back on the party and stared into my drink.

Time passed in different bass rythms and with the feeling of too many eyes settling on me. Eventually, my phone buzzed. Just a simple message from Colton at 11:55 p.m.,

It's time. Upstairs.

I thanked the bartender, Bill. He wished me luck, nodding at the council room. Apparently, Kia was right, and everyone did know about the council.

A catwalk strung four yards overhead. I stared at it and visualized landing with my long coat snapping like a true badass. *Fuck it.* And I leaped

Intention had been Colton's first lesson. He had a hunch I could do more than an average human but wouldn't get far as long as I believed my blood was useless aside from taking me off the vampire snack menu.

Apparently, my intention was too strong because I overshot, grabbed the other railing, and had to haul myself back onto the catwalk.

A few people still pointed as I straightened my hat and mask —one more story to add to the Nightmare's reputation. I melded into the shadows, and the throng spread before me. I gripped the railing, my chest tight. Vampires sucked blood in the open while others watched. Fey played tricks, making humans, weres, or halfbloods think they were animals—pawing and squawking. The more aggressive packs and clans of nonhumans chose mates for the night and marked them. Even though it was against club rules, little groups of fey created dark spots—which my blood allowed me to see into—where anything could fuck anyone anyhow, for a price. Of course, anyone could also watch through the dark for another price. I texted the dark spot locations to Caleb Isaac and Crispin, though Colton would have told me to leave it.

The more usual club troubles happened steadily: drugs traded, drinks magicked, bodies touched without consent. All beneath several veneers. For the humans, it was a roleplaying event where, for an exorbitant price, some guy in a vampire costume might pretend to bite them—until it was too late and the very real fangs were in their necks. For humans living on the Darkside, they got to party with most of the nonhuman high rollers from here to Vegas. For the vampires and others, it was an opportunity to pretend we were all just animals in a variety of stories, some good, some bad, some food.

I only sensed Colton behind me by the smell of his leather, turned musky by horse sweat. He'd been outside, riding, in the past hour. He hadn't stayed to dance after all. I glanced over my shoulder, eyebrows raised.

Sweat gleamed on his dark skin, and he dabbed his forehead with a faded handkerchief. "It's different up here, isn't it? When you stand on that floor, it swirls around you, but up here, you see how shallow it is, how broken by time."

I rubbed my thumb over my scarred wrist. "Just looks ugly to me." Most of the other Saints employees looked forward to tonight because they enjoyed the fantasy, but I couldn't see past the normie college kids in their plastic masks flirting with literal monsters.

"You are standing in the middle of your young life, just like you stood on the dance floor earlier. In a few years—decades—you will outgrow humanity and start to see the paths that brought you here and the paths others will take."

I narrowed my eyes. Colton had a philosophical spin occasionally, but why now, right before a council meeting? Why had he been on a horse? "Are you suggesting you know my path?"

"I once thought so."

He ghosted past me toward the observation room, the two-way glass, mirrorlike, distorting the party below into funhouse horror.

He held the door for me.

A long table split the room. Since the occupants weren't human, only chilled bottles of blood were set at intervals. Two vampires watched at the window, one dressed in a fur-ruffed cape with a wolf mask, the other masked by a hooded cobra. A zoo spread around the seats, and nobody removed their masks, though I assumed they knew each other. The most important vampires west of the Rockies sat in high-backed chairs in simple masks and basic, though expensive, suits. Their seconds, positioned behind the chairs, brought the flair. A woman was dressed in an actual tiger's pelt, and a man donned almost a full peacock tail. Living snakes clothed another vampire, twisting over their face for a mask. I recognized Clarisse behind her mother, mostly foregoing the animal theme for a lacy black party dress and playboy bunny ears.

I gingerly stepped behind Colton's chair. I'd attended various meetings before, but not *the* meeting.

With the music silenced and my senses heightened by the quiet—dead bodies are near silent—the southern itch seemed stronger. More than an itch, a pressure like a marble had been buried at the base of my neck. I didn't dare move to touch the spot.

Colton opened the meeting with some sort of Vampiric chant while the others bowed their heads. This was also new—usually, the meetings were in full chatter mode before Colton entered. Of course, I couldn't understand a word. Part of becoming a vampire meant learning the sacred Vampiric language, supposedly more complicated than any human or nonhuman tongue. A nonvampire could never become fluent because of something about not needing to breathe. Colton had explained it, but as I had zero interest in learning Vampiric, I blanked it out.

Now, I wish I hadn't. Colton's chant ended, and other voices leaped into the silence. Something felt wrong, like walking into a friend's house when their parents were arguing. I scanned the room, but the masks kept facial cues nonexistent, and a vampire could hold stiller than a deer in headlights. The language droned on, steady as a bad wind. Listening made me way too conscious of my bodily need to breathe.

Clarisse's mask consisted of a stripe of makeup across her eyes, so I watched her face as she watched her blood mother, the woman who turned her and matriarch of the Vegas vampires.

Across the table, the lion mask's voice snapped like a whip, and Clarisse's eyes darted to mine, then down to Colton.

His shoulders had hunched, and his neck was strained, the muscles defined against his collar. This type of anger I'd only seen reserved for people who mistreated his staff.

The spot at the base of my neck throbbed until my head ached. I broke protocol and rubbed the back of my neck with a sense of surprise when I did not touch a goose egg. Colton glanced back when I moved.

He grinned, his fangs grazing his bottom lip, then stood hard enough that the chair legs screeched along the floor.

The vampires flinched.

"Why don't we ask her, eh?" He spun the chair toward me. "Join us, Gin. Have a seat."

My stomach clenched, and a hard throb at the back of my skull made me sway. Colton took the moment to step on my foot and shove me into the chair.

Through the shadowed masks, eyes glinted. Colton crouched, which was somehow creepier than if he had stood over me.

Their windy language rose to a roar, and several vampires stood. The sudden movement felt jarring after the coffin stillness.

My chest started heaving, but Colton's voice rattled in my head. *Control your breathing, control your fear.* I counted my breaths until I could stare at the lion mask across the table. Two years ago, I'd been drunk and surrounded by vampires ready to drain my blood. At least this time, I wasn't a meal.

Didn't mean I couldn't be dead in an hour.

Colton hitched his thumb at the group. "These cowboys here think you got something else under that skin. They think I've taken too much of an interest in you, our dangerous little mystery."

The brand pressed against my hip as I leaned into the chair. Part of my brain begged for it all to stop, just like that night. Had anything really changed? I'd chosen to be here, and I'd even been happy about it at first. What millennial wouldn't want to step through the wardrobe or into Goblin City? Platform 9¾? But on days like this, I just wanted to be a senior in college, studying something safe—like economics.

Beneath the table, Colton squeezed my knee. "They

already voted, Gin. If I don't follow their unanimous decision to turn over your wardship, I lose my position at this table."

Something about his touch, his switch to English, made me pause. He'd already made a choice, though. He gave me his seat and made it clear that he didn't want to follow their order. I offered him a slight nod.

I shifted my gaze to those still seated around the table, repeating four simple words in my mind several times before my mouth finally moved, "Why do I matter?"

The lion mask slouched in his chair and rested his chin on his fist. "Everyone matters." His sandpaper voice fit his choice of animal.

I narrowed my eyes. "But you're afraid of Colton"—their wind-words rose and creaked through the room—"so, my...my wardship must mean something." I'd have to ask Colton what this ward bullshit was about later. There was a reason I'd picked a college eight hours away from my parents.

The lion mask shrugged one shoulder. "We can't drink your blood. Very few other creatures share such a trait. Mostly gods and fey."

I dragged my gaze along the rest of the table. "I'm not a vampire, so I don't see why I should listen to you."

Several vampires tittered like chirping birds.

Clarisse's mother was one of them, the sound almost metallic. "You misunderstand the order of things. In human terms, we are the one percent. Your face isn't even on a milk carton." She swiveled in her chair, motioning to Clarisse and saying something in Vampiric.

Other vampires shifted toward us, and their seconds edged toward the door.

As Clarisse lunged around the table, Colton threw the chair—with me in it—through the window.

12

Falling a couple stories into a magically-decorated club was the worst sort of rollercoaster, one of the pitch-dark ones with an unexpected drop. Even though I'd tensed for something to happen...Well, I knew vampires were strong, but not *that* strong.

I flailed out of the chair, kicking it away just before I crashed into the concrete floor of the club. I rolled on my shoulder and tried to stand but cracked my spine falling down again. I couldn't breathe and wheezed like the dying. Colton dropped beside me, an elegant shadow that would have the crowd believing in Halloween magic.

The vampires throwing themselves through the window looked less graceful and much more feral. They clawed over the shattered glass, most likely desperate to claim Colton's head—and mine.

Colton hauled me to my feet, and I screamed as the bones in my shoulder popped. He shoved me forward, and. I only just kept my feet under me, sliding in spilled wine. Well, red stuff).

He dragged me by the wrist as the crowd parted. The

messed-up humans probably thought the vampire's wind-roaring was just part of the LARP, but anybody nonhuman cast their bets either by shifting from Colton's path or slowing us down.

The first person who tried to stop us—some snot-nosed baby vampire that might have been turned that weekend—got his throat ripped out by Colton's fangs.

I leaned back as he tried to haul me through the gore. "What is this!?"

Shadows stalked through the crowd, tall and unmasked. One pulled a pistol from under his suit jacket.

Colton spun around and sliced the brand from the leather sheath. He shoved it into my hands. "I'm not letting them take you! Either keep up, or you'll be another body on the floor."

I squeaked something, but Colton ripped me aside by my collar, swiping through the throat of a fey about to slide a dagger between my ribs.

The young vampire's body still pooled cold blood at my feet. I gritted my teeth, stepped over the body, and leaned into my first swing.

The brand flashed cherry and gouged a charcoal hole in a vampire's throat. He clutched at the ashy skin.

I visualized finishing him by plunging the glowing red end into his wet mouth, the teeth still stained bloody from the night's *festivities*, but my arms trembled. Sure, I'd killed things for Colton—cursed coyotes, rabid deer, talking raccoons. I'd beaten up swindlers and gamblers and tech bros. I'd gone after warlocks or fey who tried to charm Colton's employees. I had blood on my hands.

But burning someone's eyes out?

When the vampire stopped pawing his throat and raised a gun, I reacted. I swung the brand like a baseball bat and *thunked* the jackalope horns into his brain.

Going in was easy, the skull crackling beneath my adrenaline-strong swing. But wrenching the horns out, the smell of burning brain thick as charred meat, the pulpy snap of bone—my stomach churned.

My hand dropped to my side, the dangling brand scraping sparks against the floor.

Colton slammed into my back, and I stumbled forward as a vampire pushed us. I braced against the brand and levered Colton as he grappled. As soon as Colton's weight lifted off my back, I twirled the brand and stabbed behind me, and the metal dug into meat.

A scream was silenced by a gurgle. Colton whipped around, skin stuck in his teeth and blood dripping down his chin. "Good."

He shoved me into a run, straight at a trio of vampires from the meeting, Clarisse included.

Colton yelled as he rammed into the trio.

Clarisse shot him three times before he tackled her, ripping open the side of her face with one clawed hand. As another vampire swung for his back, I chopped at his arm with a massive overhand swing. The forge-hot horns sliced to the bone.

The third vampire sunk fangs into my already shredded shoulder but immediately threw his head back, spitting. Before he could tear me open, Colton stuck a hand through his throat.

He ripped out a fistful of flesh. "Go, Gin!"

I stumbled over the bodies as Clarisse curled in on herself, clutching her ruined face.

13

A four-wheel-drive truck with a horse trailer attached waited outside the casino. Franklin waltzed around the front and tossed the keys to the sprinting Colton. He saluted two fingers at me as if murdering our way out of a club was the norm. Maybe it was now.

Colton cruised through Reno, edging past the speed limit. It's not like it mattered. He'd just convince a cop to release us with his old vampire ways and the right look.

He merged onto 395 toward Carson City, and I watched the casino lights grow smaller.

"Where are we going?"

"South."

"After...after the zombie things?"

"Of course." He reached across me, and I flinched. He pulled a bag of jerky from the glove box and tossed it onto my lap. "You used a lot of energy. Eat something."

I thumped my head twice against the headrest. "I've done a lot of shit I didn't like for you. But I killed people back there."

"They were neither people nor alive. You just ended their existence."

My chest ached, and I breathed through my teeth, trying to control the shakes. Putting my brand through their head certainly wasn't making them more alive. My hands quaked, and my legs felt like deadweight dangling over the seat. I couldn't stand, let alone run if I had to.

Colton glanced at me. "You are going into shock. You've felt these symptoms before. Work through it and relax."

The suggestion to relax rang through me, and I acted like the scared human I was. Fuck whatever was in my blood because it didn't stop me from being afraid. "I can't *ever* relax! You took that away from me two years ago! I was doing good. Got out of the trailer park, had a couple jobs, and was paying my way through college. Then I went to some party, and you showed up! Yeah, I know you thought you offered me a choice. But after some twenty-year-old kid learns that vampires and all these other monsters are real, plus you offer more money than her parents make in five years, what did you think would happen? It wasn't a choice, Colton! You bought me to add to your collection. Another oddity for your casino. Apparently, it was a good investment because now all the other vampires want a piece of me! That's what you're good at, assessing people's value and taking it—whether it's money or their body or a skill—and then you sell it off."

My breath came in gasps when I finally shut up. Already, I regretted showing my hand and all the frustration I held close.

By then, we'd turned onto Route 50, heading east. Federal land stretched on both sides, silvered by the full moon. No headlights bobbed in either direction.

Colton stopped on the side of the road and turned off the truck. "If you were human, I would have made you fall asleep as soon as you sat down. If you were one of my kind, I would have fed you blood to make you stronger and reassure you we are in this fight together. With you, I can't do either." He rapped the driver's side window. "If you go ten, twenty miles south, you'll enter wild horse territory. The horses will help you get wherever you want, and if you can pass beyond the Rockies, you should be all right as long as you lay low. Or you can stay with me and search for the origin of whatever attacked the club. Either choice is, most likely, as dangerous as the other."

I propped my feet on the dash and hugged my knees. Stripped down, the choice was to trust Colton or not. A similar offer to when we met.

I rested my chin on my knees. "Can I get the truth on something?"

He rolled his shoulders, staring out the windshield. I took that as a yes.

"Why me? You're a powerful vampire, and I'm twenty-two-year-old white trash from rural Nevada with nothing to my name. I've got nothing to offer you."

He smiled, his fangs catching the moonlight. "That's an easy answer, Gin. You're a mystery." He twisted in his seat, facing me. "I thought I knew the ins and outs of this world. You reminded me of what it felt like when I first learned about what walked in the dark—when I found the vampire that turned me hiding deep down in a silver mine. And you helped me remember what it all felt like when it was new and strange. I want you to have a better time of it than I did."

He turned on the truck, though he left it in park. "Do I wish you were a hundred years older, could stop thinking like a human, and would actually listen to what I say instead of thinking you know best? Of course. But you will grow into all those attributes. Time means very little to me, so I'm willing to wait. For you."

Part of my brain poked holes through his pretty words, pointing out how he was still just using me. But wasn't he describing the first step of friendship, trying to help and wishing the best for another person...er, being?

I opened the bag of jerky and gnawed on a strip. Colton dipped his head, and we hit the road.

Part Two
Roughing It

"[*Anatomy of the Nevada Test Site* leaves] much of the history of the region untold, but even so, [it] clearly reveal[s] a startling, simple fact: the place that hosted the United States atomic testing program was a rich and complicated environment home to a remarkable assortment of life and a diverse group of human inhabitants who valued this landscape and knew it as home." – *Doomtowns: The People and Landscapes of Atomic Testing*

14

We found the next zombie on Extraterrestrial Highway. The asphalt led straight to a line of mountains. Even in early November, heat distorted the yellow lines and shimmered the pan-flat desert.

It shambled along the road, sweating blood beneath the high noon sun. It came toward us from the south, and the closer we approached, the faster it attempted to move. A lilting step made it appear as if one leg grew much longer than the other.

Colton slumped on his horse, his skin hidden beneath layers of clothing, but the sun still sapped his strength. Even so, he only rested every other day, though I reminded him we were horse meat if vampires found him so weakened. He just growled.

I dug the binoculars from my saddle bag. My horse, Spook, nipped at a fly on her shoulder. The corkscrewing pain at the base of my skull felt sharper than last time. We'd been following it like a compass needle, but it hadn't grown worse or changed in any way to suggest we'd encounter a zombie that day. It had been the horses that had alerted us to something up ahead.

Colton had packed me a hat, which I used to shade the binoculars I squinted through. With the sunlight limiting Colton's senses, I kept lookout. Heat wavered from the pavement, distorting the zombie. If you could call it a zombie. The body was rotting and looked like the creature had pieced itself together with other dead animals pinned to gelatinous flesh. A deer's hind leg was mashed into its hip, causing the lumbering gait. A coyote's lower jaw hung slack at his throat, the tongue dangling black and buzzing with flies. Instead of hands, pronghorn antlers were jammed into the wrists.

I described the zombie to Colton.

He slid off his horse. "Well, that isn't good." He whispered to the stallion before slicing a vein and sipping blood. The horse flicked his tail as if Colton were merely a fly. He licked clean the incision, then crooned his thank you, resting his forehead against the horse's.

The first time I saw him take blood from the horses, I couldn't believe they let him do it so calmly, and I said as much. He'd laughed and replied, "But you would do it if you could."

I'd snarked back something like "you wish." But really, I was no better than the horses. If I could offer a vein, I would, especially after these past four days. Other than my crush growing worse and my dreams getting interesting, nothing special had happened. Colton and I just fell into step. The silence felt comfortable, not filled with the anxious, awkward feelings that tightened my chest when we walked down a long hallway and left me scrambling for small talk.

Sometimes, talking felt like sacrilege, especially in the quiet dawn and dusk. Even Colton seemed reluctant to break the silence, motioning instead as we crossed the rocky stretches that glowed orange against the bruise-purple mountains. Once the dark came and he felt better, he'd tell stories of mining silver in Virginia City or riding the early Reno rodeos in the twenties. On these nights, I only listened. He'd lived through my interesting stories and didn't ask me to share.

The possibility of him getting hurt while fighting a zombie meant something different now than four days ago. He'd become more than a boss, the guy who ordered me around, but a partner in figuring out this mystery. I'd seen him weak, had taken over guiding the horses when the sun became too much and followed my instinct rather than his judgment. He trusted me, and I wanted to trust him back.

I urged Spook forward, blocking Colton's path. "Look, it can't move fast. Let's backtrack and kill it at dark."

A black bandanna hid his face, but I swore he grinned. "Take a look down the road."

I glanced over my shoulder. The Extraterrestrial Highway was one of the loneliest roads in the US. It was just our luck to glimpse a windshield glinting in the distance beyond the zombie.

I tipped my head back and groaned.

Colton patted my leg. "Let's go to work."

I drew the brand from a saddle holster while Colton palmed his pistol.

The glinting windshield had turned into a metal speck.

Colton tugged down his hat. "We need to draw it away from the car."

"I go right, and you drive it after me?"

He nodded, then kicked into a gallop. I asked Spook with a gentle heel nudge if we could follow, and she assented. Asking usually worked best with her.

We made a dust cloud pounding along the shoulder, racing toward the car as it steadily grew into a larger smudge on the horizon.

I reigned Spook off the shoulder into the desert, and the zombie thing turned toward me before stumbling to face Colton. His stallion reared, forcing it off the pavement. Circling back, I snagged its attention, and its head swung around to follow me with fly-swollen eyes. It lumbered into the desert, its coyote jaw clacking.

I asked Spook for a burst of speed, and she put a bit of distance between us and the zombie. Once we were far enough away, by my guess, I pulled her up short and dismounted. She took one sniff of the air and trotted deeper into the scrub, still glancing over her shoulder periodically. Good girl.

I passed the brand between my sweaty palms, and the end burned red hot. The creature loped toward me, and Colton drew back, keeping between the zombie and the road.

Wait, he didn't expect me to face this thing alone, did he?

The zombie howled, the coyote tongue bloated and lolling between its teeth, then it dropped onto all fours and lunged.

The mashed-on deer leg and pronghorn antlers for hands somehow made it faster than the two-legged gait. The awkward lumbering down the road made me think it would be slow in a fight, but it'd gone full predator. I tripped sideways, but it slid into a turn and leaped. I raised the brand, spearing it through the chest, but the hot end melted through skin and soggy bone with almost no resistance. Momentum slid the body up the shaft as I staggered backward, trying to wrench free my only weapon. The deer leg churned the sand, and the zombie's heavy torso crashed against me.

A sage bush sent me sprawling. The coyote jaw snapped at my throat, but I caught the teeth on my fist as I beat at the jaw, my blood dissolving what little muscle remained. I levered my bitten fist and popped off the whole jaw, flinging it chattering into the dirt.

The butt end of the brand bruised my stomach, but I still

had one hand on it. With a scream, I threw my weight into the rod and pushed it upward.

The metal pulsed white as lightning, and the zombie split in half from the waist to the top of its head.

Rotten flesh, congealed blood, and stinking bones—all worsened by a burned flesh smell—soaked me.

Still screaming, I fought my way from under the remains, crawled a yard off, and vomited over and over. Each breath brought the smell coating my tongue and nostrils, so I heaved again.

That's how Colton found me, covered in zombie guts and puking.

"Well done," he said.

I couldn't find the willpower to decide if he was being sarcastic, as I was entirely focused on ripping off my clothes. Gore clung to my arms and legs, and I scrubbed sage over my skin until blood welled. The smell still clung to my mouth and nose, even worse than the puke, so I chewed on a frond, the sour taste making me gag. I probably looked worse than the zombie, standing in the desert along Extraterrestrial Highway, in a sports bra and lady briefs, munching on sage.

I turned away from Colton and the zombie I'd split, hugging myself against the warm wind. The more I tried not to think about the sun-hot splashing guts, the more I gagged. I tried to wipe my boots semi-clean in the sand. The memory of fleshy resistance shook my hands.

Colton appeared beside me in that silent vampire way. I flinched. I prayed he wouldn't say anything, just let me stare at the bright desert until I stopped trembling—then he could ream me out for being sloppy again.

He shrugged off his long coat and, careful not to touch me, draped it around my shoulders.

I clutched it. It carried no warmth other than the sun on

black leather, but it smelled like the Saints casino—cigarette smoke and liquor, the perfumed cleaning solution, the sour smell after the vacuums ran. I tucked my chin inside and breathed deeply.

Spook meandered toward us, and I picked a path to her. The rocks and goathead thorns cut up my feet.

She nibbled my hair, then snorted. I scratched her neck. "Yeah, I'm grossed out, too." I unpacked the second pair of clothes Colton had brought me: stretch jeans material, a black undershirt, and a leather jacket that wasn't mine and smelled musky.

I rode Spook to the crime scene. Colton poked at the gore splat with my brand, sorting the pieces into different piles—human and nonhuman. I slid off the horse's back and forced myself to pull on my spattered boots.

"Impressive show of strength." He stabbed the brand between the zombie's two halves. The skeleton looked like a tree split by lightning, black and curling apart.

I handed back his coat. Layered shirts and long gloves hid his skin, but he swayed in his crouch. "I can't tell if you're being sarcastic."

He tugged on the coat and clasped it. "You've fought two of these creatures now. What did you notice?"

I pulled my T-shirt over my nose, but Colton grunted as if to say *have some class* and handed me a bandanna. It must've been scented with something because a sharp, minty smell coated the back of my throat. I took my brand and braced it between my knees. The rough grip felt comforting between my laced fingers.

The body seemed more rotten and grotesque than when it had been on top of me. The skin bubbled and twisted across misshapen limbs. Bone splinters and sticks pinned the deer leg in place somehow. I nudged the seam with the brand, and it burst apart, maggots wriggling free.

I turned away and swallowed bile. *You can do this, Gin. Just focus.* Hell, I'd killed the thing. That was harder than examining the body.

The skin had a deathly grayness, but it almost seemed blistered, even in places where I hadn't burned it. Lumps bulged over one shoulder. I hooked the wrist with the brand's end and held it up. At first, I'd assumed the hands were gnawed off by scavengers, but the ragged wrist stumps looked tortured rather than chewed.

I wrinkled my nose. "Body looks tortured. These things don't seem sentient enough to sew themselves up with animal parts, so someone else is doing it—maybe?" I pointed the brand at the lumps. "These almost look like tumors. Maybe they are experiments? What were you and Franklin going on about last time—radiation?"

Colton straightened and stared toward the road. "Nevada has a nuclear history—and we're in the middle of it." He hauled me upright by my jacket. "We need to go." I tried to twist away, but he shoved me forward. "The car has been watching us."

"Yeah, that's what tourists do. Stare at things."

He pushed me toward Spook before swinging onto his stallion. "We'd do well not to be stared at."

He urged his horse into a gallop but only made it a few strides before he fell off.

15

At the motel, only the bathroom didn't have a window. Colton stumbled inside and hadn't come out, even past dark. I'd knocked once, and he'd just growled. The Little A'Le'Inn only had a room with a single queen available, but since Colton seemed intent on staying in the bathroom, I dozed, jerking awake when headlights beamed the window or a nightmare pierced my brain.

Colton had acted like an embarrassed old man when I caught up to him. His horse kept nudging his shoulder, and he'd hauled himself upright with a stirrup.

"Don't say anything."

"The sunlight is getting to you."

He'd struggled into the saddle. "What did I just say?"

"The town of Rachel is nearby. We can rent a room and get you some rest."

He'd bared his fangs. "We keep going. I'll replenish my strength come nightfall." He bent over his horse's neck, whispering, then bit. After a few sips, he wiped his mouth. "Ride!"

I just stared. At the casino, I had a bad habit of reimagining every argument. Even the imagined, weaker version of Colton that I could always outsmart and outtalk in my head never sounded like this—exhausted.

"We need to stop traveling during the day."

He twisted in the saddle, stared down the car still idling on the road, then kicked his stallion into a flat run.

I watched the car for a moment more. Three college girls got out and started snapping selfies.

He was scared. The thought passed me like the whiff of roadkill. In the past two years, I'd never seen him truly scared. Why now?

He'd seen something in the body I hadn't. As usual, Colton held all the cards. Even after days of riding horseback together, he didn't want to show me his hand. I rolled out of the squeaky bed and scribbled a note, shoving it under the bathroom door. The sun had set, so he shouldn't be quite so sick. No need for me to keep hovering. Time to win a few rounds.

True to the name, the attached bar and lounge was alien-themed and partial to the big-eyed, green-skinned type. In the dim lounge lighting, some of the aliens glowed chartreuse. I slid onto a bar stool and ordered a Budweiser. Before everything went to shit, Colton had encouraged me to see if my blood offered anything other than increased physicality. Maybe I could be an exceptional liar or turn people to my will—who knew? The last thing I wanted was a silver tongue, not after seeing vampires order humans to their knees. That kind of power was too heady, and I didn't need it.

The bartender set a bottle on a napkin. "Where's your friend?"

"Resting. We've been riding for two weeks straight." Better not to tell the whole truth just in case Colton was right to be afraid.

"Of course. What an adventure." She polished a stein. "It's

the type of thing my husband and I always talked about, but on a good day, there's plenty to see up there." She glanced at the ceiling, and for a moment, I wasn't sure if we were talking about God or stargazing; then I remembered the aliens.

"You see anything on your ride so far?" she asked.

"UFOs, no. But, there's this one thing." I took a long sip of beer. "We thought it was a coyote, but it seems almost human-shaped. Head, arms, legs, upright for the most part."

She stowed the first stein and started wiping down a second. "Oh yes, they are the latest addition to ET highway. We aren't sure what to make of them yet, but I saw one while walking the dogs the other morning."

I almost choked on my beer. She talked like someone who straddled day and night. Maybe out here in a town with no gas station, it was a required skill to understand the weird.

She worked on a third mug. "They just lumber along. We've been leaving them alone since they look pretty nasty, and so far, they've left us alone."

"You must be curious," I said.

"Oh, curiosity only gets you so far out here by Area 51."

The door opened, and two of the college girls Colton and I had seen from the road entered the bar and leaned on one corner. They looked nearly identical in button-ups, tan down vests, and high black boots.

The bartender went to take their orders. I sipped my sweating beer. At least Colton and I rode in the right direction. If these things walked in daylight all the time, why hadn't we heard something before now? Then again, this part of Nevada remained pretty deserted.

I reached over the bar and snatched a wad of cocktail napkins. I scribbled the different pieces on separate napkins: *Something coming from the south, Zombies, Radiation???, Saints Casino.* I put the Saints in the center.

I finished my beer, tapping my pen on the bar top. Why come *into* the Saints, though? Starved out of the desert?

Unless these zombies functioned like scouts. Searching for something—safe passage, a specific place, a lot of food? Colton? Maybe that's why he'd run on Halloween, not just from the council but from whatever had found him in the Saints. Then why take me with him?

The bartender set another beer in front of me. "Courtesy of that lady down the bar." She winked.

I looked up as I felt for the brand I'd left back in the room. Damn it! One of the college girls waved, baring her fangs, as the door creaked open, and the rest of the posse strolled in. Leading the pack was a familiar if newly scarred face. Clarisse smiled, licking her lips.

I gripped the pen. At least they couldn't drink my blood—though that wouldn't stop them from, you know, killing me.

The vampires circled behind as Clarisse sauntered over and took the stool beside me. She ran her fingers along my arm. "You made me lose a bet, Gin."

I flinched, still staring behind the bar. There had to be something I could use as a weapon. I'd beaten up vampires before, but usually, they were intoxicated. Maybe if I screamed loud enough, Colton would come.

The humans in the barroom kept watching the TV, sipping their beers. Colton had mentioned older vampires sometimes had talents like this—glamour nets, telepathy, camouflage. Clarisse had brought the big guns.

"I bet we'd have you at mother's feet in twenty-four hours."

I faced her. "I thought you had different plans for me."

Three long lines cut from her temple to her lip. Even her vampiric good health couldn't erase that night's scars. "Oh, Gin, I'm not going to disobey my blood mother just to get laid."

I cupped a hand over hers. "Sure we can't make a deal? Just twenty-four hours head start, and you can do whatever—"

Other hands latched onto my shoulders. "Yeah, Gin. I'm sure."

All right, now or never. I gripped the bar, ready to push back and hopefully topple the two vamps behind me, but a deep *thud, thud* stopped me.

We all looked toward the door. It hadn't sounded like a knock, though. More like two birds hitting the window.

It came again, four separate hits.

Clarisse took advantage of the distraction and grabbed a fistful of my hair, smashing my head into the bar top. The next few seconds came hazily, my sight going in and out. Clarisse yelled something about taking care of me while the others—

But six zombies piled through the door. Two more crashed headfirst through a window, the glass shivering apart their bodies.

The noise broke the vampire glamour, and the humans shrieked and called to Jesus. The room erupted in movement as the vampires faced off against the zombies while the humans clambered for any way out.

I struggled to stand, twisting against Clarisse's grip. My vision blurred, and memory overlaid reality. I was drunk, slumped, and pressed into a chair while Clarisse pulled my hair, forcing my head back and exposing my neck.

I fought her now as I wished I could have fought her then, and I punched her in the throat.

She reeled, then ducked a second before the gunshots registered. The blast disoriented me as much as the head blow. The bartender pumped a shotgun at a stumbling half-bear, half-man. The wrist stumps were punched through two coyote heads, the jaws somehow animated.

It swung one lumbering arm at Clarisse and me. I dove

away, a blast of shotgun balls catching my arm. Unlucky again. I screamed something, maybe "fuck" or "watch it."

The zombies sliced apart on the window tried to stand, sliding in their own gore and stitched-on limbs. Another zombie swung through the window, landing on cat's paws. Big paws. A rotting long tail flicked, splattering the walls with chunks of flesh and pus.

It straightened and turned a golden eye on me. A cougar and coyote skull had been mashed together, the stitching and slate pins obvious down the center of the face. It shrieked and sprayed blood.

I scrambled behind the bar as it lunged, catching on a chair. The bartender had fled, taking the gun. I snatched a vodka bottle and swung it at the cougar-zombie perched on the bar top. It dodged the blow but pinned down my wrist with a bony paw. Snatching another bottle with my free hand, I broke it over the thing's grip, and the rotten bones splintered.

Didn't matter; it had held me long enough. Two of the human zombies scrambled over the bar and dogpiled me. I kicked away, sliding in the broken glass and liquor, but one distended its jaw and latched onto my calf. The other sunk claws made of bone shards into my guts then snapped at my throat. My blood sizzled against their skin, sloughing it off, but their bones still stuck in my flesh. I slammed a fist through the mouth, puncturing the back of the head. It still tried to chew through me even as my blood burned away the last bits of tissue.

"Quick, get her, get her!"

Two of Clarisse's sorority girls leaped onto the bar top—one beat apart the cougar-zombie with a chair leg, the blood splattering me.

The second vampire just laughed. "Maybe I'll leave you there awhile."

I bellowed as I plunged my hands into the zombie's chest cavity. I tore it in half as black blood and guts spilled over me. I wrenched my leg free of the second zombie, but its head, boiling from my blood, separated from the neck, with the teeth still serrating my muscles.

Clarisse shoved over the chuckling vampire and swung next to me. She crouched, her knees on my chest. "Sorry, kid."

And she ripped open my throat.

16

In the haze of blood loss, I finally accepted that Colton wouldn't save me.

Even as I was bleeding out, they fed me their blood to keep me alive.

"Hurry, get her some blood. She's fading."

"Then you give it to her! I need it if we are going to get out of here!"

"Shut up!"

My head lolled forward, and a current of hair blocked my gaze as one of them hauled me out of the bar. Clarisse's ass bobbed a few feet ahead.

Headlights zig-zagged. A horn blared. Bones crunched.

"I swear, Jesse, if she's dead—"

"Fine, fine!"

A wrist weeping blood pressed into my mouth. My head jerked back, and gravity drew the blood down my slack throat.

The night brightened. A glimmer of strength trickled through me. I gathered my legs beneath me, and I lunged for

Clarisse. Something tripped me, and through the bleary fog, I heard them laugh.

Clarisse screamed at them to shut up as a zombie tackled her. She tossed it to the ground and curb-stomped the head.

I dug my fingers into the dirt. Something dripped off my nose. Blood or tears, I wasn't sure. I should have listened to Colton and focused on my powers rather than being pleased whenever I made a bad move, and something new sparking in my blood kept me alive.

Then again, Colton promised to keep other vampires away from me. That's why I signed onto the Saints, that promise of shining a light in the shadows.

I gripped a fistful of rocky desert. Things went wrong so fast. If I'd just told Colton as soon as I felt the warning from the south....

I struggled to my feet. Vampire blood pulsing in my veins trembled along my arms. The night ached with a noon brightness as the blood mingled with my inherited night vision.

The Walmart-sized parking lot that was Rachel, Nevada had become a George Romero movie. Half-human, half-animal —all dead—zombies crawled, limped, and galloped around the lot. A mustang-turned-centaur with a human body shoved on top snatched one of Clarisse's posse and dragged her off, screaming.

Three vampires left, plus Clarisse. They circled closer, always several hands touching me.

I clutched the Nevada soil. *Please, whatever gives power to my blood, please give me some juice.*

Clarisse wrenched me forward. "Move!" She guided me by a fistful of hair, and her fingers looped through my belt.

The blue Mustang that had watched us from the road waited at the far end of the parking lot. Apparently, a vampire had been left on guard because she hung half out of the driver's seat, gnawed to chunks.

The vampire blood settled inside my veins. My legs remembered how to walk. My lungs stopped gasping. The ground felt good beneath my feet. As if each step were medicine.

The others flanked us and beat back the zombies as they caught up or charged from the shadows. One went down. Then, two more. Only Clarisse and I ran for the car.

A whistling cut the night. The sound of something falling through the air.

Instinct made me dig my heels into the dirt and hide my face in my arms.

I didn't have to, though, and I wouldn't next time. My power knew not to hurt me.

Blinding light and the shockwave happened simultaneously as if a sunset had dropped from the horizon. Clarisse blew backward and away, even though my clothes barely fluttered. Dirt and rock mushroomed and scythed through the air but parted around me. The Mustang exploded, and parts sailed overhead, embedding in the Inn and the pavement and the far desert.

I turned around. So close to the center, the light burned my shadow in four directions. Particles in the wind tore apart the zombies and charred whatever flesh remained.

Scorch marks peeled over the Inn, then it burned. Cars melted into the bubbling pavement.

The *boom* washed over me like a pleasant pressure. My ears popped.

I hadn't realized that the world had slowed around me. With the release of the pressure, time caught up, and I stumbled into it.

Fire crackled. Plastic popped like a toy gun. Beyond those

initial sounds, a deep silence cloaked me, like when I'd stood in the vampire council. A lack of breath coming from bodies, animals...everything.

My fingers went slack, and the Nevada soil sifted to the ground. I spat congealed blood and pawed at my throat. The slash had closed, just sticky now.

Had...had I?

The aloneness felt so wrong it wrenched me out of my fear. "*Colton!*"

I ran for the smoking Inn. The hallways and rooms had been blown back, unnaturally spread like a bird's broken wings.

I shouldered into our room. The roof had collapsed, and I wadded through the rubble.

The bathroom door was bent double as if trying to hold up a heavy weight. I kicked it down.

Empty. Dried blood splattered over the surfaces as if a zombie had exploded. Except for the mirror.

The glass remained clean except for an image drawn in blood. Not the congealed, fetid zombie kind.

Somebody had drawn a dick in blood. Like the kind scratched on bathroom walls or doodled in notebooks.

I frowned. In the midst of a zombie apocalypse—at least for Rachel—somebody had taken the time to make a dick joke? I slid to the floor, smearing a bloody trail along the wall. I rested a hand on the side of the tub, the last place I saw Colton. He wouldn't have left a dick pic, but why would anyone?

Except Clarisse. She must've seen us at the Halloween dance. Maybe they captured him first before coming for me.

Then he would have been in the Mustang already blown to smithereens.

I launched upright and sprinted outside.

Clarisse had been gusted to the edge of the parking lot, and she crawled toward the nearest corpse, a dead human clutching a rifle. I stepped between her and the body.

She collapsed on her stomach, panting. Burns sandpapered her skin, and something bulged underneath her singed shirt. With enough blood, she might survive.

She bared her fangs. "If you're going to kill me, do it." Her words hissed with disgust.

I swallowed hard and winced at the soreness. I rubbed a hand down my face. "I don't want to kill you."

She spat. "Bullshit."

"Did you take Colton?" An edge hardened my voice, making me sound more like him.

She laughed. "Something else must've got him, sweetheart."

Trusting Clarisse was never a good idea, but she could have split my world even further by telling me Colton was dead, blown up with the Mustang—and she hadn't. Nothing to hide if he were dead, so perhaps he was still out there, in the desert somewhere.

I dragged the dead human closer to Clarisse. "Tell your mother to leave us—to leave me—alone."

17

I searched the rubble and found my brand, scavenged a week's worth of food and a few days of water. Now, I just had to find my horse. I whistled for Spook, and it took a few minutes, but she galloped out of the desert. No saddle or halter, but I tossed a blanket on her back and jury-rigged saddle bags by strapping together reusable grocery bags.

Colton's horse didn't come. Would he have galloped in to die beside Colton? More likely, a zombie got him.

But if I believed in likelihoods at this point, I'd be dead. With the same hope I'd whispered to whatever lived in my blood, I asked Spook to find Colton.

She trotted into the scrub as if she understood.

Even though Colton wasn't riding at my side, his voice echoed in my head. *Always eat after you use the power in your blood. Rest if you can.*

I chomped through my week's worth of supplies in an hour. I forgot to account for magic hunger. I weighed going back, but Clarisse would have been snacking, too, and whatever magic thing had happened, I had no idea how to repeat it.

Spook picked paths through the sage. I just held on. No zombies followed us. My only plan to avoid the vampires was to sleep on Spook's back, leaning forward and tying myself around her middle.

It sort of worked, but after seventy-two hours of little sleep, I fell out of the saddle when Spook sped into a trot.

Adrenaline flooded me, and I rolled to my feet, scrabbling for the brand tied to my back. Spook stopped a few yards ahead and looked back, nickering.

I blinked, focusing my night vision in the dusk. The desert stretched empty around us, except for some hunched structures ahead of Spook. They spread like a town, but something about the air, the quiet, suggested otherwise.

I limped to Spook's side. My thighs bled from riding sores, and my feet throbbed in my boots. After two tries, I struggled onto Spook's back. She meandered toward the not-town.

We paralleled a broken, weedy road. A graffitied wooden sign read *Adaven*. Something about the word seemed familiar, and I rolled it around in my mouth as we walked down Main Street. Oh yeah, Nevada spelled backward.

Broken foundations spitted the sky. I slid off Spook. The road continued into the red rocks, but the ghost town lived up to its name, silent and watchful. Forget whatever could be hiding in the sun-bleached buildings, I had to get a hold of myself. Fifty percent mortal meant I could still starve, and for the past day, I'd been licking crumbs.

I pressed my face into Spook's neck. "I gotta sleep. Please wait for me."

I slung the homemade saddlebags over my shoulder and stumbled over the wreckage into a brick building with one wall still standing. In the corner, I dragged a mostly intact door (though something like ax marks marred the center) and created a weak lean-to. It made me feel safer even though I wasn't.

I dreamed Colton woke me up the next morning, a mug of coffee under my nose, except he'd been zombified with sheep legs and cougar paws and had bubbling skin as if burned.

Instead, I woke to piano music and Nat King Cole's voice echoing through the ruins.

The music was equally nightmarish in a ghost town. I crouched slowly. My lean-to had vanished, the door returned to its hinges.

Cole crooned, the vocals too pure and loud for a stereo. I walked across the now clean floor—apparently, this place had been a restaurant, judging from the tables set for dinner. I peeked around the shimmery, restored door.

The lyrics sounded like "Orange Colored Sky," a song Colton had banned from playing in the casino, even when tourists requested it.

The buildings had been repaired in the night. Sort of. The original remains appeared solid, but the returned bits looked like a mosaic, hovering, about to join. Sunrise knifed between the pieces.

A voice joined in, howling over Cole's on the chorus, almost rageful.

I pressed on the new wall blocking my exit. It bulged and then the pieces snapped together. All right, then, through the door.

I gripped the brand. I'd blown up a zombie hoard and vampire hunting party. I could walk outside. Even though some terribly strong magic had reanimated a ghost town. The music faded as if moving away through the town.

I glanced out the windows as the music blasted from farther along the street. The now populated street. People stood frozen, staring at shop windows, driving 1950s cars, chatting on the sidewalk. They all faced toward the music.

Okay, *really* powerful magic.

I took a deep breath and rested the brand over my shoulder. *Showtime, Adaven.*

I kicked open the front door because it made me feel more badass, and I stepped into the sunlight.

Nobody turned at my spectacle. I pulled low an Area 51 trucker cap I'd stolen from the inn. A man wearing a dated suit and a retro-looking woman in a yellow blouse and knee-length skirt huddled near the restaurant window.

The music played ahead, but I couldn't see a source, just more still bodies.

"Excuse me," I whispered, touching the woman's shoulder.

Unnatural stiffness made me jerk back my hand. My motion made the woman wobble. I poked her, and she toppled forward. Her posture remained frozen. I circled in front of the man. His features were painted on, frowning.

The music squealed to a halt.

"Who did that!?"

I whipped around and held the brand like a sword. The tip burned volcanic.

A moving figure separated from the still mannequins. He wore all white, even his shoes. Plastic sunglasses sparkled in the morning light, and a cigarette dangled from his lips.

Twenty yards off, he paused, settling his weight in a slouch. He whipped off his sunglasses and hung them from his collar. "Why, hello, gorgeous." He sauntered forward, his gaze taking me apart an inch at a time.

A guy looks at you like that, you cross the street, duck into a coffee shop, and call a friend. I turned slightly and shifted my weight to my toes. Heat wavered off the brand. "Stay back."

He stopped just out of reach. "Baby girl, don't look at me

like that." An almost plastic smoothness brushed his face, like a colorized photo, though his skin was bone-bleached white. Full, pouty lips led to high cheekbones led to wavy chestnut hair. He shoved his hands in his pockets. "I made all this for you. Don't you like it?" He shrugged as if gesturing to the town.

I did the one thing Colton always said not to do. I took my eyes off my opponent and glanced at the once-dilapidated buildings, now a mosaic of completeness.

He somehow dodged my brand and crushed against me. His teeth smashed against my lips, and when I opened my mouth to scream or gasp in surprise, his tongue slid over mine.

I tried to activate my strength, but my muscles strained, and my strength seemed ordinary again as I shoved against his chest. In his arms, nothing happened. I became a fully human girl, just like I had wished—except I absolutely did not wish it right now.

So, I bit his tongue. Sour, hot sludge burst into my mouth, and I gagged.

He reeled back. "You little bitch." He spat, and the yellowish liquid bubbled and smoked , eating a depression into the ground.

I stumbled back until I hit a mannequin. I wiped my mouth on my sleeve. "Who are you?"

He prowled forward as I retreated through the mannequin crowd. The brand burned cherry between us, heat wavering off the tip. A steady stream of *fucks* threatened to short-circuit my brain. I had to get away, but how? This guy had some sort of magic or power, and I had nothing compared to all this.

I needed more info—to keep him talking. "Look, just tell me your name, and maybe we can start over."

He frowned, watching me from under sculpted eyebrows. "Mike."

"All right, Mike. Wh-what are you?"

He raised his hands as if in total frustration and stomped among the mannequins. At least he wasn't coming at me. Running became an option, but if he caught me and my powers vanished again, the odds weren't in my favor.

He shook one of the dummies. "Goddamn!" He punched another, and it cratered a building. The magic burst, returning that structure to ruins. "You, of all people, should know who I am!" He stomped a child mannequin in half.

I kept inching backward, my tone easy, like when I tried to cajole a drunk into ordering an Uber. "Give me a clue."

He smirked. "Just for you, baby." He snapped his fingers.

A mushroom cloud bloomed behind him. A shockwave burst over me, dusting the town. Much like at the inn, the surrounding area succumbed to the hot wind—the pressure, the dirt turned to shrapnel—but a protective cone opened around me. Maybe this explosion burned brighter because heat singed my skin, and the wind made me sway.

As the dust settled, his outline appeared in front of me. I sidestepped, but he caught my wrist and jerked me close.

Instead of the James Dean knockoff, he now seemed bigger. A wool suit emphasized his broad shoulders and chest, and his hair was slicked down and shone in the dust-dulled light. He looked like the scarier version of my grandpop, I realized with a jolt.

I pointed the brand at his gut. The wool suit singed. "Let me go."

He engulfed the head in one fist. "Well, now." He levered it from my hands. Again, whatever extra strength my blood usually granted me evaporated.

He released me and spun the brand, testing the weight. It glowed in his hands. I glared at it—*traitor*.

"Been a while since I saw this old thing." His voice had changed, replacing silkiness with pure confidence. He swung so the brand whistled through the air. "Came from Los Alamos, did you know that?"

I nodded, then glanced over my shoulder. Spook was nowhere in sight. Who knows, he could have killed her. I closed my eyes. *Now would be a real good time to not be dead, Colton.*

"Speak when you're spoken to, now that's a good girl."

When I opened my eyes, all the mannequins had twisted toward me. Their fun-loving faces were at odds with the moblike posture.

"Fuck you."

Clacking and chittering came from the buildings' shadows. I whipped around. Zombies lurked in the dark corners, their mutated faces leering. Well, that was one mystery solved—I at least knew where they came from. Now, if I could get out of here alive.

He sighed. "The history books forget how *bored* we were in Los Alamos. The sex wasn't that interesting at first—everyone feeling the jitters after their first or second affair. It got better once I arrived." He swung the brand like a showman. "I called this device the Paramour. Oh, I had those bitches begging for it."

I swallowed, but my mouth had turned as dry as the desert beneath my feet. So far, we'd gone from bad to worse, and things wouldn't turn around at this rate. At least if I ran, I'd know that I'd tried to escape during whatever happened next.

He inspected the glowing brand, bringing it close enough to his face the wafting heat distorted him. "They begged for the heat of it against their backs. Why, I remember this one secretary who—"

I split. I screamed for Spook as first one mannequin, then two tried to snatch me. Four boxed me in, but I shouldered through them. Only a few more rows before the open desert. The pale dot of Spook galloped toward me, I thought, I hoped.

A mannequin tripped me. I rolled to my feet, but my momentum had slowed just enough. Three jumped me and dragged me to my knees.

I stopped screaming for Spook. "Colton! Help!"

A fourth kicked me in the face. I collapsed on my side, still calling for him even though I knew he'd already broken his promise to keep me safe. Two more kicks broke some ribs, which wouldn't have hurt so fuckin' bad if my blood decided to start working again. What a damn time to quit.

A heel dug into my nose, and I spurted blood. At least I'd tried to escape with all the human strength I had left. I'd gone down fighting.

The mannequins tumbled off, clattering to their feet and circling me. Sunlight blinded me until he stepped into the rays.

He tugged off his belt. "You need to learn some proper manners." He wrapped the end around his fist twice, leaving the buckle hanging. "On your hands and knees."

I skittered backward and banged into a wall of mannequins. Did—did he really want to whip me with his belt? Like I was—

A child. Wait, he said I should know who he was.

I pulled myself into a crouch. It couldn't be, though. Mom would have told me if I were adopted and I did look like her but —uh-oh, not much like my dad. Colton always said my powers came from heritage. My mind reeled as the pieces fell into place.

"Dad?" The word brought back the sour taste of him. What kind of fucked up father was he?

He knelt on one knee. Somehow, he seemed even bigger than before. "Yes, Juniper. Now be a good girl and come over here." He patted his leg, the belt still wrapped around his fist. "You will respect me, understand?"

If he thought I was going to let him touch me with that belt, he had another thing coming.

Sweat trickled down his jaw. One lock of hair went limp over his forehead. "Obey your father!"

I stood, casting a shadow over him. "Hell no."

He smoothed back his hair. "Boys."

Their splintery hands snatched my arms and legs as I kicked and screamed. They forced me toward Mike.

A flash like dark lightning cracked against him and cratered the hardpacked earth.

Clarisse stood over him, panting. An iron beam rammed through Mike's—my father's—chest. The iron grew hot, and Clarisse ripped her hands away.

He snickered, then chuckled as the iron reddened where it pierced his chest.

Clarisse hauled me up by the front of my jacket. Black clothes armored her against the sunlight. "Repeat after me! Neutron hits uranium-235."

I stared over her shoulder as molten globs dripped from the beam. Mike laughed, his head tipping backward.

Clarisse slapped me. "Say it!"

"Neutron hits uranium-235!"

"By our blood, I banish you!"

"By our blood, I banish you!"

Mike blinked out of existence.

The mannequins collapsed into splinters. The town crashed apart, each mosaic piece returning to where time had left it as if pulled by puppet springs.

Clarisse dragged me into the desert with vampire speed and strength. "We might only have thirty seconds!"

I willed my blood to match her speed rather than thinking

about my feet bouncing along the rocks. Speed flickered down my legs like static, just like it had whenever I willed it the past two years. In moments, I outpaced her. Whatever had just happened seemed to bring my strength back along with it.

We sprinted into the deep desert. As my power pulsed stronger through my legs, my broken ribs snapped back into place. At least he hadn't done anything permanent to me other than add another nightmare to my collection.

I glanced back at Adaven. Clarisse had been right. Less than a minute later, the town had puppeted to life again.

He just stood there, watching as we ran.

18

Usually, when I ran for my life, the sprints lasted less than a mile. The Saints had always been a safe spot, and at my speed, I could be there in seconds.

Across the desert, my body settled into a rhythm I'd never felt. My initial burst slowed to match Clarisse's pace. We must've covered a hundred miles before Clarisse peeled off and bounded over a rock formation. A strangled cry echoed, and I raced after her.

She crouched in the shade, a black-tailed deer beneath her. She gripped the throat in her fangs as blood leaked down her chin, staining the dark clothes shielding her skin.

Once the deer stopped struggling, she released it and licked her lips. "Eat."

I wrinkled my nose.

"I'm too weak to give you blood. Eat." She sunk her fangs into the juggler. The soft sucking sounds made my stomach clench. I looked away.

She raised her head and licked her lips. "You child. He let us go! Get your strength back. Now!"

I reached behind for my brand. Only when my fist clutched air did I remember. He still had it. Hell, it sounded like it belonged to him.

"Who is he?"

Clarisse took a long suck. "According to your witch-friend, he's at least part god."

"What?"

She quirked an eyebrow while sticking her fingers into the fang wound and licking off the blood.

I grimaced. "You talked to Leia?"

"Yeah. That's how I saved your ass."

Leia came from a long line of witches and conjure women, and she had completed her degree in two years, joining a magical master's program afterward. I couldn't help but compare myself to her since we'd been on track to graduate from college in the same year—if we hadn't both chosen magic. At least it'd paid off if she could banish whatever Mike was.

"What did Leia say?" I asked.

Clarisse tore open the guts and picked through the organs. "I called my mother after your little show at the inn. She spent a favor with your friend's coven. Turns out, Leia's been researching unusual god activity in Nevada. Her hypothesis: the state ended up with a new god post-1950s nuclear testing, which suggests—"

"The bombs created the god."

Clarisse sucked the heart into a withered pit. "Or something like that."

"So, what was the whole blood banishment thing?"

She peeled out the lungs like pieces of wet lettuce. "Stands to reason if you made a mushroom cloud and had weird blood, there might be a connection. Gods are notoriously horny. Could be you're his granddaughter or something."

I rested my head in my hands. He was my dad—he hadn't

been lying. But how could Mom never tell me? Maybe that's why she and Dad—not my newly discovered biological father—divorced after all. Here I'd been blaming the poverty and stress of raising a kid on food stamps. Somehow, a god wasn't better. "Fuck."

"That's what I said."

I took a deep breath. "I guess you have no idea what happened to Colton?"

Clarisse squeezed the lungs like a sponge, the blood dripping into her mouth. "I thought you'd planned something and outsmarted me."

More like he'd outsmarted all of us. All the times he promised he had no idea what twisted my blood. Something this big, he had to know. No wonder irradiated zombies showing up on his doorstep had scared him. But why keep it from me? Colton must have gained something. "What now?"

"If your dear relative let us go, he wants something. What happened before I arrived?"

I described the scene as Clarisse butchered the carcass.

She wrapped the backstraps and cut clean a thigh. "Your dad, huh? Well, that's worse than I thought. What's your gut say?"

I shook my head. "He was upset I didn't know who he was. Next time, I need to know how to act around him before I try to slit his throat."

Clarisse shoved the bloody thigh into my hand. "Blow on it and imagine a good venison stew. I got a feeling."

I rolled my eyes but tried. The meat crisped. Clarisse smirked and settled against a rock, licking blood off her fingers. I ripped into the meat. Colton's chiding about letting my powers save me rather than learning how to control them ghosted through my thoughts, but I shoved it away.

"Something tells me a library isn't going to cut it," she said. "Who would know more than a book?"

I bit my tongue as the realization hit me. "Mom. But you can't—"

"That's what I was thinking. That should be our first stop."

I stood and wiped my greasy hands on my pants. The protein settled hard in my stomach, but I didn't feel like a shaking stray puppy. "You're thinking? I'm not going anywhere else with you." I pointed my thumb at my still wound-red throat, even if my blood powers had mostly healed it. "You ripped me apart."

She stowed the raw meat in her pockets. "And I repaid it by shoving an iron beam through your dad."

"As if you care about my life."

She flinched. I'd actually struck something. "Yeah, I do."

I stepped into her. "Except when a higher vampire wants my blood."

She picked a piece of meat from her left fang. "My mother didn't want you dead. Just in better hands than *his*."

"Colton and I get along just fine."

She spread her arms. "Then where is he?"

My jaw clenched. She was the last person I wanted to save me. I turned on my heels and marched into the desert.

19

My mom lived in Yerington, about forty minutes outside of Reno. She'd moved after separating from my dad—shit, adoptive dad—for the tenth time. It wasn't abusive or anything—well, physically abusive. My dad believed in Jesus Christ to a worrying degree. Mom was Catholic, and therefore, "of the devil." I don't know why they got married.

After dark, we pulled into the driveway of a double-wide trailer I barely remembered. I'd helped her move in right after I quit college. Rather than remembering the move to the trailer, I remembered the shame of lying about classes and grades and all the friends I'd made.

The car Clarisse stole after we walked from the desert ticked as it cooled.

Clarisse drummed her fingers on the steering wheel. "So, we going in or what?"

"Wait here." I swung out of the car and slammed the door.

The cool valley air felt good on my skin. I took a deep breath as the porch light flicked on. Dogs barked. Huh, Mom hadn't been much of a dog person.

I stepped onto the porch just as the door opened, and three pit bulls burst onto the small deck, spilling a cat litter bucket full of crunched PBR cans.

They circled me, slobbering. I offered my hand, and they licked me. "Hi, fellas." I smiled.

My mom stepped onto the porch, kicking aside cans. "Long time, no see. Who's your friend?"

"My friend?" I asked just as Clarisse threw her arm around my shoulders.

"Girlfriend. Good to meet you, Mrs. Straid! I've heard so much about you."

My mom pressed a fist to her mouth. I turned on Clarisse, ready to shout about how my mom had lived in rural Nevada for way too long to just out me as a bisexual.

My mom hugged me, sending the pit bulls into a barking fit. "I'm so glad you are finally acknowledging who you are!"

My arms hung limp at my sides. "What?" This continued to be the weirdest week of my life—and I had a long list of weird experiences. I eased my arms around my mom. At least it wasn't all bad.

After wrangling us and the dogs into the double-wide, my mom insisted on feeding us and put a Papa Murphy's pizza in the oven. Two long-haired cats, black and tiger, lounged on the table, glaring at Clarisse. Mom shooed them every few minutes, but they leaped up as soon as she turned to check the oven. The house had a lived-in feeling—and a second carpet of pet hair— since the last time I'd visited. Pictures of me hung in the halls beside thrift store finds of forest glens or tumbled-down barns that seemed at odds with a fancy-framed "Home Means Nevada" lyric print.

I scratched the black cat's chin while the other head-butted my shoulder. "When did you become such an animal person?"

"Always was." She propped her hip against the counter. "Your father was the allergic one."

The pit bulls sat around me, their wide tongues lolling. A black one refused to leave Clarisse's feet, and she rubbed its belly with her foot.

"Speaking of Dad," I said awkwardly, glancing at Clarisse. She nodded. "I, um...know you had an affair around the time I was conceived." I winced, waiting for the explosion.

The timer dinged—Clarisse and I jumped—and my mom pulled the meat lovers pizza from the oven. "It was a long time ago. I'd rather not talk about it." She set paper plates with double slices in front of both of us, then cracked a PBR.

I twisted in my chair. "Mom, I need to know."

She cupped my head. "It doesn't matter. You will always belong to me and your father, dirtbag that he is."

I rolled my eyes as Clarisse cut in. "I think what Gin— Juniper is trying to say is we have a heritage project for this sociology research methods course. We're arguing that blood isn't necessary to family, so Juniper's dad technically being her adoptive dad is important to our research."

My mom turned around a kitchen chair and folded her arms on top. Damn it, so that's where I picked up that trait. She swirled her beer, drained it, then tossed the can into a recycling bin beneath the sink. "Well, in that case, let's see." She jumped into the story so fast her reluctance must have been a show. "His name was Michael, but he told me to call him Mike. He looked so much like James Dean one person took a photo. It was summer in Vegas—hot. We met at this bar called Doomtown, named after all the testing, you see. Anyways, Mike says he'd been working out at Yucca Mountain on scouting containment sites but made enough cash he could just travel on his bike for a while. He asked me to come with him—we were very drunk—and I said no. Settled for a quickie in the alley. Honestly, I don't know what came over me." She let out an exasperated laugh. "At the time, I loved your father, and we'd already done a courthouse wedding because he couldn't wait the six months to hop in bed. Just, somehow, Mike got to me."

She sighed, not regretful but dreamy, and popped another PBR. I forced myself to count to a hundred before interrupting.

"Mom?"

She shook her head. "Yes, Junie?"

I could sense Clarisse's grin beside me. "I asked you not to call me that. You never saw him again?"

She drained the can and crunched it. "Nope. Trust me, I wouldn't have made that mistake twice. I'd have left your father in a hot minute if Mike came around again."

I winced. "You always told me to stay away from guys like that." I'd largely followed the advice—except for Colton. Still, even he didn't compare to Mike.

She packed the pizza leftovers in yellowed Tupperware. "Sometimes, you gotta live a little."

Because she's still my Catholic mother, Clarisse and I had to sleep in separate rooms, which meant I was stuck on the couch. I tried to argue that Mom had just admitted I was the product of an affair, but she cut in about how she was going to raise me right, blah, blah. I would have slept on the floor, anyway, but Mom treating me like a teenager still pissed me off. Did she know how many times I'd nearly died? Of course not, and if she did, she'd dig a basement and chain me up down there.

I thought I'd crash as soon as I hit the couch, but my body went taut. Pressure built behind my eyes, and my legs still ached from the desert run. Just thinking about it turned my tongue to sand.

I rolled to my feet and went to the kitchen for a glass of water.

Clarisse stood at the counter, watching out the window. I started and reached for the brand that was no longer slung across my back.

"Jesus, Clarisse."

She flicked on a light. "Afternoon for me, Junie."

I glared and took down a glass with a worn Corona logo. "Don't even start."

She smiled but without showing her fangs. "I think it's cute."

I downed a glass of water. City water sucked compared to the well water out here. I sighed. "It's always different when it's your mother."

"Tell me about it."

I leaned against the counter. "So, when do you head out? Don't you need to pretend to be hunting me?"

"Unless I convince you to come with me."

My fist tightened around the glass, and it cracked. I carefully set it in the sink. "Listen, I'm with Colton—"

"Who clearly left you behind."

I stepped into her, baring my teeth like I had seen him do so many times. "You don't know that."

She dipped her head, staring at my lips. "You're angry because you believe me."

We stood way too close. I retreated, but the oven brushed my ass. Clarisse followed, bracing one hand on either side of me.

"You had god blood in your veins, so he played you."

"He didn't know." It made sense, actually, that he wouldn't know. I didn't have any specific species traits to suggest I had a fey grandmother or some old elf blood from way back when. Just a general sense of power, which seemed very godlike in hindsight. "Nobody knew where my powers came from, not even you and your mother."

Her body was another cold shadow, but somehow, that made my heart beat faster, like the chill that came from passing a dark wood.

She leaned closer. Her breath held a salty tang. She bared her fangs. "Are we going to kiss or not?"

If she'd just done the deed, I would have pushed her off. Something about that question felt right for us, like enemy soldiers trading cigarettes.

I leaned into her, but my last kiss flashed over my tongue, the chemical flavor of Mike. Clarisse's coppery taste felt too similar and even more dangerous.

I pulled back, but she pushed forward. Her hands slid beneath my shirt, and their deathly cool touch made me take a shaky breath.

My thudding pulse and prickling skin dulled the ache of instinct. Only when a black bag dropped over my head and another set of hands took me in a chokehold did the warning wash over my senses.

20

Whatever chemical they'd doused the bag in made my blood traits work overtime to barely keep me conscious, but I couldn't do much else, weak as I was. Simple plastic ties were enough to bind my hands. Colton would laugh if he saw me.

Don't think about him. If he were here....

But he wasn't.

When the hood came off, I sat in the All Saints' council room. The window overlooking the club was still broken. I took a deep breath, washing the chemical taste from my mouth. My senses cleared as the familiar Saints' smells of alcohol, cash, and stress rushed over me. Home.

They'd cut the plastic ties, too.

"Take a moment to recover your strength." A woman's voice.

I blinked and rubbed the crud from my eyes. Amenities spread on the conference table: tissues, a damp towel, a water carafe, fresh fruit, deodorant.

I stared at the stuff until my stomach settled and my legs

stopped shaking. I glanced around the room. It seemed so plain compared to a few weeks ago. No magnificent costumes, no bass beating against the now-broken window.

Clarisse was still there, though, standing behind the small woman seated across the table. No other vampires sat in the room.

The woman seemed the same size as the costumed vampire from Halloween. She emanated strength from her posture, bright eyes, and a thick braid of black hair, but her body seemed a husk, her light-brown skin draped over her bones. Vampires aged so much more slowly, so she must be ancient. She'd be strong, though. Older vampires weakened physically while other abilities grew, like illusions or telepathy. Which meant the physical threat would be Clarisse, and I'd beaten her already.

"I am Eve," the woman said. "You may call me Evelyn."

I focused on Clarisse, but she stared at her shoes. "I'm Gin. You can call me Juniper."

Eve's lip twitch—maybe a smile? "All right, Juniper. Our methods previously were coarse, a nearsightedness of my own. We did not realize what you were."

I poured a glass of water. My mouth tasted coppery, and the Reno water didn't help. I had no idea what Eve meant, but she seemed to be operating on at least two levels above my knowledge.

I tilted back the chair and propped my heels on the table. Clarisse's nostrils flared. A familiar smugness, like when I used to tease Colton, made me feel strong.

"I'm glad we're on the same page, but I'm not interested in chatting until I know Colton's safe."

Eve frowned and glanced back at Clarisse.

Shit, I'd blown my hand somehow. Over Colton. C'mon, Gin, when are you going to learn.

"We assume," Eve said, "that he's with your father."

Clarisse finally looked at me. "He knew who you were, Gin."

"Well, yeah, he must have known something. He talked to my mom right after I came here. He told me that back when I started working for him and said she didn't know anything. He wouldn't have lied about my—my dad. What good would that have done him?" At least, I hoped he hadn't known. Otherwise, I'd always and only been a pawn. There had to be more to me than that. The Saints had to mean more—had to *need* me more than just another poker chip.

Eve clasped her hands on the table. "He kept you docile, didn't he?" Somehow, she must've signaled one of her underlings because a vampire brought in a glass of something red. The metallic smell meant blood. Clarisse tasted it first, then handed it to Eve.

Eve swirled the glass and sniffed it. "Did Colton tell you how he won this casino?"

I lowered my feet. "No."

"How long do you believe he's owned it?"

I sighed, trying to calm my jittery brain enough for subtraction. "This place was built in the thirties, so maybe the forties?"

She smiled. A pink-tinged fang peaked out. "The year you were born."

Shit, of course an ancient vampire would know more than me, but she held all the cards. The information would be valuable if I could trust her. Colton had never told me when he purchased it, but it seemed like more than two decades. Different legends said the fifties or the sixties, depending on who was talking. Nothing so recent.

"We never discussed it."

"He won the contract by finishing a great feat. He captured a newborn god named Mike—your father. They aren't as rare as you might think. Which makes you?" She inclined her head as if waiting for me to respond.

"A demigod?" My voice squeaked, and I hated myself for it. I couldn't breathe, so I pushed back the chair and bent over. Saying it out loud in front of a centuries-old vampire made it seem so much more real. A desert rat couldn't be half-god. *What if* Colton had known? Why wouldn't he tell me? We could have learned about my powers together. I wouldn't have abandoned the Saints just because of half-godhood. He had to know how much I loved the place.

Which meant there was something else going on. There had to be.

But my status as a demigod would explain why I wasn't chained to a chair with a naked lightbulb overhead. Why Eve apologized for her methods. I'd become more than a weirdo half-human or even the great-great-great-great-grandchild of some horny Greek deity.

A hand touched my shoulder. "Gin?"

I rocketed out of the chair and punched Clarisse. She took it and just stared as I panted.

Eve laughed. "She sniffed it out first that you were more than Colton let on."

I ground my teeth. "Great, now if I only knew how to smite her."

Clarisse smirked. "I knew you'd like being a god."

I sunk into the chair. How often I'd wished for more. Respect, power, control. I could have had it all along but had been convinced I was a nobody. "What happened next? With Colton."

Eve sipped the blood. "Colton beat the god. Many versions abound regarding how. A wild west shootout, a game of wits, brute force. He stuffed him in a nuclear waste barrel, one of the few things that can contain Mike." She said the name with a sneer as if it were too common for her. "Four weeks ago, my scouts noticed the undead coming from Yucca Mountain. Now, let's tell this story from another angle. A vampire is sent to destroy a newborn god. Instead, they make a deal. The vampire will capture the god and then release him once the god's daughter has reached maturity. Both receive what they want. The god has his daughter served up to him however he wishes, and the god helps Colton solidify his power over Nevada, or maybe the whole West Coast."

"No," I said. "Colton would have told me." I didn't believe the words as I said them. He always kept secrets, right from day one. My past would be no different.

Eve tapped the table with a long fingernail. "Your loyalty is a gift, child. One my clan would cherish. We are a matriarchy. You have no fear of gods with us."

"Who said I was afraid?" Terrified would have been a better word, but I'd practiced bluffing quite a bit over the past two years.

Eve stood, and Clarisse pulled back the chair. "My clan currently holds the Saints contract for now. Make yourself at home. You are free to leave—indeed, we would be powerless to stop you doing whatever you desire—but I would not advise it. We do not know the whereabouts of Colton or your father." She turned toward the door, and Clarisse offered her an arm.

As soon as the door shut, I leaned over and rested my elbows on my knees. They had it wrong. Colton wanted me to learn everything about my powers. It was my lazy ass that didn't try.

Then again, Clarisse continued to lie. Why should I believe her mother?

But Colton didn't always play straight with me, either. Must be a vampire trait. I had to confirm something—find a cornerstone to build from. Nobody better to ask than the true overseer of the Saints.

~

I found Franklin in his usual spot, a booth on the casino floor, his papers making a tablecloth. While the casino accounts remained online, he kept anything magical on paper.

He smiled as I walked over. "Well, well, well, mi trago de ginebra." He hugged me, but I wished for something stronger than his frail arms. He motioned for me to sit, and I slid into the booth.

"They were smart enough to keep you on."

He smoothed his mustache. "No reason to stick a wrench in the works."

I leaned forward. "So, Colton is just gone, then? The Saints isn't his?"

Franklin sipped his horchata. "Sometimes, business calls a vampire for long periods. In that case, the vampire's business holdings are transferred in trust to another clan, with the contract stating minimal changes will be made. Until more information is received, the Saints continues."

Yet again, more things I didn't know about living on the Darkside. At least nobody was going to lose their jobs. One of the waitresses, Shelia, brought me an Icky IPA. "Good to have you back, Gin. Colton coming soon?"

I raised the beer. "Hopefully." When she left, I let my head fall against the booth. I had to be better for them. All these people in the Saints were counting on me. "I'm only twenty-two, Franklin. I don't know how to do this."

He took my hands. "Twenty-two going on a thousand. You are more than your age now. Never will you know everything, and that would be a poor existence if you did."

"Yeah, I guess." I hunched forward and lowered my voice. "What about the others? Crispin, Caleb Isaac? Who's still here?"

He let out a dry chuckle. "Everyone's here, Juniper. Crispin and Caleb Isaac are on administrative leave for now. All the employees are doing exactly what they are supposed to do. Keep their heads down and ride out the storm. No coup d'état, no sabotage. Don't get ahead of yourself." He pressed his smartphone into my hand. "Now call your mother. She's worried sick."

I raised an eyebrow. "How do you know my mother?"

"Because she keeps calling here asking for the manager."

"First, I need to ask you something."

He closed his eyes and whispered in Spanish. "I know you talked with Evelyn. If Colton made a deal with a newborn god, he didn't tell me."

"Did he ever tell you what I was?"

Franklin sighed. "We guessed many things, including a distant relationship to some sort of god, but he never told me if he knew or not."

I sipped the beer, another taste of home. "I don't know who to believe, Franklin."

He gathered a stack of handwritten notes. "That's above my paygrade, but you have friends here, Gin. People who care about you, and if I dare say, people you care a great deal about. That hasn't changed."

I nodded and washed down the thickness in my throat. "Evelyn said I wasn't a prisoner here. That true?"

"As far as I know. Once they put the pieces together about your heritage, their attitudes changed." He winked, then flipped open a hefty folder. "Now call your mother."

21

After I reassured my mom that Clarisse and I had left early for the city and were staying at the Saints, I checked out my room. My clothes spilled over the floor, the bed tilted off the mattress, and the fridge door hung open, leaking water. The one shelf holding stuff from my human life had shattered—my *Naruto* mug crunched on the carpet as if some heavy boot had stomped it.

My shoulders slumped. I needed a drink, but desert funk would get me kicked out of a bar or worse—labeled a Burning Man attendee.

I showered, soaping and shampooing twice, then tugged on a pair of tight black jeans turned loose after my week as a fugitive and a baggie black hoodie. All I needed was an abundance of eyeliner to relive my senior year of high school. I'd lost my phone somewhere, but my old iPod still worked. I turned up *The Black Parade* by My Chemical Romance. I wanted a night of just feeling normal, just another human girl drinking away a breakup.

I tested Evelyn's goodwill by marching out the front doors.

No wards shoved me inside, and neither of the new door people tried to wrangle me. I let the music overwhelm my thoughts. *Just be human for one night.*

I walked to the Reno Public House. The crowd suggested it was a weekend, but I had no idea what day it was. I snagged the last bar seat and flipped up my hood. If some guy hit on me, I'd probably punch him.

Six Sierra Nevadas later, I felt like crying. Usually, I'm an even keel drunk, but...everything. I glanced around the full taproom. Voices merged, too loud. Candles and moody tungsten lights kept the corners dim.

The sense of being watched prickled my neck. I slid off the stool. It had to be Evelyn's spies, but what if Mike had followed me? Clarisse had been right; he'd let us go. Would he come for me on my home turf?

A hand clapped my shoulder. "Gin?"

I whipped around, smacking away the hand. Winston stood behind me, confused.

I fell into his arms. "Thank god, Winston."

He wrapped me in a strong hug, and I buried my face in his chest. He smelled of coffee and cigarettes—not the most changeling of smells, but oh-so-human.

He kissed the top of my head. "Let's get some fresh air, eh?" With a wave at the bartender, he guided me to the patio. We sat on a picnic table, feet on the bench, and smoked cigarettes. I finished two before he spoke.

"Are you sure you should be out and not on your toes at the Saints? Word is there's a god around."

I laughed. "Correct. Except he's not just a god, he's my motherfucking dad."

"Ah."

"That's all you have to say?"

He rubbed his arm. Even in the November chill, he only

wore a T-shirt. According to him, fey-land felt much colder. "It's not that unusual, Gin. Like being a redhead."

"Oh sure, just like being a redhead."

He stubbed out his cigarette. "Bad example."

"No shit."

He touched my back, and I leaned into his chest. "Are you okay?"

"I don't know."

He rubbed small circles between my shoulders, and I tucked my head under his chin.

"I never wanted any of this," I whispered into his chest. "I'm sure some kids want to be magical. I just didn't want to be poor."

He stroked my hair and hummed a lilting tune, drifting in and out of lyrics. The words sounded like summer wind and a stream glinting in a meadow.

The moon had shifted when he straightened. "Let's get you warmed up. I see now why you need to get sloshed. Consider me your wingman for the night."

As we drank our way through Midtown, the story came out in pieces. At first, I lied and pretended to be courageous about how scared I felt, how Colton made me feel, the stabbing pain of Clarisse's betrayal, or the fact that her tactic worked at all. How could I have trusted her? After whiskey at Ceol's Irish Pub, I caved and talked about Mike—apparently my real fucking dad—and how he'd tried to hurt me, or worse. I never wanted to be alone with him again. Winston promised I wouldn't, but a fey-raised human couldn't really promise protection from a god, though I didn't say that out loud. It lingered unsaid between us like our cigarette smoke.

Around three, we ended up in Roberto's Taco Shop because even though the bars stayed open late, the kitchens didn't. Inhaling tacos sobered me enough to realize I'd been white girl trashed. Considering it had been over twenty-four hours since I'd eaten, the food alone evened my perspective.

"Thanks for putting up with that."

Winston stole one of my churros. "Nothing to put up with. S'all good." The slight slur made me feel better. "So, what's next for you, Gin?"

"Um, music? Where's that fey bar you've been talking up?"

He shimmied in his seat. "I'm all about it, but what I meant was the sun's gonna rise, and we're going to sober up."

I tipped back my head. The darkness spun when I closed my eyes. I blinked. "I'm no match for this."

"Most folks aren't. You need help. And I don't mean Colton." He pulled a scuffed-up smartphone from his jacket. A thorny fey sigil scratched the case. He pressed it into my hand. "Call me next time. I call you a friend, and I mean it."

I rolled my eyes and made a show of examining the phone because my throat thickened. "You're everyone's friend, Winston."

He took my hand. "I'm here with you right now."

And tomorrow, it'd be someone else, another sob story. Winston had a talent for dragging people up, but it was unfair to shame him for it.

True to his word, we kept on drinking, and after a few pliant shots, he agreed to take me to The Solstice. We headed toward the casinos' neon auras but turned down East 4th Street, then up Valley Road to give the Saints a wide berth.

Winston slung an arm around my shoulder. "You do know they are following us, right?"

"Figured."

He turned around and walked backward, waving into the shadows. "Hello, vamp friend! Want us to buy you a round next time?"

The shadows gave no response as we snickered.

Like most of the major dark fauna, the fey had a hold on the casino industry and reserved about half of the Circus Circus for their games. While the fey-operated casino bars had their own flavor, the local fey and fey-adjacent preferred The Solstice— across the railroad tracks, excavated under Bibo's coffee shop by campus. The local fey organizations had spent a lot of magic to keep the university from expanding over the bar.

Across from Bibo's, flyers fluttered against a graffitied community board. An oak tree hunched over it, the preferred spot to sip cold brew and smoke a cigarette before class. A wave of "should have stayed in school" anxiety made me swipe Winston's cigarettes from his back pocket.

He stepped behind the community board to knock on the trunk. The tree groaned, and the roots slithered aside like tentacles. A ladder made of smaller roots dipped into the soil.

Winston jumped into the hole. I opted for the ladder.

The tunnel opened like a funnel, and we stooped, then crawled to a door made of living roots thin as spiderweb. Winston whispered, and they parted, wriggling back into the dirt. He squeezed through first, then dragged me behind.

As soon as I passed the living barrier, magic washed over me. I always heard the fey preferred tapping and manipulating a place's inherent power. Vampiric magic came from blood heritage. Weres connected to the moon. Humans used intent unless they could get their hands on a fey. This place felt uncanny, like the moment before thunder rolls.

We stood in a small café with worn wooden tables and candle chandeliers. Smoke hung around the rafters, seasoning the smells of herbal teas and coffee. Music played, but not the tinkling fake Enya I expected, but coarse acoustic. Rather than breakup songs, the lyrics sounded like guttural chants. Bookcases sliced the room into more private areas with couches and skin rugs made from unrecognizable species. Fey and other nonhumans packed the seating, even sitting on the floor or leaning against walls. All looked young and wore human clothes. Band T-shirts explained the music: Mastodon, Russian Circles, at least three Being as an Ocean. Some wore more traditional fey clothes—fancy suits with enough velvet to line a coffin or the faux-natural leather-and-ivy look.

I slipped an arm through Winston's. "I thought we were going to a club."

"This is a club. Just a different sort. If you want the sideah debauchery, we need to go to the casino."

I stuck out my tongue. "Let's not."

"I'll get us some drinks if you find a seat. Try in the back." He winked. "There's lots to see."

I sidled between the tables and among the bookshelves. The coffeehouse stretched deeper and deeper. Each time I mazed through another little library, I expected a wall, but only more seating appeared. This far from the bar, the patrons changed. They chatted in small groups, frowning when I passed. Some played cards or dice. Other huddles seemed more romantic, the candlelight dimming in those corners. Aging paper and musky candles muddled the tea shop scents.

In one alcove, the flames burned bright, but a single woman paged through a tome.

She looked so much older than our freshman year. No more baggy animal shirts and boy's jeans. A well-worn suit, forest green with dark elbow patches, turned her professorial, except for the combat boots. In this space, I only recognized her because she felt like Leia—a quietness that stilled the clutter of knowledge and clinking glasses.

Her gaze flicked up from the page, caught my eyes, and scanned me—my oversized hoodie, jeans that should have been tight but weren't anymore, my dirty Converse shoes.

She tucked a silk ribbon between the pages. "That grunge look won't help you blend in down here."

I wanted anger to flare in my gut. No hi, hello, how are you? Just giving me one of those Leia looks like when I'd come late to class or helped sneak weed into the dorm. We weren't college kids anymore. My troubles meant dead bodies. My shoulders slumped, and I shoved my hands into my pockets. Why would she care, though? I'd ruined our friendship with too much drunken shouting—and her dislike of Colton.

"I'm not trying to. I'm just a mess."

She steepled her fingers. "I heard you were in trouble. I didn't expect you to be drinking and"—she winced and took a deep breath—"I mean, want to talk about it?"

No extra chairs invited visitors into this alcove, so I went to the next section walled off by bookshelves and took a chair from some amorous folks. Leia put aside her book when I dragged in the oversized armchair.

"I could have requested one," Leia said.

I flopped into it. "I wasn't sure you would."

"The number of times I barged into your dorm room, I would have consented." She wrinkled her nose. "You smell like you stuck your head in a bathtub of Jungle Juice."

"Not a bad idea."

"I thought you'd stopped dealing with your problems through drinking."

I rubbed my forehead. I needed another shot. "Yeah, well, shit changes when a god is hunting you. Guess you wouldn't know what that feels like."

She sighed. "I still have plenty of surprises of my own."

"Yeah, like finding out your father is a god? What would you do about that?" Taking out my frustration on her was the last thing I should be doing. I pinched the bridge of my nose. "Sorry."

She nodded at the bookcases. "I'd find out how to kill him."

Before I could ask what she meant, Winston returned with an ornate silver tray bearing shot glasses.

Leia smiled and stood. "Winston, I hoped Gin wasn't wandering The Solstice alone." She snapped her fingers twice, and a third overstuffed chair appeared along with a small table.

Winston set down the tray and then loosely hugged Leia. "The barkeep said you two had found each other. Sent you another cappuccino."

"Wait," I said. "Did you bring me here on purpose?"

Winston grinned. "Leia invited me to drop by after what you said about wanting to come. I just didn't mention you."

I reached for a shot glass. Purple liquid swirled like a galaxy even though the tray remained still. I knocked it back, and a frosty bite coated my tongue; the refreshing chill slicked my throat and settled in my stomach. I sat straighter. "Well, us together is usually a buzzkill these days."

That'd always been our joke about Leia in college, that she never let herself go too far. At the time, I'd liked her best out of all our friends—that kind of freshman group that ends up together because of dorm layouts or trying different clubs but fades by senior year. Later, when I found out she was the daughter of the local green witch coven leaders, her reason for staying behind made sense.

Winston hefted Leia's tome. "*On Creation* by the Fourth Mountain. Heavy reading."

"I want to know what we are up against."

Whatever I'd knocked back continued to clear my head, but it also created a soothing, cool space inside like I'd swallowed a canister of Altoids. "What are you two talking about?"

"Let's just say the reports of your god are..." Leia seemed to roll a word around in her mouth. "Malevolent."

"He's not *my* god."

She crossed her legs and clasped her hands over her knees. "Your power supply, then."

I bit my lip. Couldn't argue with that. "I didn't ask for this." I stood, facing Winston. "I came out to forget about this whole mess for a night, not—"

He caught my hand. "I brought you here to meet someone."

I glared at Leia.

Winston scrambled to his feet. "Not just her. C'mon." He took my hand and pulled me through the bookcase maze despite the squeak of my Converse as I dragged my feet. Leia followed, her combat boots making a solid *thud* on the floor.

The twisting turns abruptly ended with the bookcases shifted away from a center point, leaving scratch marks and an open space on the floor. A group of café-goers crouched or knelt around two folks seated on cushions. A length of parchment covered the floor, and the players set down what looked like *Magic: The Gathering* cards. Other observers stood nearby, whispering as the players deployed cards.

Winston murmured, "That fey is one of our best gamemasters in the state. The man across from him is the grandson of a god out of Vegas, a card shark."

"Are they really playing *Magic?*"

Leia stepped behind me and crossed her arms. "The game matters less. It's about the strategy, the ability to game the system, to read a situation. But yes." She grinned.

We watched. I knew the basics of *Magic,* so when noises rippled the crowd, I could guess which big monster had entered or what deploying so many counters meant. After ten minutes, I tugged on Winston's sleeve and raised an eyebrow. He waved me off, focused on the cards.

A minute later, the crowd cheered, and the card shark spread his hands, smirking. The fey, an older one judging from the long ears and lichenous undergrowth peeling off his skin, bared sharp teeth. He evaporated in a hurricane of leaves and cards.

"Sore loser," said the card shark.

The observers closed in around him, bringing drinks and asking strategy questions, while we faded into the library.

"Okay?" I asked. "Your point?"

Leia scanned the shelves, pulling out small volumes and dusting them off. "Stop moping."

I glared at her. After nearly dying, after being saddled with defeating a god, she thought I was *moping*? "I have a feeling his god relative didn't try to beat him while trapped in a nuclear ghost town."

Leia gathered a stack of books tucked under her arm. She placed her hand on my shoulder. "Feel what you are feeling. Be angry, but don't ignore your blood—don't ignore that you have to *do* something to survive. Figure out a way to channel it." She handed me the books, all basic primers on everything from poetry to calligraphy to card tricks. "Find something that works for your magic. Maybe you already know what it is." She turned and sauntered toward the front of the shop. She raised a hand without looking back. "Bye, Winston."

I held the worn books against my gut. "Is that really what you wanted me to get out of that show?"

He took half the books. "Sort of. More like, try to find what's fun about it."

Fun was something you did on a long weekend or at Chimney Beach in Tahoe. Or with some hot person in bed. Reading dusty books to discover how magic might save my ass was not my type of fun. Leia's response being "study more" just felt like the same judgment from a few years ago, that the only way out was keeping your head down and a nose in a book. Sure, it worked for her, but that's not what I was trained to do, not by Colton or by my father.

We wandered the maze until we found our alcove with the drink tray. I set the books on Leia's seat. Winston gestured at a green-colored shot.

"Try that one."

"Why?"

"Just trust me."

I downed it, a spruce-y flavor washing over my tongue. While refreshing, I felt floaty and settled into the chair, my feet propped on the small table. Winston took a shot of the same thing and copied my pose.

"What is this stuff?" I asked. A silence seemed to settle between my ears, like being in a snowy forest long after dark.

"We call it *The Lovely, Dark, and Deep*."

I slid into the crisp sensation. My eyes drifted closed. The candlelight shimmered through my eyelids, comforting, like sitting by a woodstove.

I crunched through the snow spreading out at my feet; my legs never tired, and the cold never too intense. My breath clouded the air, drifting away from the deep woods. Wind wove through the trees and brushed my hair forward as if tousled by a ghostly hand.

Gin.

I turned around. Only my footsteps marred the snow. So, I kept walking.

Gin...Gin!

I scanned the trees, unzipping my coat. Sweat suddenly trickled between my shoulder blades. The voice sounded like Colton, but Winston had concocted fey magic to bring me into this dreamscape. He wouldn't have included Colton, not after everything I had told him.

The trees thinned, and ice glinted ahead. I kept walking.

The wind kicked up and began to thrum, bending the trees toward the brightness.

GinGinGinGinGin—

I broke into a run, my feet punching through drifts. I stumbled onto the rocky shore. The mountain bowl of Lake Tahoe opened before me, icy and blinding. Except Tahoe, under normal circumstances, stayed too warm to freeze.

The ice stretched like a different kind of desert, still dry but cold and glimmering with starshine. A dark spot cracked the silver-blue. With the intuition and surety of a dream, I knew the dark spot was Colton far out on the frozen water.

A crack echoed across the lake, and a chasm split the impossible ice.

Colton vanished underneath.

22

The chair under me smoked, and I snapped out of the dreamscape and shoved myself to my feet. A fey had paused mid-step, a book lying open in their hand, to stare at me.

"What?"

They clicked their teeth. "You—you looked like a blast of light. A candle flame."

I ran a hand through my greasy hair. "It's normal."

They glanced at the charred chair, then hurried on. I sighed. My powers were always unpredictable but not destructively so. Nightmares had never triggered my blood. Maybe whatever fey magic had twisted that last drink activated something.

Winston had slept through whatever I'd done. He was curled in an armchair, one leg on the floor, the other tucked to his chest with his arms wrapped around it. His green eyeliner and lipstick had smeared. I whispered his name, and when he didn't stir, I dug in my pockets for a scrap of paper and left a thank you for the night.

I wandered after the smell of coffee until the bookcases

opened into the café. A few fey settled at the tables, nursing coffees and pastries. The card shark from last night played solitaire.

I hesitated and watched him for a moment too long. He glanced up, then did a double take. He tipped back his hat and motioned for me to join him.

Not interested in having a demigod show and tell, I flipped up my hood and hurried for the entrance.

I crawled out of the tree roots into the dry air. Even in November, the sun warmed the high desert fast, and I stripped off my sweatshirt, tying it around my waist. At Bibo's coffee shop across the alley, college kids clustered on the patio, and the line curved out the door.

I stepped toward the shop, but behind me, someone coughed.

"Already got you one."

I glanced back. Leia sat on a log beneath the community notice board, smoking. Two coffees trickled steam beside her.

I stalked over. "Let me guess. Sun's out, so Evelyn hired the coven to keep a daytime eye on me?"

She blew a smoke ring that twisted into a winking fox face. "You're getting better at tracing the web."

I snatched a coffee, slopping some. "Didn't think you were politically inclined."

"Wasn't. I always thought magic meant freedom, but turns out there are just as many rules and regulations as the rest of the world."

I crouched, my back to the sunlight. "Since your coven is working with Evelyn, do you know why they are trying to take over the Saints? It's gotta be more than me."

Leia glanced at the hidden entrance to The Solstice. "Let's walk."

We cut through the university campus, our lowered voices

screened by the students' morning chatter. The normalcy made my hands shake. I took a big gulp of coffee. I looked so much like any of these students, and I knew I could walk right into the library and nobody would blink. My stomach turned to acid. A day like this, and I knew I'd made the wrong choice to quit my life and join up with a vampire.

Leia filled me in on the magical gossip. The Saints had always been lucrative and a coveted contract, but the Tesla and Amazon complexes meant a population increase, thus more stock for vampires. A revival in non-sanctioned vampire hunters made Portland and Seattle less appealing, and like all creatures, the California wildfires drove more nonhumans east. The Saints could become a headquarters as big as Las Vegas or San Francisco.

I tossed out my coffee as we neared the historic quad lined with oak trees. "So, it's about power."

Leia shoved her hands in her trousers. "As always."

We walked past the pond and turned down Virginia Street toward the sun-dulled casinos.

"You have power," Leia said. "It will be in demand."

"No chance of living in a van with a dog out in the desert?" Right before our friendship imploded, that had been a mutual fantasy when school felt like too much—go nomad and live where we wanted when we wanted, not tied down to parents, grades, or the nine-to-five. How easy it was to imagine all that.

Leia smirked. "You can try."

"All right, spill it. You were always telling me what to do in college."

"Yeah, not my best moment."

We passed the Circus Circus with the outdated creepy clown sign. The casino smell of cigarettes, stale air, and salty buffet food suffused the street. My chest tightened with a homesick pang for the Saints.

"Really, though," I said. "I'm lost. I don't have a coven to give me advice. Not like I can ever go to Colton again."

We paused outside the Saints' pumpkin-colored round-about. Leia nodded to the door people. "It seems simple to me. You have power. Use it."

Leia made taking control of my power sound easy. Then again, maybe it was. If I understood the origins of my power, maybe I could tap into it easier. Colton must have had a plan. If he knew what I was, then my training was more purposeful than it had seemed back then. Maybe he'd let me slack off so I wouldn't progress too quickly. He'd been a hardass, but I'd also been a brat sometimes.

I still wanted to believe there was something salvageable with Colton—and what I had at the Saints. I couldn't give up my home after all this. And now there was all this dream stuff with Colton in my head *again*. Fey magic or no, Colton still had too much of a hold on me. If there was any way to stay at the Saints, I had to set some boundaries, somehow, with a hundred-year-old vampire. Not my strong suit. But first, I needed to know what Colton had on me.

I went to Colton's office. Like my room, Evelyn's vampires had ransacked the place. They'd stripped the books off the shelves and tossed them in a corner. Bookshelves had been knocked down, and the hardwood sundered. They'd taken his computer, of course, and smashed apart the desk. The drawers' contents carpeted the floor.

I let out a long breath, thinking how angry this mess would have made Colton. The room didn't even smell right anymore— sour instead of Colton's leather and copper smell. I rolled over his desk chair and started sorting everything into three piles: useful, not useful, and maybe.

I'd never spent so much time alone in Colton's office, and I kept glancing toward the door as if he might stomp in and snarl at me. If only he would. I shook the thought from my head. Just like two years ago, my world was all broken up again. I'd survived learning what lived in the dark; I could survive taking control of my powers—with or without Colton.

A file caught my eye as I organized the books because a Polaroid stuck out from the corner. I glanced at the office door, then peaked into the hall. Nobody around that I could see, but even I didn't know all the cameras Colton had positioned around the place.

I flipped open the file with the toe of my boot.

A baby picture. It looked like me.

My palms began to sweat. I swallowed hard. Of course, Colton would have a file. He wanted to understand my blood just as much as me. That would mean research, and he had talked to my mom after he found me. A baby picture wasn't that usual. He probably had dossiers on all his employees.

I picked up the folder and set it on a wobbly chair. He'd written the notes in cuneiform-like Vampiric, but the pictures told enough of the story. Childhood photos of me, then some from when I attended UNR—these photos more clandestine, probably taken across the quad while I walked to class. After these photos, pictures of nuclear devastation: mushroom clouds, flash burns, fake towns ready to be blown to smithereens. The last documents were news reports from the *Reno Gazette Journal* about the Trump administration sending a nuclear waste shipment to Vegas this summer. And a few weeks later—zombies appeared.

I turned away and bent over, my elbows on my knees.

Colton knew. Maybe not everything, but enough that he should have told me. Evelyn had told me the truth.

Hate so hot and sour pulsed over me. He'd wanted to control me, keep me ignorant until he had me drinking the Kool-Aid. Hell, he'd been close. I'd fallen right into him and the life he offered. Now, the little show at the Halloween ball made sense. He wanted me stupidly crushing on him so I wouldn't see the signs. Wanted me to believe it was us against the world, the living and the dead. And I had.

Sweat dripped off my fingertips. A red glow outlined my veins stark beneath my skin. I hid the glow, hugging myself. Leia was right. I needed to learn how to control this power and use it, but Colton had kept me ignorant of my actual strength.

I left the office and slammed the door. The *crack* echoed along the hallway. I took the stairs to burn off my anger. Once my hands stopped going nuclear, I turned on the cell phone Winston had given me. Only two numbers were programmed: his and Leia's.

I texted her: *Help me learn magic?*

A few seconds later, the phone vibrated. *Self-care first. Not teaching you hungover. Eat something and get some real sleep.*

I responded, *STFU.* But Leia might be right. Hard living and magic seemed like a bad mix.

I ordered two wedge salads and a steak from room service before running the tub. I slid into the hot water and realized how sore and wound up my body had grown over the past few days.

Exhaustion pooled in my head, and I closed my eyes.

A chill stirred the water, and the light beyond my eyelids turned bluish.

I opened my eyes and stood again on the Tahoe lakeshore. The impossible freeze burned blue under a full moon. The Sierras surrounded the lake like fangs sharpened by snow.

A shadow stalked over the ice toward the mountains. Wind gusted his long coat.

I screamed for him to come back, but I couldn't speak. He kept walking. At my toes, the ice cracked, splintering toward the shadow that dream logic declared was Colton.

The cracking echoed among the mountains.

GinGinGinGinGin—

My eyes snapped open. I huddled in a dry tub. The water floated over the edges like a splash radius. Unmoving, frozen into still-life.

I gasped, and the water fell. Only about half *slapped* into the tub. The water had somehow turned icy, cold as the lake against my naked skin. Frost flecked the tub's sides.

I shivered so hard that I almost slid on the wet floor. I snatched a towel and hurried from the bathroom. The shaking wrenched my body, and like a child with a fever, I cocooned in the covers and wrapped my hair in the towel.

I fumbled for my phone on the nightstand. According to the clock, I'd closed my eyes for thirty minutes. No way could the water have cooled that much. Things could be worse— turning water from hot to cold seemed less dangerous than almost burning up a chair. At least I dreamed about Colton and not what happened in the desert. But why dream about him at all? This time, there was no fey magic in shot glass to blame. It had to be a sign. He'd been experimenting on me with his vampire dream abilities before everything went to shit. Maybe he was calling to me. Didn't mean I had to answer.

Another shiver made me clench. I dragged the covers over my head and breathed warmth into my cloth cave. It'd been over a year since a scary piece of magic or a new monster had reduced me to hiding under the blankets.

My phone buzzed. The blue light hurt my eyes and reminded me of the icy moonlight. I took a deep breath. Just a text from Leia.

My mom wants to know if you're still alive.

The punctuation made me huff. *Glad to know you care.*

Leia responded, *I'll report your well-being.*

On impulse, I wrote back, *Can't close eyes. Powers are going to shit.*

As soon as it sent, I groaned and hid my face in the blankets. Heat crawled up my neck, which felt better than the shivering. The last thing Leia needed to know was how much I sucked. She'd always had a grip on everything—school, relationships, fitting in as a witch and a normal person.

My phone buzzed. I opened one eye.

Fourth floor, usual spot.

For some reason, the message made me smile. We'd been good friends back in the day, but everything had splintered like a cup with one crack you kept trying to use. Working for the casino had been a big problem, but she'd always aced everything that had me struggling. Even now, if she'd been given these powers, she would probably already have Mike dealt with —and here I was, hiding under the covers. Now, I could see she had her own problems, which I'd been a dick to ignore, but maybe that was why we couldn't quite fit, too much of a power struggle.

By usual spot, she meant the university library. Since she used to commute from Sun Valley, she'd spend all day and late into the night on campus, often hunting through the library stacks. Her favorite spot had been a wall of whiteboards. We'd map out our problems or to-do lists or brainstorm thesis statements.

I took a deep breath and typed back, *Sure*.

An instant response buzzed as if she were also staring at the screen. *Coffee PLEASE!!!*

I kicked off the covers. After dressing in yoga pants and a hand-stenciled *Food Not Bombs* hoodie I'd bought from Winston, I opened the door.

Clarisse crouched in the hallway. She glanced up through her blonde hair. "I thought—"

I slammed the door. I should have stayed in bed.

A gentle knock made me flinch.

"I'm on bodyguard duty. I thought being obvious was less stalker-y than just following you."

I flipped the lock on the door and left through the window. She'd know, but I didn't have to make it easy. So far, she'd lied, manipulated, ripped open my throat, and lied again. Saving me from Mike in the desert didn't give her a pass. Acting cute wouldn't have me eating out of her hand this time.

Campus was less than a mile off, so I reached the library in a few minutes. Like when Leia and I crossed campus yesterday, I blended in with the other students. I picked up two black coffees, then took the elevator, hoping to throw off Clarisse.

Students bent over the desks and clustered around the computers. In alcoves, whiteboards covered the walls, all of them crowded with STEM students, except for Leia's. She slumped in a chair, her fingers steepled, staring at the blank board. When I neared, she glanced over her shoulder. Her lips twitched into a thin smile, but her eyes brightened. I felt it, too. The barest desire to be friends again, for better or worse.

Her almost smile switched to an arched eyebrow. She nodded toward the stairs.

Clarisse leaned against the railing, staring way too hard at her smartphone.

I stalked over to Leia's alcove and shoved the coffee toward her. "Bodyguard duty."

"What gives? I thought she saved you—"

"I'd really like to tear her guts out right now. Can we focus on something else?"

Leia motioned to another seat. "You texted me."

"Not at first."

She took a long sip of coffee. "You know what I mean."

I told her about the last two times I fell asleep—about the burned chair and the water. When I described the dreams, she rolled her eyes.

"I see you still have an unhealthy relationship with Colton—"

"Don't start."

She raised her hands. "I'm just saying you might be in a different type of mess if not for him."

I sighed and waited for her to get it out of her system. "I know how you feel about him."

She pinched the bridge of her nose. "Sorry. We're not here to talk about him. You need to be able to sleep."

"And not kill someone."

She pushed herself out of the chair. A slouchy tweed suit and scarf made her look like a professor wandering Princeton. It worked for her.

She snapped her fingers and wrote on the board with her index finger. I glanced around, but she didn't seem to care if anyone saw.

She drew a stick finger with a frown and wiggly arrows going in all directions. "I'd guess you are experiencing overflow."

I snorted, and she glared at me.

"Like you draw any better. Pay attention." She drew a cone around the stick figure, directing the wiggly arrows to a circle with Xs for eyes. "You need something to focus it on. Like giving a screaming child a TV."

"Wait, am I the screaming child, or is that my deadly magic?"

Leia glared. "Inherited power like yours usually leans toward a certain Fidget."

"A what?"

"Remember that girl in our history class who would knit the whole time but got hundreds on all the exams?"

I nodded. It'd pissed me off since I had to write down every word to get a B-.

"That's an example of a Fidget. That's what I call it, anyways. It's the subject of my thesis."

"Give me some more examples. Like biting my nails?"

"My research indicates it's usually something creative. Whittling, drumming—movement-oriented. I've got this friend over in San Francisco who inherited a connection to the wind, and he's a masterful b-boy, always moving."

I drew my knees to my chest. "Well, you know I can't dance. I just blow stuff up."

"It could be a new skill," Leia said. "Your inheritance revolves around science, power, fire, and war."

I winced. "Thanks for the reminder that I've got genocide in my blood."

"You can't shy away from the truth, Gin."

"I don't see how this helps. What? Should I take up playing with matches?"

She tilted her head. "Not a bad idea, actually." She patted her pockets and then opened a canvas shoulder bag. She tossed me a worn lighter. Interconnected runes vined across the metal. "You know the annoying kid from the *X-Men* movies? Welcome to your new persona."

I slipped the lighter into my hoodie pocket. "Great, just what I always wanted."

"Light a candle with that and leave it burning all night. If you still have trouble, I'll bring you a blessed candle tomorrow."

"Is that all you got, Doctor Leia?"

"That's Doctor Professor Leia to you. And yeah, that's my best idea."

I shrugged. "All right, cool. I'll let you know if it works."

She smeared off the whiteboard with her fist. "You don't have to go. I've got research to do, and I could suggest some reading for you. If you want."

I glanced at Clarisse, still waiting by the stairs. "Sure, why not." Going to the Saints meant maybe destroying another part of my room or worse—another Colton dream.

Leia dug into her canvas bag, her arm disappearing way deeper than the bag's dimensions. She hefted a book titled *Encyclopedia of Deities*. "Time to learn about your cousins."

23

Leia shook me awake a few hours later when the library closed. I felt like a child being roused from a nap. It'd been years since I'd fallen asleep with my face in a book. At least I hadn't turned the library to ash.

Clarisse must've joined us after I fell asleep. She examined Leia's rune work, scrawled over the whiteboard like algebra. Leia erased the board and promised to check in at sunrise. I left the library with the last few stragglers, Clarisse still following me. I allowed her to walk with me as we returned to the casino since I'd lost the will and energy to make her leave. At the door to my room, she blocked it open with her boot.

"What?"

"I overheard you talking about your dreams with Leia."

I swallowed a yawn. "You ever heard of the word privacy?"

She removed her boot. "I assume Colton has explained that when vampires age, they do become physically weaker, but they also develop extra abilities. He's pushing two centuries, so his power might have manifested. That's why I came early to Halloween—I was supposed to see what I could uncover about him. Some vampires are dreamwalkers. They can sort of communicate telepathically through dreams and are powerful manipulators. Colton always kept his talent close, but that's what I suspected. We don't know what he can do." She returned to her crouch against the wall, thumbing her phone.

I shut the door, then cracked it open again. "Thanks."

Part of me wanted to take my keys and head to Tahoe that night and confront Colton, but part of me wanted to listen to Leia and ignore him. He'd lied about all that I was—how could I believe anything he said? If I were being honest with myself, the dreams were probably a trap, too. He'd probably tested his powers on me back before Halloween for just this type of thing. But the Saints was his, and he cared about it more than Eve's coven ever could. It was my duty to figure out how to get him back. I owed it to all the other employees—all of my friends— who counted on the casino. He still held too many of the cards, but I had a few of my own now. If I went looking for him with a clear head, I could establish boundaries.

Still, at fifty percent human, I needed to take care of myself. I set an alarm for six a.m. and then lit a candle with the lighter Leia gave me. Just because I was going to go chat with Colton didn't mean I wanted him in my dreams. The flame burned straight and steady.

Abnormal dreams flitted at the edge of my sleepy haze when the alarm blared Kendrick Lamar's "HUMBLE." four hours later. Ice and water and drowning, and no Colton. More importantly, no spontaneous combustion. Maybe Leia's lighter and candle had worked.

I rolled out of bed and texted Winston about driving to Tahoe. He hadn't responded by the time I dressed and laced up my boots, so I headed for the garage.

Colton kept a variety of sports cars, but I snagged the keys to a 4WD Jeep.

At first, I wondered if I'd lost my followers, but going up Mt. Rose Highway, the lack of traffic made the motorcycle rather obvious. A motorcycle would be harder to lose, though. Whatever Colton's messages meant, the last thing he'd want would be Evelyn's watchers following me.

At Incline Village, I pulled into a sports rental shop run by one of Winston's snowboarder bros, Joey, who just nodded along as I dashed past the counter, asking him to cover for me. I slipped out the back as the motorcycle turned into the parking lot. I sprinted into the woods toward the lake.

As part of my training, one of the first things Colton taught me was how to run. Not how to cover the distance I had with Clarisse—that type of running was a whole different thing—but we spent several weekends racing up the Mount Rose summit in the middle of the night. Sometimes, I'd could flip the switch in my legs and keep up with Colton's speed. Other nights, he left me gasping in the pines. Nearly dying several times and my long haul through the desert must have taught me how to access the weirdness in my blood since the last few times I'd sprinted like something inhuman. Today, while not out of pure joy, zigzagging through the trees to lose a tail felt pretty good.

The ground turned steep as I neared the lake, and I grinned as I half-slid, half-fell toward the water. Running downhill, my body instinctively trying to stay upright, always felt the best— plus, whatever bruises I received thrashing at full tilt down a rocky incline would vanish in a few hours.

On the shore, I crouched behind a boulder, a thin line of water swirling between my feet. I closed my eyes until my heartbeat and breathing eased. As my senses widened beyond my pounding pulse, the forest brightened, like cleaning a dirty window. Steller's jays chittered at each other. Water slapped against the rocky shore. A squirrel skittered up a pine. Incense cedars and ponderosas creaked. The pungent-sweet smell of sap, loam, and sage filled the air as the sun warmed the mountainside.

A vampire could hide in this terrain—Colton had avoided me often enough—but I hoped the forest might sense the disturbance. A superior predator wandering the woods usually caused something to cry a warning.

When first exploring whatever power lived in my blood, Colton had nagged me about meditating. It hadn't done much except once when I settled into this trance for hours, my body perfectly still, my breath so shallow I felt as if I were suffocating. Except I couldn't wake myself up, like sleep paralysis. When Colton found me six hours later, he called it a success. I preferred the term *nightmare*. Colton wanted me to practice it, but I'd never wanted to feel that powerless again.

I hadn't been meditating that day in training, but when he'd taken me into his dream, I had frozen up. Such a state might call to him.

I settled my shoulders against a rock, tucked from view. Hopefully, it would be comfy for a few hours—or longer.

I cupped Leia's lighter in my palm and closed my eyes.

The trance stole over my skin like frost. My lungs ached for more air, but my body refused. All turned cold, but with my body locked, I could look beyond it. I crawled onto the rocky shore. No, not me. I still sat against the rock, my lungs barely lapping up oxygen.

I stood even though I had no legs to stand on. Well, at least I seemed to be getting better at this whole god-powers thing.

The world had turned to ice and frost, to blue light and glistening crystal. The water held so still it appeared frozen—like in my dreams. The oversized moon hung just above the mountains' rim, even though it should be daylight.

Behind me, the trees bristled black. Moonbeams splintered

between them before fading to fog. Their tops, capped with snow, gleamed like spears.

This dreamscape of Tahoe felt separate from the peaceful place where I sat against a boulder. Dark and cryptic, this place felt like a dangerous fairytale while I associated Tahoe with glittering sunlight and water so clear nothing could hide. Even so, I'd come here by choice, not dragged her against my will. If Colton wanted to meet, then I had questions he would answer first.

In the stillness, my name cracked like breaking ice.

Gin.

I faced the water. A shadow stretched before the moon, a long reflection. It grew smaller and coalesced into a figure, standing on the frost-bitten water.

Colton, it had to be—just like in my dream. He waited on the water.

I stepped onto the lake. Instead of pressing through the icy membrane, the water felt solid. Not like ice but not a liquid, either. More like the moment when you jump off a bridge or cliff when the water seems to stretch taut before swallowing you.

I walked across the lake.

The wind grew stiff, tugging at whatever made this form. Colton's silhouette became clearer with each step. His coat flapping, one hand raised to keep his hat in place. A black bandanna hooked over his nose.

He tipped his hat, and my next step seemed to bring me yards closer. Suddenly, I was in his arms, his body as cold as the ice. I wanted to punch him, shove him away from me, kick his shins, scream *Why did you leave me?* Except I was supposed to be mad at him for more important reasons. He'd lied to me over and over again.

His arms held me against his broad chest—real and solid.

Not a dream unless I'd become dreamstuff, too. *I knew you would come.*

I relaxed against his ice-crusted long coat. Maybe he hadn't really left me, or else he wouldn't have contacted me through these dreams. Maybe he still had a plan. *What's going on?*

He tipped up my chin, and his touch felt so real I took a sharp breath. *You sensed my call.*

The dreams?

Exactly. Long ago, all vampires could communicate in this manner. Now, dreamwalkers come rarely to our kind.

I leaned back from his grasp but kept my hands on his arms. *Why did you bring me here now? Where were you in the desert when—when I needed you?* Not the question I should be asking, but if he could just explain why, then maybe, just maybe, everything could go back to the way it was, and I could shrug off this responsibility like a bloody jacket.

His grip tightened. *Oh, Gin, except you are here now. Proof you didn't need me.*

Wrong answer. The lake darkened. A cloud dissected the moon. A sound like rocks grinding reverberated through me.

I tried to back away, but Colton drew me closer as the wind gusted over us. He wrapped me in his coat.

Relax—I've only arranged a meeting.

The cold seeped into me, pressed against his unliving body. Here it was, a trick within a trick. Colton didn't want to meet with me, at least, not just me—there was always something more. I'd never see through his bluff if I couldn't give up on him being the boss I wanted him to be. Those days were gone.

The shadows deepened. A tall figure blocked the moon. It slowly shrunk as it approached.

A chemical slick washed over my tongue as I tasted Mike on the icy air. I shoved at Colton. *Let me go!*

His lips brushed my hair. *Trust me, just one more time, and I'll tell you everything.*

The shadowy figure remained undefined as it came nearer. Darkness wicked off the body like smoke. Red coals replaced eyes.

Colton tipped his hat. *Here she is, as requested.*

The shadow rippled. *This is only the dreaming part of my daughter.*

I shrank back, but Colton gripped my shoulder. He hadn't called to me through the dreams to check on me or to explain himself. He wanted my father to find me and—do whatever he intended. Colton was still trying to fulfill the bargain, get whatever had been promised between them. I'd turned into a pawn again.

His fingers bit my skin like ice shards. *She grows angry. I'd suggest speaking your piece.*

I tried to break his hold, but he pulled me into a vice, my arm twisted behind my back.

I fucking hate you, Colton! I'm going to tear you apart as soon as I get out of here!

The shadow bloomed like a mushroom cloud, and a deep laugh boomed over the lake. Embers smoldered in his shadow. *Now you sound like my girl.*

I stilled, and Colton loosened his grip. *I am not yours. I want nothing to do with you.*

The shadow drew closer and seemed to kneel, the coals level with my eyes. *You are a part of me. We are bound together whether you wish it or not. If you learn to obey me, I will show you our power.*

I don't want power. I don't want your blood. I don't want any of this!

I am a god of balance, Juniper. I heal as I destroy. I am

chemo and Fat Boy. You are part of that balance. Without you, I am a totality of destruction.

Colton released my arm and gripped my shoulders, pressing his thumbs into my tensed muscles. *Consider your future, Gin. You will live long, and such power makes for a better life.*

I ducked out of Colton's grasp and away from them. Two types of fathers—one by genetics and one by knowledge. Both saw me as needing them like a child they didn't want to grow up.

Why do you want me, Mike? A half-human must look like a pathetic excuse for your bloodline.

The coal eyes burned white. *You are, for now. Once I transform you into my image, you will become strength itself.*

Okay, fuck this. Time to go. Forget Colton and his *trust me, and I will tell you everything* bullshit. If he'd united with this creep, I needed to leave the lake and hope Evelyn's tail had stuck around for a quick escape off the mountain. I closed my eyes. My body felt far off and stiff. I stretched my feelings outward, imagining the Steller's jays' cries, the slap-lap of the water, the boulder's cool grit.

Gin, wait!

I wasn't sure who called for me, Colton or Mike, but the water cracked, and I plunged into the cold.

Except no icy water stole my breath away, submerging me in darkness. I fell into the club—the Nightmare. There I sat, two years ago, somehow looking so much younger as Clarisse sucked on my neck.

Except I watched it happen—felt an uncanny fear staring at myself through the eyes of another. Colton's thoughts washed over me like a puff of cigarette smoke. He was so afraid he had the shakes, and I felt them in my own hands.

Now, he wedged himself in the doorframe, ankles crossed

and thumbs hooked in his belt to hide his trembling. His thoughts skittered around me, the skinny white girl currently being drained by Clarisse. He wasn't afraid of me. No, it was that I had arrived at all. Fate, or the will of a god he had long ago locked up, had somehow found him all the way out here in Reno.

His hands spasmed into fists, and his fingernails cut his skin. A little blood oozed. Maybe he guessed wrong. He'd lost track of her at five years old when her mother had passed among friends for housing. He'd been distracted when Clarisse's blood-mother and ruler of much of Vegas had made a bad bet on the Sacramento werewolf club, asking Colton to clean it up. That year had been a wash in more ways than one, and losing his grip on the girl had been the least of his worries.

Until now. Now, it gave him shivers worse than his first sip of blood. How had this girl come here? Dirt poor in a southern corner of Nevada, and now she was underage and drunk in his club, not that legality mattered. Still, how had she come to be here?

Clarisse swung off the girl and wiggled down her black leather dress that barely covered her lacy thong. She glanced at Colton and licked her lips. "Didn't expect to see the Cowboy here. Thought this wasn't your scene."

She bent over, flashing her lace, and licked the line of blood dribbling down the girl's neck.

With heightened hearing, he caught the girl's moan, and her head sagged forward onto Clarisse's shoulder. Clarisse smoothed her hair. "All done, baby girl." She snapped her fingers at the attendants. "You can take her away now. Don't think anyone else should drink her for a bit."

Colton motioned for them to wait. He stepped into Clarisse and gripped her wrist. "Why her?"

Clarisse looked at his hand, then at him. "What's this,

Colton? You know women have their own rights in this century."

"Good thing you're a vampire in my club. Why her? She's average, and you prefer slutty."

She tapped his wrist. "Language, cowboy."

He squeezed. "Answer the question."

Clarisse swayed. She ran a hand over her bloody lips, smearing red. "She's different. Got a spark. Like the burn of sun on your skin." She stumbled into him. "Remember that?"

Colton swung away just as she bent over and vomited right where his boots had been.

The other vampires stopped, even as their drugged, drunk, or spelled humans begged and bucked for more. Colton's casino had a good reputation for clean drinking, and if someone had given Clarisse a poisoned blood bag, well, those were some high stakes.

Clarisse's head snapped up. Her eyes were clear and glaring. "How dare you? When my mother hears about this, your little casino is dust!"

Colton hooked his arm through hers and turned her toward the girl. "Relax, you aren't poisoned. Her blood—just doesn't agree with you."

Clarisse shoved him off. "What do you mean?"

He signaled for his attendants to cut the music and raise the lights. "A hunch." He knelt in front of the girl, who stank like a distillery. How much alcohol had Clarisse or his club runners plied her with? It didn't matter; the blame was with him. This was his casino and his party.

He took her slack left hand, then tilted her chin up. Her eyes swung around the room before slowly settling on his face. "Are you next? You're hot." She grinned as if Clarisse hadn't just drained a pint of her blood while humping her. Goddamn, he hated when kids like this ended up in his club.

"None of that, now. What's your name, kid?"

"Juniper."

"Well, you do smell like a gin bath. How old are you?"

"Not telling that."

Colton sighed and tipped back his hat. "We need to have a talk. How's some steak and eggs sound?"

"I don't have any money."

He straightened and offered his hand. "It's on the house."

She shrugged and tried to stand. He caught her.

Clarisse stomped her foot. "Just take a bite already. Or are you going to vanish the evidence?"

He tucked the girl under his arm. "I do not allow poisoned blood bags into my casino. You're fine. Go drain another girl. Over twenty-one this time."

"I want answers, Colton."

He guided the girl out the door and toward an elevator. "And I'll let you know when I find something interesting."

Clarisse flashed her fangs, but he swung into an elevator before she could snatch at the girl. Somebody would be pounding on his office door for these answers before long, but he didn't want to bite the girl without asking for some sort of sober permission.

She nestled into his side, gripping his coat. "Is this part of the game? Am I winning?"

It took a moment for him to remember the vampire "role-playing" event meant to entice the humans like her to the club.

"You might have just won the lottery."

My muscles spasmed as I unfurled my body. Tingles burst over my skin, shivering shook me, and I curled on the sand, trembling. A ringing in my ears subsided, and the night noises grew louder and replaced it. I made a strange grunting as I shook in the sand and clamped my mouth shut hard. What the fuck had Colton done to me?

After two tries, I struggled to my knees and leaned against the boulder. "See, you can do this," I whispered as I got my feet under me, crouching in the boulder's shadow.

"Not likely."

I stood too quickly and fell over, banging my knees on the rocky shore.

Colton stepped from the trees. Unlike the dream version, he looked ragged. Mud and sand splattered his coat, and one shoulder seam had torn. Briars and thorns prickled the hem. He'd lost his hat, and his bandana was tied around his forehead like a bandage.

I stood slowly. "Stay back."

He raised his hands. "I'm not here to hurt you—"

"Oh, fucking right. You're just here to turn me over to dear ol' dad, who you made a deal with or knew about or who the hell knows! What was I, the big pot to lure him in?"

He rubbed his eyes. "Gin, stop—"

I stomped into the trees, but wobbling and stumbling into the trunks ruined the effect. "There's nothing you can do to make me listen. You trapped me in your head!" My eyes watered, and I sniffed hard. He'd sent me to that night even though I told him not to—even though he knew how much it hurt.

Air gusted past me, and he pressed against my back, one large hand spread over my stomach while his other arm crossed my chest. "If we didn't play his game, he would have nuked the Saints. He would have destroyed everything you loved so you would only love him."

My mind screamed at me, begging me to struggle, but my

body sagged against his familiar form. "There's no we. You left me with him. He wanted—he wanted to hurt me."

"I was there. If Clarisse hadn't arrived, I would have stopped him."

Heat flushed my face, and tears blurred my vision. "But I didn't know that." My voice thickened.

He loosened his grip and turned me. "I made a mistake. I couldn't let you wake up and run away, so I—"

"Trapped me. Again."

His hands lowered, and he stepped back. "I wanted to be honest with you. I figured the moment you met me was the most honest I could be right now. That night changed everything for me, too."

The fear overlaying the memory had been real, a fear I'd never witnessed in Colton before. His choices had come back to haunt him, and he'd felt trapped. A deal with a god he regretted making, a human life in the balance. His first thought hadn't been how he could use me but rather about getting me away from Clarisse and the other vampires—about getting me some food and sobering me up so I could understand what was happening. He'd sent me into the dream, so maybe he could control what I saw, but still, that was the Colton I thought I was working for these past two years. Maybe there was still some truth to that.

I looked up into his dark eyes. For a moment, memory turned the air golden, and we stood in the Saints on Halloween. "I still don't trust you." Did I believe that? If he told me to swim across the lake right now, I'd pitch a fit, but I'd still be in the water. Then I'd curse myself when I nearly froze to death—the same cycle.

He cupped my chin. "Let me make you feel safe."

"Why, when it's all lies?"

He leaned closer. "Then let's be honest, from here on out."

His rich, metallic scent washed over me. I wanted to believe him because then I could forget it, leave it all in his hands. Just like I wanted to get drunk and wander the city for a night. I wanted the safety of vulnerability, even if he shattered it the next night.

He still cupped my face. I stiffened. Either I would lean into him or run. He'd lied over and over, but he'd shown me what life really was, the light and the dark. He'd protected me from monsters and taught me to protect myself. He'd given me a home, not just the Saints. You couldn't have the Saints without Colton—he meant home, too. His smile with fangs that dimpled his lower lip, the way he laughed with his bartenders, checked in with his waiters, and knew the staff's birthdays and families. The copper and leather smell of him.

He pulled me close again and held me until I only smelled him. He took a breath as if imitating a human. "Come with me, and I'll tell you everything."

We passed silently through the gray forest as dawn cracked the mountains.

24

Alight burned among the trees as we climbed the hill. The lake became a blue disk below.

A house materialized through the dawn haze—an A-frame that faced the lake with windows turning silver as dawn grew stronger. An oil lantern flickered from a hook by the door.

He stepped onto the wooden porch and offered his hand. "Only Franklin knows I own this house. We'll be safe here."

I stepped beside him, suddenly close on the narrow porch. His fingers were laced with mine. I shook myself, pulled my hand free, and crossed my arms. Sure, a part of me wanted to believe him, to save the Saints together, but he needed to give me answers.

"I found the folder, Colton. You knew all along what I was, even if you somehow 'lost me.' And you knew that Mike was back before the zombie ever showed up. That thing that hurt Kia wasn't my fault—it was yours. And you let me believe it was my fuck-up."

He traced a design on the door, and the wooden grain glowed silver for a second. He gripped my shoulder. "I know. I

187

played the hand I was dealt and played it poorly. Let me make it up to you. Your home—our home—is the Saints. I'm not giving that up."

He swung open the door and took my hand, pulling me inside. For a second, the cabin was dark, then all the lights flicked on at once. I blinked until my eyes adjusted.

A slight woman sat on an armchair, her legs crossed. Evelyn. Clarisse stood behind her.

Colton dropped my hand, and I shoved my fists into my pockets. Of course, they'd think we were here for other reasons, not just the answers I wanted.

He tipped his hat. "Well played, Eve."

She smiled, but it looked more threatening than friendly. "What else did you expect? Or did you forget you brought my blood daughter here once upon a time for a similar tryst?" She glanced over her shoulder at Clarisse, who smirked at me.

I expected anger to explode, but disappointment settled like a noose around my neck. Another lie, promising a safety Colton couldn't offer. Of course he and Clarisse had fucked here, and she would guess he'd bring me here, too. I'd never be able to stay one step ahead of these vampires, not if I kept thinking like a heartsick human.

If I could have manifested the power in my blood to go invisible or shape-shift into a bird, I would have. Instead, I wished to be as far away as humanly possible. Perhaps drowning in the Atlantic Ocean.

I vanished from the cabin.

Part Three
Fallout

"We will begin this hearing, which focuses on the findings of the National Cancer Institute report on radioactive fallout from nuclear testing at the Nevada Test Site in the 1950's and 1960's. [...] Atmospheric nuclear bomb testing in Nevada yielded significant amounts of radioactive fallout. [...] Hot spots where the iodine-131 fallout was greatest included many areas far away from Nevada, including New England." –Senate Hearing 105-180

25

Wind screamed over me.

I had no control, no sense of my body. My skin felt stretched taut as a parachute but also thin as a sieve. I tumbled and spread apart until I felt lost in the dark, then riffled together like the pages of a book.

I *splashed* back into my body.

Something crusted my skin and stiffened my clothes, and my hair formed a matted curtain. Grit stung my eyes. I tried to move, and the ground shifted beneath me. Sensation returned to my fingers. Sand. I palmed handfuls of sand.

A wave of freezing water submerged me, and I flailed, struggling to my feet as the sand and water pulled me off balance.

I crawled out of the ocean and over the water line.

I panted as the water dripped off me, darkening the sand. This wasn't a tropical beach, though, and felt colder than Tahoe. The shivers began, but if I curled into a ball, I might never move again.

Gray skies spread over the water. In front of me, a boardwalk stretched left and right. Even in the cold, people were out and about, hurrying along.

A winter jogger kicked up sand a few yards ahead and made a wide loop around me.

I stood. Nothing felt broken, just exhausted. Sand crunched between my teeth, and I spat.

A new skyline cast neon over the clouds: Bally's, the Golden Nugget, Harrah's, Caesar's. My wish had come true. This had to be Atlantic City.

This one statement—my wish...had come true—kept repeating in my head as I swayed in the sand.

A woman ducked from under the boardwalk. She wore a puffy Eagles coat and tight jeans. She waved, and I shifted my slack-jawed look from the casinos' lights to her.

She came a few steps closer and lit a cigarette. "You 'right?"

I sniffed. Snot had left a long trail down my face. I shook myself and wiped my face on my sleeve. "This—this is Atlantic City?"

She nodded and came a few steps closer. "That's right. You want a smoke?"

"More than anything."

She tossed me the pack. I pulled out the lighter Leia had given me. It warmed my palm and magically sparked, just as I would expect of Leia's gift.

The woman stood beside me, out of reach, and I leaned closer to return the cigarettes. "I like to watch the ocean, you know. Clears my head. You see lots of shit come out of these waters. I've even seen some bodies. But you, I watched you slowly wash in. Just a little bit at a time." She side-eyed me.

I took a long drag and closed my eyes. "I don't know what happened."

She ground the butt in the sand, pocketed it, then lit

another. "You need anything? Food, water? I got a few shots of gin left."

I whipped toward her at the mention of gin, and she jumped back. Her humanness struck me—wrinkles, chapped lips, limp hair. Aging, which wouldn't touch me for centuries. She was not a plant or some sort of spy all the way out here. Just a human being nice to what she saw as a lost kid.

Tears welled up, and I looked away, focusing on digging in my pockets. I pulled a soggy twenty from inside my jacket. "To replace the cigarettes."

She shook her head. "I think you need it more than me, hon."

I laughed, though it edged into either maniacal or broken. "No, I don't. I'm one of the rich bastards living on the top floor. I try not to be, but I am."

She took the twenty. "If you say so. Keep away from the water, 'kay?"

I shoved my hands in my pockets and trudged toward the boardwalk.

Colton had friends in every gambling city. Here, a vampire clan owned a squat building opening onto the sand called Paradise Found—these damn vampires and their puns. Odds were, a magic user had sensed whatever power I'd expended to come here. Colton might already know my location—on the other side of the freakin' country.

I walked the boardwalk until I found an empty pizza parlor called Grotto's that made my stomach growl. I ordered a large pizza before asking to use the phone. It took three tries before I remembered one of Winston's numbers. Leia, with her magic, would have been a better choice, but she obviously worked with the vampires. At least Winston pretended neutrality.

The call went to voicemail. My throat thickened, and I coughed. The cashier kid faked scrolling on his phone. I turned away and slouched against the counter, trying to sound normal, as if I hadn't lost that skill over the past two years. "Hey, Winston. Just wanted to let you know I ended up going to Atlantic City. Um, I'm not sure what to do here. I guess I'll hang out at the Paradise for a while since Colton's buddy owns it. I'll call from there."

I slid into a back booth and took my time eating. The calories cleared my head.

The door opened. I resisted the need to watch whoever came in. At least for a little longer, I'd become a regular twenty-something partying at the beach—and I had to act the role.

Footsteps and the metallic tap of a cane approached my booth. I focused on shoving two-thirds of a slice into my mouth.

A stooped, elderly man stopped at my table. He leaned on a cane. No—not a cane.

I pressed into the vinyl. I hadn't seen dear Dad in the flesh since the desert. But in this form, he looked like a great-grandfather. Checkered shirt, slacks held up with suspenders, a wide-brimmed Vietnam veterans hat. Arthritis rounded his knuckles, and his skin stretched thin and pale. I only recognized him because of the cane—my brand. I'd used his—our—power to come here, so of course he'd find me first. Didn't seem like the trip had done either of us any good.

He eased into the booth with a grunt. Part of me screamed to run, but I also wanted my weapon back. Besides, if he were at full god-power, running wouldn't help, but some instinct said this elderly version wasn't an act.

"Hello, Juniper."

My mouth dried, and I felt for my soda, almost knocking it over.

He set the brand on the table. "Aren't you going to greet dear old dad?"

I slurped with all the teenage disdain remaining in my bones. "You aren't my father."

He huffed. "As if the man who raised you did any better."

I stirred the ice cubes. "What do you want?"

"Come home."

"I might."

He bared yellowed teeth. "There is no *might*. If you make one move to leave, I'll kill them all. I'll crater the casino. Bet on it."

I pulled a napkin from the dispenser and wiped off my hands. I had to think. This wasn't some fey deal Colton wanted me to sort out. Something had spooked Mike. Perhaps me escaping our home state. I needed time and information.

I settled into the booth. "All right. If you're my father, then tell me about my heritage."

He picked up a congealing pizza slice and took a bite. Somehow, his decrepit body was real. "What do you want to know, sweetheart?"

My jaw twitched at *sweetheart*. "Where were you when I was a kid?"

He picked at his teeth with a dirty thumbnail. Grease stained his mustache. "The bastards were afraid of what they created—my older brothers and me. They wanted our power without the violence. That's what scared them. They hired your vampire friend to stuff me into a barrel, but we made a deal because I knew you were growing in your momma's belly." He reached a knobby hand toward mine. I hid them in my lap.

His lip twitched. "Except he betrayed me. He never came to wake me up like he promised. So, I'll make him pay, along with the rest of them who buried me underground."

"Who's 'they?'" I made a mental note of the mentioned brothers. Apparently, I had uncles to worry about.

He smiled. "The gamblers and the ditch-diggers"—his voice

raised and spit flecked his splotchy beard—"and the river-runners and the blood-drinkers and the wing-flappers and the dirt-eaters and the spell-weavers! I had only begun my creation, and they called it destruction!"

I glanced toward the counter, but nobody seemed to listen. They repeated their pizza shop duties over and over, boxes piling on the counter but nobody coming to pick them up like automation run amok.

He gripped the edge of the table, joints popping. He took a deep breath. "But you. I created you. They didn't wait to see my finest destruction."

I leaned over the table until I could smell his acridity. "You had *nothing* to do with me."

He patted the brand. "Oh, sweetheart, your legend begins with my mythology."

A laugh bubbled like soda fizz. Even though I shared his blood, I could choose what to do with it. I was still part god, so why was I sitting here listening to *this*? I had less patience for guys that I kicked out of the club. If it wasn't this fucker calling himself my dad jerking me around, it was Colton or Eve. Here I was, a demigod, still acting like a teenager with a curfew. I'd let them drag me around, but if they all wanted me, then I had a choice.

I drew the brand to my side. "I really don't give a shit."

"You will when the Saints is a pillar of fire."

The brand heated in my hands. The tabletop smoked and blackened. "Didn't you just hear what I said?" I stabbed the brand through his chest.

I expected him to vanish in smoke or lightning. Instead, the brand seared through meat. Bones cracked. I leaned into it.

He gasped, then bared his yellow teeth in a grin. "You can't win 'em all."

I wrenched back the brand. Charred meat and burned hair made me gag.

He fell forward over the table.

I watched the body and sipped my drink. When he didn't move after I counted to one hundred, I slid the brand into my belt and left the shop with my final pizza slice.

If dear dad had figured out my location so quickly, Colton and Eve couldn't be far behind.

I paced the boardwalk, muttering. I'd probably logged a couple of miles before a calf cramp drove me to a bench. My body still felt dragged down by exhaustion, even though I really needed some super endurance right about now.

I couldn't pull the pieces apart. Did Colton know where I was? Did it matter? Could I disappear? Sure, Colton would cut off my accounts eventually, but if I had god-blood, then I could probably get an even better job, right?

The sun dipped behind the buildings, the last rays cutting across the ocean. I took a salty breath. Once night came, something would find me. Colton kept Reno reasonably safe after dark, but with the stories I'd heard, other cities sounded like horror shows.

The Paradise Found hunkered beside Caesar's, but waltzing inside meant game over. I needed a plan, a persona, a reason. Something. If I returned to Colton, I wanted a choice in the matter. God, why did I act like such a silly kid around him?

Exhaustion seeped down my spine, and my stomach churned from scarfing a large pizza even though I needed the calories. My blood should prop me up, but maybe I'd spent too much power on however the hell I'd gotten here.

A cold gust spraying sand pushed me from my stupor. I massaged my calf. Most folks on the boardwalk hurried toward one casino or another, bundled in puffy coats. Which made the crew coming toward me conspicuous. Long and tattered coats paired with straw cowboy hats made them look like a parody of a vampire gang.

That was my cue. I hopped the boardwalk railing and ran. Sand sucked at my feet, and I stumbled. "C'mon, c'mon." I imagined taking off like deer, but my legs ticked like a dead car battery. No more juice.

The vampires dropped into the sand, silent as the shadows they didn't cast. "Juniper, ward of Colton, we have a warrant for your capture!"

I faced them, mainly because running away from vampires at night usually got you a broken bone. Here they went with that ward crap again. If Colton and I had any salvageable relationship after this mess, we were going to have a talk.

I drew the brand and leaned on it. I didn't have to pretend to pant or shake with exhaustion. I bent double, hands on my knees. Something wasn't right. I hadn't felt this weak in years, even before I met Colton.

The vampires formed a crescent around me, five to one. A woman stepped forward. She wore a purple straw cowboy hat. "Gin, we met once before at the Saints. Delilah, remember?"

I didn't, but nodded anyway.

She took a step closer, her hand outstretched. "You've had a shock. You spent too much energy. It's time to come in and let us take care of you."

I set my feet wide and cocked the brand over my shoulder. "Leave me alone."

The brand grew hot. Heat radiated from the head, warming me. I ground my boots into the sand, leaning forward, ready to run and hack and slash.

The other vampires backed up. The female vampire glanced over her shoulder and retreated a few steps. Except they weren't looking at me. My heart pounded as I steeled myself to turn around.

I didn't need to.

Clarisse padded beside me. "Strange how I never met you, Delilah. Sure you've been to Nevada?"

Leia sauntered to my other side. She lit a cigarette with a snap of her fingers. Her thrift store professor vibe should have been out of place on the beach, but between me in my dirty jeans and leather jacket and Clarisse in obscenely tight pants and crop top, she balanced us out.

The vampires retreated to the boardwalk but hovered over us. Clarisse made a shooing motion.

Leia hugged me. I dropped the brand and leaned into her.

"Please don't tell me Colton or Evelyn or your mom sent you."

"Nah, we're free agents."

Clarisse crossed her arms and cocked one hip. "Where's my hug?"

I rolled my eyes as I pulled back from Leia. "How'd you find me?"

Clarisse hitched a thumb over her shoulder. "Winston knew—damn it!" She whipped around and scanned the board-walk. A lone vampire still tracked us. "Shit, he must've gone into another club."

"What are you talking about?" I asked.

Leia hooked an arm around my shoulders and guided me toward a set of stairs. "Winston took us through some hell gates to get here, but he got a little excited. All that fey magic."

"I'll find him." Clarisse jumped straight from the sand to the boardwalk.

Slogging through the sand seemed to drain me further. "What's going on, Leia?"

"You scared the living shit out of everyone, that's what."

"He—he followed me."

"Your dad?"

"Yeah, but he was . . . weak." I paused, sagging on the brand.

She raised an eyebrow. "Like you?"

"I feel very human."

"You don't have to be speciesist."

I shook my head. "You know what I mean."

She tugged at my arm. "Talk later. If we can get you out of here before Colton's spies surround us, it will be a miracle."

We climbed the steps. I half-pulled myself up by the railing, panting even though we were at sea level rather than Reno elevation. "Why did you come for me?"

"Clarisse saw you vanish, and Colton and her blood mother squabble over whose fault it was. In her words, they just wanted to chain you up like some toy mascot. She's not about that."

On the boardwalk, I sagged against a bench. Two crotch rocket motorcycles were parked at the top. They glistened with some sort of fey glamour, but my blood helped me to see through it, though with less success than usual.

I swallowed hard and swayed. "What's wrong with me?"

Leia steadied me with a hand on my shoulder. "Sometimes magic is fixed to place. Maybe your place is Nevada."

"Then how did I end up here?"

Clarisse hauled Winston out of an alley. His lipstick was smeared, and a human followed them, waving.

Leia swung onto a bike and motioned for me to join her. "Have you ever looked at a map of hotspots from the Nevada nuclear tests?"

I slid behind her. "Why would I?"

"Turns out, New Jersey got some fallout. Particularly along the coast. Maybe you traveled along the same lines."

Clarisse gave Leia a dirty look, and for a moment, I wasn't

sure why, then realized how the small bike forced Leia and me together.

Winston said something in a fey tongue. His eyes sparked lightning over his cheekbones and curled around his eyebrows.

I waved at him. "You okay there, man?"

He licked his lips. Clarisse slapped his shoulder.

"Focus, you have to get us back to Nevada."

He jumped onto the second bike, and Clarisse climbed behind him. The bike rocketed way too fast for the narrow beachside streets.

Leia gunned the engine. "Hold on!"

26

Traveling the gates took most of the next twenty-four hours, but the closer we jumped to Nevada, the stronger I felt. We reached Virginia City around dark, dropping out of a random doorway and sitting on an embankment devoid of any houses. They drop-tested Leia's skill on the bike, and we skidded sideways onto a paved road. I jumped off but managed to rip open my jeans below the knees. Somehow, Winston kept their bike upright, idling on the road. Clarisse still clutched him with her face buried between his shoulder blades.

I limped over to Leia, though already my asphalt-burned leg had stopped bleeding. Mountain ranges rolled into the twilight, and a large, softly-lit *V* built into the rock outlined Mount Davidson behind us. The thin air felt fuller than by the ocean. I took a deep breath, and the trembling exhaustion fell away beneath the Sierras. Maybe Leia was right. Maybe I couldn't escape Nevada. Not that I ever really wanted to.

I hefted the bike off Leia. She panted, her clothes dusty but in one piece somehow.

I helped her sit upright, then she waved me off. "Just give me a second."

Clarisse swung off Winston's bike. He revved up and down the empty road, popping wheelies like a toddler too full of energy.

"What's wrong with him?" I asked.

Leia leaned back on her hands and took a deep breath. Clarisse crouched next to her, a hand hovering behind her back as if to support her. "Nothing," Leia said. "All the gate travel reminded him what it's like to live as the fey again. Winston might not choose that life permanently, but he does love it." She waved her hands over the leg that had been trapped by the bike. She muttered some words and traced symbols over her clothes. "All right, I'm starving." She shook her leg out, then stood.

Clarisse narrowed her eyes. "You called yourself a bull-headed apprentice."

Leia grinned, dusting off her professorial suit. "Doesn't mean I don't do my homework."

We rode the bikes onto C Street, the tourist destination that looked half like a dumpy mountain town and half like a Clint Eastwood set. After finagling some parking, we followed the smell of pizza. Winston's sparkling fey-ness had calmed down, and now he only stumbled like a drunk. Clarisse kept him upright with an arm wound through his. Considering the number of bikers with plastic cups, he blended right in.

We snagged a back booth at the Red Dog Saloon. Judging from the number of tourists meandering the wooden walkways and the band setting up on the indoor stage, I guessed it to be Saturday night. How long had it been, then? When had I gone to Tahoe searching for Colton?

In the saloon's dim lighting, we looked shook up. Leia ordered the pizza since her clothes were dusty but in one piece.

Clarisse seemed frayed—not older, but worn, the sharp bite of her sanded off. Winston fidgeted with energy that seemed to be too much, like anger ready to spill over. He poured salt on the table and drew designs in it while his leg bounced. I slumped against the cracked vinyl. The itch at the base of my skull had returned, twitching whenever I faced toward Reno. I rubbed my neck. Exhaustion dragged me down, but at least I no longer felt a crumbling emptiness like in New Jersey.

Leia returned with a pitcher of beer. "I know we are biking down the mountain, but I needed something to get me through the rest of the day."

Clarisse propped her chin on her fist. "If we return to Reno, there's no hiding her."

I poured the beer. "Who says I want to hide?" Thing was, my father probably knew I was back in Nevada already.

Winston threw a pinch of salt over his shoulder before brushing the rest onto the floor. "You aren't strong enough, hon."

"I never will be. He's a god."

Leia tipped her glass toward me. "So are you."

"Half-god," Clarisse and I said in unison.

"Suggestions, then?" Leia asked.

I slurped my beer. My best idea involved running headfirst into whatever dear Dad had coming and hoping he didn't capture me alive. Saying it aloud seemed counterproductive after they'd come so far to rescue me.

Winston scratched his head for too long before shaking himself. "I could ask the fey to hide you. Chances are they would, for a price."

"I just said I don't want to hide."

"You need to grow stronger," Clarisse said. "Hiding for a decade wouldn't hurt you. Age can't touch you, remember?"

I expected her tone to turn flirtatious, but she just stared at her hands.

Leia folded her arms on the table. "Why does anyone have to fight him? We are looking at this like a war, but—"

Clarisse bared her fangs. "You didn't see what remained of the town of Rachel."

Leia stabbed a finger at me. "Half of that was her fault, and if she tries it again, then Reno's toast. She can't win a war."

"Not alone," Clarisse said.

I wiggled my fingers. "Um, I'm right here."

The waiter came over with a large pizza and two dozen wings, stretching the awkward silence as we waited for him to leave.

I tore into a chicken wing, sucking the meat off the bone. "Listen, he wants me for all these bullshit balance reasons. If I keep him out of trouble and get to be a god, maybe that's not a bad trade-off." As I licked sauce off my fingers, I felt rather proud of how adult the idea sounded. How reasonable.

Leia rolled her eyes. "Yeah, that's the same shit you said when you signed up to be Colton's maid."

My jaw popped. Ah, yes, that's why our friendship dissolved. "Yeah, well, maybe if I'd known my friend was a *witch*, I wouldn't have taken the first chance at safety and considered my options instead."

Leia rolled her eyes but raised her hands. "If you want to play savior and fight by yourself, fine, but you need to have a better plan than spilling your guts on the Saints' carpet."

Clarisse dipped a finger in Winston's beer and flicked it at us. "You're worse than hungry cats."

Winston nodded out the large windows. "All the land around here is federal and empty as hell. Plus, I know a few fey dens. Let's just camp out—"

I spoke around a mouthful of chicken. "Until the radiation zombies eat our brains?"

Clarisse watched me eat, and I remembered for the hundredth time that she needed something other than greasy food. She licked her lips. "It might give us an extra day. Thirty-six hours tops."

"Unless your dad's tired of pushing you around," Winston said. "Maybe he'll take a break for a week."

Leia snorted. "He's a god of nuclear power. Pushing is what he does."

Not to mention, I'd pissed him off by shoving a brand through his chest.

27

We all had our elders to face, even Winston. Apparently, he needed a permit to travel more than a thousand miles by hell gate. Who knew? Leia's mom and coven leader had ordered the witches to stay out of it, which left Leia with a dozen angry voicemails and magical correspondence. Clarisse had double-crossed so many people nobody knew what side she was on, least of all me. And at the center of the shitstorm, me—a half-god who just learned she was a half-god a few days ago.

After downing the first pizza and ordering a second to go, we walked a half-mile until we had trekked far enough away that the federal land turned all to desert silence. Winston found us a hollow clean of wild horse shit while Clarisse went to catch herself a blood bag.

I half-sat down before Leia hauled me up by my coat. "We don't have a second to waste."

"Great, cut to the training montage."

Leia's clenched her jaw. "Clarisse told me what happened in Rachel. You need to do it again, but be in control this time."

I recoiled, scuffing up the grit. "And incinerating Virginia City in the process. What the hell are you thinking?"

"I said *control*."

"I don't know how! You think I can out-blast a god of nuclear power?"

Winston stepped closer, fidgeting. "Um, this isn't helping."

I crossed my arms. "Fine, if that's what you want, then let's just have Clarisse tear my throat out and force-feed me digested vampire blood, and we'll see what's left standing after I go nuclear."

Sweat trickled down my back. My feet felt hot and swollen. I angled into a lower stance. The ground beneath me cracked like broken glass.

I raised a boot. Heat waves wafted from the dirt, and rock and sand burned to obsidian.

Leia whispered something like "fucking hell."

I kicked dirt over the shards. "Let me guess, you're gonna give me the speech about how I shouldn't access my powers by being angry, blah blah blah."

Leia grinned. "Gin, they've been telling us not to be angry since we could talk. You really think I'm going to let that go?"

Winston raised a hand. "Just speaking from experience with angry fey, but maybe there's another way? Nuclear power doesn't have to blow up. It can be used for energy, too."

"Which creates toxic waste," Leia said.

"Better than annihilation."

Leia paced in a circle between sagebrush. "What about mutation? Clarisse described some pretty fantastic zombies."

"And what, unleash them on the casino?"

Leia groaned, digging her fists into her thighs. "Fine! You figure it out!"

"I'm trying!"

Winston popped open the pizza box and gnawed on a pepperoni.

"Give me one of those." I snatched a slice, the half-congealed cheese sliding off. I ate the cheese with my fingers. "I don't know what to do—about any of this. Colton, Evelyn, Mike—they all want a half-god, and I don't even know how to be a functioning human. That's why I wished myself away." Admitting it out loud made me feel even more helpless.

Leia stepped beside me and nudged me with her shoulder. "We can't keep wishing, Gin. No living in a van with our dogs out in the desert. We got shit to do."

I wiped my greasy hands on my jeans. "Except I don't know how."

Over a rise, sand gritted under boots, but the wind carried Clarisse's scent. I motioned for Leia to relax as she whipped toward the noise.

Clarisse dropped a black-tailed deer onto the sand. Blood stained her chin and trailed down her shirt. "If we need a beer run, I'm not an option." She grinned. Her tongue swiped blood off her fangs.

My breath shallowed, and I tried to hide it by shoving half the slice into my mouth. Leia swallowed hard and pretended to inspect her pizza. Glad I wasn't the only one.

Clarisse wiped her mouth with the back of her hand. "Any progress?"

Winston scratched his head. Leia muttered about not getting dandruff on the pizza. "Avoid destruction. Maybe creation? Mutation?"

"Congratulations, you've attempted a crossword."

I dug my bare toes into the sand. "I won't be as powerful as him, but I don't know what else to do other than rush him. He can't be reasoned with. He's about power."

Clarisse picked deer hair off her shirt. "Then be his opposite. Give away power." She sauntered forward. "The way I see it, you are the nuclear waste. He made you. Now make something better."

I leaned onto the balls of my feet so I didn't feel like I'd retreated. "I know you're old and all, but I still don't appreciate sexist bullshit. He didn't make me."

Leia snorted.

Clarisse tilted her head. "I think we can agree he's responsible for everything special about you."

I gave ground and looked away as I considered saying for the hundredth time that I didn't want this, that I wanted to be a normal kid in college on the way to a normal life of drinking too much, trying to find a partner, getting a divorce, and all the other things my generation stumbled into. But hell, even that wasn't true. I needed to stop lying to myself. I had made my choice in Atlantic City. I wanted that Nevada soil under my boots.

I could have hopped a plane to anywhere from New Jersey, but for the first time in ages, I had felt human—powerless—and I did *not* like it, even after all the complaining about just wanting to be normal again. Plus, I'd totally wanted to fuck Colton and maybe Clarisse, two relatively ancient, dangerous, dead beings. Hardly any of my friends were human, and those that were—Kia, Bobbi, and Leia—rode the line between human and magically-altered. Hell, Kia and Bobbi would trash their humanness the moment someone offered the otherworldly. I'd given up that normal life. Pretty emphatically, it seemed.

Giving up on being human hadn't transformed into embracing my inhumanness, though. Even though Colton had ridden me about it, I never focused on my powers. I usually learned about it by doing it. Oh, hey! I can jump pretty high because I just had to outrun a werecat. Thank god I can heal fast, or else those claws would have bled me to death. That kind of thing. The nonhuman therapist Colton had shelled out for said stumbling into my powers like that was self-destructive.

But I was scared. I'd lost a year to booze for the same reason. Another side-effect of nuclear power. Fear.

I took a deep breath and looked Clarisse in the eye. "I'm afraid." It felt good to admit it.

Leia stepped forward. "Yeah, no shit—"

"Not just of Mike. Like yeah, I'm scared shitless of what he wants to do to me. But I'm afraid of who I am, what it means that I'm going to outlive generations." I glanced at Leia. "Outlive you. I'm scared that I don't know what I can do. What if I blow up the state in my sleep?" I motioned to the three of them. "I'm afraid of you all. What it means to be your friend if we are that. What it means that you are going to call on me for help like I called on you. And what if I'm so fucking afraid I can't help. I wasn't prepared for the regular world, let alone this world."

I stared at the Virginia City vista, the moon illuminating the mountain ranges, with the tall rock lump of Sugarloaf in the foreground. I toed off my boots, then my socks. Warm sand cupped my feet, and I dug in my toes. The musky scent of sage clung to the crisp air. Nevada had always felt like home to me, even if the rest of the nation thought it so worthless that they detonated their bombs and dumped their sludge. Truth was, I couldn't beat Mike. We both pulled our power from this stolen land, except he'd been doing it a lot longer than me. I couldn't stop him, but what if I could contain him? He'd been stuffed in a nuclear waste barrel before.

"Wait, wait. Maybe I have an idea. We're going about this all wrong. He's a god. Killing him is way out of our league. What if we trap him?"

Clarisse crouched beside her deer carcass and slit open the chest cavity. "It would buy us time."

Winston nodded. "He was trapped before."

"Or not," Leia said. "My coven thinks Colton and Mike made a deal—that he went willingly."

"Doesn't matter. We could still trap him."

"In what?" Leia asked.

I tapped my chest. "Me."

Leia shook her head. "Oh no, we aren't doing this martyr shit—"

"Listen, listen." I grasped her hands. "I'm his opposite. I haven't blown up any cities—well, if we don't count Rachel. I can balance him out by trapping him inside me. Then, when your coven or Evelyn or the fey figure out how to get rid of a nuclear bomb, we can get him out."

Leia gripped my shoulders a little too hard. "Listen to yourself. Until then, you *will be* the nuclear bomb."

"But that's what I am already. That's my heritage."

Leia groaned and stomped away. Winston slid off the rock and joined me, slinging an arm around my shoulders. "To be honest, we don't have any other ideas, L."

She rubbed her chin, pacing back and forth. "I know, just give me a sec."

"I'm cool with this, really."

She nodded past me at Clarisse. "I have no idea how to do this, do you?"

Clarisse dug out the deer's heart and picked off a few hairs. "There are only two ways to kill a god. Either the god loses power and dissipates because they've been forgotten—run out of energy, essentially. Or they are subsumed. Incorporated into another god. That's just what we are going to do. This will work." She sucked a mouthful of blood, then wiped her mouth.

"We're going to need some containment spells, I think,"

Leia said. "If you really want to do this. At least something to help guide your power since you don't have any training."

"Yeah, good. Then you will already be tapped in if something goes south. You can try to contain—whatever happens."

Leia shoulder bumped me. "Nothing is going to go south. We've got to figure out some spells to make sure he doesn't just possess you." She paced again. Clarisse returned to her dead deer and ripped off a leg. Winston sat next to me quietly.

They would know the spells. We would contain Mike. I could see the pattern spread before me. In some ways, I wasn't concerned about that moment. If we didn't, I'd die and wouldn't care what happened next. If I incorporated Mike, but he took me over, odds were, I was as good as dead and didn't have much to worry about. Really, it was the aftermath of winning that stressed me out, when I had to face Colton and Evelyn and learn if I would ever be safe again. In the face of all that—of finding a way to *live*—eating a god alive was the easy part. All I could do was try. Even failure would be heroic.

We talked and planned and tested spells until the mountain ranges turned from silhouettes to layered shadows. At sunrise, the instinctual itch stabbed down my spine like lightning, and I doubled over with a grunt. Leia steadied me, asking what was wrong as Clarisse and Winston hurried over. I stared into the horizon and braced myself against the pain.

As if the Saints were screaming my name, I knew something had trespassed on my turf.

28

We raced recklessly down the mountain, burning rubber on the curves. I clutched Leia as she worked to keep us upright while talking to her coven when cell service allowed. The itch at the base of my skull had changed direction. It no longer scrabbled toward the south but pounded a steady beat in the direction of the Saints.

Slowly, Leia relayed the pieces to me. The attack had been unexpected. The casino had trembled as a mushroom cloud bloomed over it. Seconds later, Colton had rushed in *on horseback* like some apocalypse herald, shouting for everyone to get out.

While smoke still clung to the building, someone had pushed the emergency button, but not the one that signaled some human interference, but an even worse alarm: bad magic; get out.

Except no one did. Leia's people thought Colton might have triggered the emergency systems, so maybe my people were safe in the shelters underneath. Either way, it seemed Colton tried to help the casino rather than Mike. We couldn't know for sure, though, since nobody had gone in—or come out.

Leia ran the last red light and braked hard enough to slide sideways. Two cop cars blocked the main entrance, and I recognized human officers on the payroll. Caleb Isaac stood talking with them, Leia's mother, and four black-swaddled figures that probably belonged to Clarisse's coven.

He did a double take when I swung off the motorcycle and shoved the others aside to jog toward me.

Leia caught my jacket. "Hey. You know who we need to be right now?"

I took a deep breath and settled my shoulders. "Yeah. I'm a demigod, and you're next in line to the most powerful magic lineage in the state."

She let me go. "Good. Now tell your people that." She jogged toward her mother and the rest of their coven.

I met Caleb Isaac under the thruway.

He clapped my shoulder. "Thank god, Gin, I thought you were in there."

"Any updates?"

"Just a giant fucking cloud!"

"I heard. But I know who did it, and I've got a plan." Nobody else could take down Mike, at least not with the place still standing. I couldn't show fear. I was part god now, and after I swallowed my father, like so many gods before me had done to their fathers, then I'd be even stronger.

Or dead. Part of me shriveled up, the same part that trembled at Clarisse, that was unable to break from Colton, that was so afraid to train my powers because I couldn't stand what might unlock next.

The exterior lights and neon lit up, a few bulbs popping even though it was sunrise. Caleb flinched, protecting his face with his right arm. "What the hell?"

At the top of the casino, the Saints' purple and orange lights turned sickly yellow and green in the mushroom cloud.

"Who got out?"

"Nobody, I don't think. But Colton—he rode in. Just after... whatever it was. It struck the Saints, and, I swear, I heard the building scream all the way in Midtown."

Leia ran over and took my right hand. She forced my fingers to splay and began writing runes along and around my fingers as if taping my hands for a boxing match.

"Caleb, here's what you need to do. Keep everyone away from the building. That emergency alert goes to all employees, right?"

He nodded.

"I'm sure some will come to help. Tell them to go home. Better yet, tell them to spend the night in Sacramento. And find out who was scheduled to work."

"Right, right. I'm on it." He pulled out his smartphone as he walked toward Clarisse's people.

Leia drew sweeping lines over the back of my hand, up my wrist, then repeated the runes on my left hand. "You did good there. These marks will help us know when you need our power. We'll be watching and casting." Already, Leia's mother dispersed groups around the building. In the general weirdness of Reno, their chalk circles and candles looked like one more performance art display.

One of the black-clad figures broke away from the front and joined us. From the stalk, I guessed Clarisse. Motorcycle gear and a helmet shielded her body from the sun. She raised the visor. "You have until nightfall, then we're taking the Saints."

My hands jerked, and Leia growled at me to hold still. "Not if he's still in there. He'll blow it up!"

"Well, at least it's not Vegas."

I grit my teeth. "All those people."

"Consider it motivation." She flicked the visor down. "I'm sorry. It would be worse if he won." She hurried toward a black Suburban with tinted windows idling in the street. I guessed Evelyn sat cocooned inside.

Leia capped the marker. "Do what you need to do. We'll enhance what we can."

"Thanks, Leia." I held out my hand, but she hugged me.

"Save your people."

"Don't let anyone come in after me."

She nodded. "I won't."

I faced the front entrance. The exterior lights flashed orange and red as if a toxic warning. I walked past the cop cars, past Clarisse's people. Just another day at work.

Caleb Isaac reached for my jacket, but I side-stepped him. "You can't go in there alone!"

"Haven't you heard?" I walked backward, spreading my arms. "I'm kind of a god."

29

I approached the Saints' tinted windows, the lights of the slot machines just a firefly flicker beyond. I peered through, letting my eyes adjust. Beyond the glass, the patrons' shadows shifted. An energy resonated through the air, the first snap of winter right when the trees dropped their leaves.

I touched the grimy wall, and it almost felt like the building groaned beneath my fingers. Leia guessed home turf advantage might mean something to me. Mike's place would be outside Vegas at the atomic testing sights, but Reno was my spot. I'd grown up here—not physically, but when it came to my powers and walking in the dark. After two years at the Saints, I knew every carpet stain, cracked mirror, and broken lock. Mike had nothing on me.

Colton would, though. With the Saints in trouble, I had to believe he was on our side.

I shouldered into the Saints Casino like I did every day.

The already dim lights seemed lowered. I took a deep breath, tinged with the familiar smell of cigarette smoke. Slot lights popped, outlining an unusual number of players for an early morning. All the gamblers sat with their backs toward me. At the bar, people hunched on the stools, but nobody served them. At this time, Katie, Sarah, and Johnny usually waited, and with this sized crowd, they'd be rushing. Nobody moved among the players. It was uncanny.

I pulled the brand free. The spiked handle already felt warm, and the head glowed like a warning. I stepped forward.

Activity rolled over the room, the lights flashed full, and the people drank, laughed, gestured—like puppets. The music dialed louder to an upbeat Bruce Springsteen, and then the slot machines whirred and jangled as the patrons pulled the lever or pressed their buttons. At the sports bar, screens strobed between different games as the betters played at betting.

A voice crashed through the noise. "Pretty cool, huh? I got this place runnin' like clockwork. Don't think I'll mind the casino business."

He was back to his whiney James Dean voice. I could imagine him sauntering through the slots, a cigarette balancing in the corner of his mouth. I prowled forward quietly, just as Colton had taught me. "Then go back to Vegas."

A dark slot machine to my left burst with light and I flinched. "But you like Reno, right, sweetheart? Then I think we should stay."

I set my teeth as another slot came alive, blaring a coyote howl. "There's no *we*. You're leaving the Saints."

The ceiling lights flickered to his voice. "C'mon, Gin, don't you see what we could create? We could nuke governments!" A slot machine exploded, and I shielded my eyes as money and shrapnel pocked the carpet and cracked the mirrored walls. "Or make all the energy anyone would ever need." The lights blared so brighz bulbs popped like gunshots. "We could cure cancer. I'll help you do that—whatever you want. I just want my daughter at my side."

Smoking shrapnel melted the carpet and crunched beneath my boots. Leia, Winston, and Clarisse had guessed he'd try the sweet lines first. "You were born out of the intention to control —the bigger stick. Nothing good comes from that."

The first row of patrons mechanically played the slots a few yards ahead. I recognized one of the regulars in her lucky horse fleece, Charlotte, who bartended at the Sierra Taphouse by the river.

"I've saved lives." Mike's voice had changed from James Dean to the deeper, barrel-chested, slick-haired executive. The face he'd worn when he'd tried to hurt me. I raised the brand over my shoulder, ready to swing.

The lights lowered, and I blinked to adjust my dark vision.

"If nothing good comes from me, then you are damned."

Another few steps, and I would be able to touch Charlotte. "I know."

The speakers squealed. "Bring her here!"

People turned from the slot machines. Glowing burns reddened their skin, and heat blisters bubbled over their faces and hands. I stumbled back and crashed into a stool. They limped like zombies as if the same burns pained their feet. Even beneath the radiation, I knew them: Pam, who came in after her gas station shift to play a few penny slots but mostly to talk. Bob, a bus driver and always had the latest construction updates. Queen, the Bibo's barista. Jesse in his cowboy hat.

We'd planned that I should go straight for Mike, ignore whatever little shows he'd set up just like this one, but I couldn't leave these people here. What if they found out I'd run off and left them? They trusted me. Most of them hadn't touched the dark, let alone knew what was happening to their bodies. I was supposed to stop that.

If Mike had turned them, then I could turn them back.

Jesse rushed me like a linebacker, and I sidestepped, but his flailing right arm slammed against my hip. I hissed. Now, I just had to figure out how to wake them up.

I spun right as Charlotte dove for my legs. She caught my ankle, and I almost smashed my boot into her face. I trembled with the pent-up fight energy. I twisted away as two more blistered patrons lunged, but I ducked behind a slot machine. They crunched into it, scrabbling over the flat top. They must've broken ribs.

I leaned into a sprint but skidded on the carpet as a wall of burned patrons stumbled forward, a hash of familiar faces. Some of these folks I'd seen every day.

The loose circle grew tighter, but a gap formed near the escalator. I dashed and slid below the grasping hands, kicking up to my feet and pelting toward the sports bar.

The lights flickered as Mike's voice slicked the speakers. "They're just addicts, Juniper. Kill them already, and let's get on with it."

I vaulted over the bar going too fast and slammed into the far wall, cracking the shelves. Alcohol shattered, soaking my jacket. I took a breath—keep control, Gin. The patron-zombies staggered after me. Maybe a ten-second buffer.

I slapped the touchscreen computer, and it lit up with the emergency signal, giving the quickest routes to exits and the lower level safe room. At least they'd had some warning. Maybe that's why only patrons and no staff had been radiated.

The first patron-zombie slammed into the bar so hard it shook—Jerry, a cross-country trucker who always stopped to play our slots. His bellowing face made me react before I could think, and I shoved the brand into the base of his throat.

His scream choked, but even as the brand burned, the radiation redness and the blisters faded. The rage twisting his face slackened, and he stumbled sideways. "Oh god, what's going on?"

If I didn't move now, the other zombies would trample him. I rushed toward the narrow escalator. It'd make a choke point, and I could—I could brand them. I choked on a sob as I took the steps two at a time. *I don't want to, I don't want to.* Was it saving them if I had to do something maybe worse? To scar them for life, a reminder of a nightmare world just a heartbeat away. I was supposed to save them, not hurt them!

So many of us already lived with scars, just like the nuked desert. If one more was enough to save them, then I would carry that guilt.

As the first patron lunged up the stairs—Kaidy, a mother of three who liked to gamble with her rich husband's money—I visualized how to snatch her arm, pin her, and brand her back.

"I'm sorry."

I pinned her against the wall and seared. At the brand's touch, she stopped fighting, and I shoved her behind me just in time to catch the next one in the gut with the brand. They came too fast—it couldn't be neat and clean.

But I was saving them. They woke up one by one.

After I freed the last one, Dillon, our mailman, I threw down the brand. All except the last few were huddled together, mostly standing. Some had already run.

I pointed back down the stairs. "Street doors are open and should be safe. Stick together and get outside as fast as possible!"

They hurried past, clutching their burns. Some said thank you, but I could only nod.

I'll fix it, somehow, I promised silently as they passed. I wouldn't leave them with my scars.

The cold brand rested on the ugly carpet. I imagined bending it in half with a sneer. Instead, I tucked the toe of my boot under it and flipped it into my hand.

Level one held restaurants, convenience stores, and bars in

addition to slots and different tables. The escalator came up between two bars—the Chainsaw Cantina and Bizarro Beers. As I stepped past their entrances, their lights, music, and animatronics blared. I raised the brand while twisting between the two, expecting another wave of zombified patrons. The Cantina played Latin-influenced hard rock, while Bizarro's featured creepy circus sounds mixed with Halloween music like "Thriller." The Cantina had a chupacabra mascot that "walked" back and forth across the awning while Bizarro's motion-activated clown giggled and juggled broken beer bottles —a clever piece of fey magic Colton had paid steeply for. The rest of level one remained gloomy, though as my eyes adjusted, the floor glistened with fresh blood still soaking into the carpets.

Glass broke, and I whipped around, raising the brand like a baseball bat. The clown slowly let the magicked bottles fall from its juggling routine. The mouth creaked open, cracking the plastic. "Last chance, Juniper."

A revving chainsaw sounded from the Cantina, and I shivered. "When guys don't take no for an answer, I throw them out." I ground the words out through clenched teeth.

The grin grew wider until the plastic split, and the jaw clattered to the floor. The juggling hands stopped, and the remaining bottles shattered on the carpet.

I turned away and walked deeper into the casino, even as the revving chainsaw sound effect made me flinch. At least Colton hadn't gotten around to ordering that wax figure of Leatherface. That was the last thing I wanted to fight.

The level opened into the ring where the Haunted House rose from the basement through the arched opening. I crept to the railing and looked down. My gaze adjusted to the dark, and I focused on a castle that spiraled upward, twisting and turning to defy gravity. When the house was running at full swing, different monsters poked heads out of the crevices and shrieked at the tourists. Tonight, the dark shard just threatened to rupture the ceiling.

The copper stench of blood overwhelmed the usual cigarette stink. Even late at night, the casino wasn't this quiet. "Hello! It's Gin!" My words echoed.

I gripped the railing, and my hands came back sticky with blood. The Haunted House was the heart of the casino, according to Colton, so I guessed that would be where Mike set up shop. I was supposed to enter the attraction as fast as possible, but all this blood—what if people were trapped? I at least had to check the safe rooms and see if anybody needed help.

Rather than take the stairs, I vaulted over the side and dropped to the next floor. Behind me, the Saints joined to the Circus Circus —now closed since the emergency signal had been tripped—with a walkway, but a sculpture depicting hell guarded the entrance. The other casinos hated it since hell was the last thing they wanted their good patrons thinking about. It featured a recreation of "Dante and Virgil in Hell" by W. A. Bouguereau, and Dante and Virgil watched two tastefully naked men fight, one tearing out the other's neck. The edgelord art students liked to come to sketch it.

Now, I just hoped it wouldn't come alive. I watched it for a ten-count before carefully turning around. To my right, light shone beneath a staff entrance door. I tried to shoulder through it and banged into a solidly barricaded door. Well, at least some of the staff remembered their emergency training.

A chainsaw revving shattered the silence, and I threw myself to the right as the metal bar hit and spit sparks against the door. It didn't have any teeth, but the bar could still be used as a club.

I rolled to my feet just as my friend Bobbi stabbed down with the toothless chainsaw. Radiation burns bloomed across their face and neck while blisters leaked over their hands and arms.

"Bobbi! It's me!" I scrambled backward until I hit flesh. I looked up just as Kia smashed a broken bottle into my face. Blood curtained my eyes as I tried to crawl away. Not my friends—I couldn't hurt my friends. I was supposed to keep them safe, not give them scars.

Kia shrieked as she raked the broken bottle across my back. My jacket took the worst of it, and I lunged away. I got to my feet and swiped the blood from my eyes.

They limped toward me. Kia's leg was mangled again, probably from walking on it, and Bobbi snarled as they revved the chainsaw. Except the hate didn't reach their eyes. God, did they know what they were doing?

I backed up, my brand between us. I had to. I couldn't keep wasting time, and the only alternative was to leave them in Mike's control. What if he made them jump over the railing or hurt themselves? Or worse, what if I couldn't trap him and I just left them like this. At least if I helped them now, they could get away.

Kia's leg twisted with each step.

I let out a cry as I stabbed at Bobbi, except they raised the chainsaw just in time to glance against my blow. I'd aimed for their ribs so they could hide it, but my brand seared into their neck.

Bobbi collapsed with a sob. Kia stumbled toward me, the broken bottle dripping blood. She held it toward me as if offering. I knocked it aside with the brand and caught her in the chest, burning a hole through her sweater.

She fell backward, screaming.

I tossed the brand aside and dropped to my knees. I wanted to hug them, but—I'd hurt them.

"Oh god, Gin." Kia gasped out a sob. Her bloody hands shook. "I'm so sorry."

Bobbi drew Kia into their lap. "We could see it—but we couldn't—it was like we were puppets. We couldn't—" They hiccupped out a sob.

I crawled to them both and hugged them, babbling about the brand, that I had to do it, and that he didn't give me any other choice. They both held me, our apologies overlapping.

The blood stopped flowing into my eyes, and I wiped off the worst of it. "C'mon. We gotta find the others." I helped Kia stand, and Bobbi acted as her crutch.

I snatched the brand and returned to the blockaded door. I took a deep breath and kicked it open, breaking a metal door jammer. The shards crunched under my boots. "Stay close. I won't let anything touch you."

This hallway connected to the offices with a private elevator going down further into Colton's tunnels. Part of the lifeblood of the Saints, the hall allowed staff to run between restaurants, slots, tables or take a break from constantly smiling at the patrons. Hardly ever was this hallway quiet, let alone empty, so the flickering lights and total silence felt just as wrong as the blood smearing the walls—sometimes shaped like handprints, sometimes like bullet spatters. *Please don't let it be any of my people.*

I inched forward with the brand raised over my shoulder, ready to swing. When nothing tried to sink teeth into me, I motioned for Bobbi and Kia, and we hurried down the hall.

Blood slicked the floor and pooled along the runners, but no bodies, only bits of zombie flesh that stank like dumpster juice. I skipped checking the office spaces and breakroom, heading straight for the safe room instead. I almost skidded into a pack of zombies banging themselves to pieces against the vaultlike door.

I backpedaled into the shadows, shoving Bobbi and Kia backward and placing my body between them and danger. The zombies didn't change targets, still breaking apart on the door. At least that meant somebody had managed to reach safety.

About twenty stitched-up zombies slowly fell apart against the door. I didn't have time to wait around for them to batter themselves to death. I waved Bobbi and Kia back, then crept closer until I was only a few feet behind the rotting creatures. I knocked my brand three times against the wall, and the metallic gong split about half the zombies from the group. They lunged down the hallway, and I danced backward, hacking one, then another into gore, slowly moving so the pack couldn't tackle me. I beat them into pieces.

Before I waded into round two, the vault door swung open, crushing two of the remaining zombies. A round of gunfire made me jump back and press against the wall. The final zombies spattered into a runny mess.

A security squad of vampires I didn't know surged past me, scouting the empty hall and pulling Bobbi and Kia into their ranks. Franklin waltzed out, still dressed in a burgundy suit, even after a god had invaded with a zombie army.

I glanced at the security crew before running into Franklin's open arms. We hugged, but I looked over his shoulder as the day crew slowly peeked around the door.

Franklin followed my gaze. "I checked the security footage —only a dozen remain unaccounted for."

"I found Bobbi and Kia. I had—their hurt."

Franklin hushed me. "You did what you had to."

The security forces retreated to the vault, posting around the door. Most wore sun gear, maybe in case they had to make a break for the sidewalk and didn't want to start smoking in front of the tourists. I had to give it to her; Evelyn was better equipped than us.

The leader barely glanced at me, then nodded at Franklin. "We will take it from here—"

I shook the gore off the brand, willing the tip cherry-bright. "Doubt it. There's a god in here, and I—"

I could hear his sneer. "I'm fully aware of what you allowed in your house."

Anger flashed through me, and I shoved him into the wall hard enough that he slid to the floor, groaning.

The lights flickered in time like applause, and the ghostly chime of slot machines ringing *winner* echoed down the hall.

I ran a hand down my face, sticky with hell knew what. "Sorry." I offered to help the vampire stand, but he struggled upright.

My face felt hot, either from anger or embarrassment, I wasn't sure. I turned to Franklin. "I'll find Colton and the others, but you all have to get out of here."

The head of security removed his helmet, cracked in the back. He had the crooked nose of a boxer and the same gray-white pallor of the walls. "I'll see to it."

"And clear the area. I'll do my best to keep the Saints standing, but...."

Franklin squeezed my hand. "You're a daughter of the bomb. That's what Colton called you."

Evelyn's security officers started organizing the day crew into the hallway. I nodded or tried to smile at so many folks I'd spent the last two years learning from. The new faces, who had no idea what waited in the dark, folks who maybe would have been initiated after a few years—they looked the most frightened, some still leaking tears or clutching to the more assured, those that knew vampires were behind those visors but that Colton or I would take out this latest big baddie.

I took a shaky breath. We'd brought this mess on them. Me, by accident; Colton, through miscalculation.

The last folks hurried down the hall, and I walked beside Franklin.

"We have people with Colton," he said. "We were cut off by the zombies. Colton took them and entered the Haunted House."

We paused at a cross-section, one hallway leading toward the heart of the casino. I hugged Franklin and whispered, "Leia and Winston will be outside. We have a plan. Just tell them I'm working on it."

"Good luck, Juniper."

I faced the hallway leading to the entrance I needed. At peak times around Halloween, the line would be zig-zagging to fill up this whole hallway. Now, the rope barriers tangled across the worn carpet.

In a lockdown, the security cameras blinked off in the Haunted House. Meant to protect anyone running for that safe room. It also kept me blind to whatever Mike might have sent to hide in the maze.

I stepped into the entrance. Cold air gusted from the arch, fluttering the cobwebs stretching between skeletal remains pressed into the pillars. I blinked to adjust my sight to the darkness, but without even emergency lights, my heightened vision couldn't breach the shadows.

I raised the brand like a torch and let the glow light a path. Something had run through the narrow entry hall. Fake cobwebs dusted the floor, and the plastic arm of a motion-sensor skeleton meant to startle visitors and prompt the first scream from the unaware was snapped at the shoulder.

The brand's candle-dull glow glistened along the floor, and I dabbed my boot in a gore slick—a zombie had taken a hard hit and spilled its guts. At least whoever had run was fighting back.

I followed the dripping zombie guts, dodging through the fake mine tunnel that functioned as the first floor before climbing up into the house. Some of the effects still flickered to life—the clanging mine cart running off the tracks—but unlike the rest of the casino, Mike didn't take control of the house. At least, not yet.

I followed the zombie stink to the exit, a pulley elevator meant to raise miners and tourists, up past empty tunnels that blew cold air or sent fake bats flying. I leaned against the bars, my hands clasped over the brand's handle. On my third day on the job, Colton had brought me through the attraction, explained the intricacies, and then left me at the heart. He'd just vanished in what I soon realized was a vampire calling card, the way they could disappear into the shadows. Colton said I could learn if I focused on training what my blood could do, but I'd brushed him off. I hadn't needed that kind of skill as a glorified bouncer. I needed the brash visibility that screamed "don't fuck with us." I hadn't thought bigger, and Colton had left me to my ignorance.

The next level was my favorite. Wide ranch land, a thunderstorm clawing the horizon, stretched toward the far wall, which, through clever optical illusions and laser technology, showed a mansion growing bigger with each step until you could knock on the door. It always made my stomach twist, like when you thought your car was moving, but it was the car next to you. While visitors marveled at the laser-mansion, the real special effects happened—something would rustle the grass, seem to run full speed, then vanish. Shrieks, snuffling, and footstep noises all activated according to different pressure sensors in the floor. I kept the brand raised so as not to set fire to the synthetic grasses.

The lasers flickered on and off, the mansion sometimes tiny, sometimes giant.

The first monster-in-the-field activated, and the rustling made me whip around even though my brain knew better. Still,

I tracked the movement until it ended, curving away with a wail. Just like it was supposed to.

When I faced the far wall and next door, the mansion lasers had changed, and I stumbled back, tripping on the tussocks meant to keep the visitors on the right path. A giant James Dean look-alike leered at me.

"You know these are his fears, right?" he drawled, the lasers flickering his facial movements against the wall. Beneath his chin, the doorway twisted the image.

I drew into a crouch and scanned the tall grass. Nothing moved, though the next trigger waited about ten steps ahead. Lasers couldn't hurt me, so better to get off this floor and closer to Colton.

I straightened and walked toward the giant James Dean. Unlike the mansion illusion, he shrank as I neared.

"Did he tell you about them?" Mike asked. "About how he twisted himself to fit in those low mining tunnels? About getting bit and moving onto the ranch? The never-ending dark of his new life almost drove him to the mines again."

The next interaction triggered, and the grass shifted in multiple trails as if rats might suddenly burst onto the path. I kept walking, staring at the door. Colton hadn't told me the inspiration behind each floor, but others working at the Saints had pieced it together over the years, over enough drunken stories and occasional explanations, until Colton had created his backstory whether he wanted to or not.

Another yard and the final interaction sprung, something running through the grass behind me. I didn't turn around.

The James Dean face had shrunk, so he stood in front of me, still about ten feet tall but dwindling with every step. "Thing is, kiddo, I'm not interested in what scares him. You, on the other hand—"

Whatever had been shaking the grass slammed into me. I hit the floor, breathless.

The zombie raked claws down my back, slicing through my leather jacket. I tried to scream but couldn't breathe.

I shoved off the floor so hard the zombie slid off of me. I whipped around, raising the brand to block any blows, but the grass parted again, and another zombie crashed into my side. They weren't the half-mange roadkill Mike had sent before, but more solid. The brand illuminated a face, a waitress named Greta who'd worked at the Saints for two decades, one of Colton's favorites, who he'd even offered to turn, but she'd chosen to remain human.

She wasn't human anymore. She broke my jaw with a right hook as I fought to get my legs under me. I dragged myself upright, even as she clung to my back. I shook her off, matching her strength, only for something to snag my feet, trapping them together at the ankles.

I dug my brand into the fake soil, trying to brake, but Greta kicked my ribs. I was reeled into the mansion while Mike laughed.

The next room was supposed to be a foyer with children's toys on a rotting rug, but I was dragged into a party. A vampire LARP—at least, what I had assumed was because who other than LARPers would dress like that and pretend to have fangs.

Mike must have been in my fucking head because the rooms unfolded just like it had that night two years ago.

I looked so much younger, just twenty with a good fake ID. A pair of Wal-Mart jeans, a slinky top from the Target sales rack, too much black-blue eye makeup, and a pair of bunny ears with attached mask I'd spray-painted black, leftover from some Easter play back when my dad had been really into church. Such a child, which Clarisse seemed to be thinking as she led me into the black light room, her dress flaring purple with fake blood spatters. She'd told me it was a VIP room, and I'd believed her.

Of course, she assumed she'd glamoured me, but it wasn't her vampire powers pulling me forward, just the energy of it all. I'd only been to one other college party, and I hadn't been popular enough to end up at any real ragers in high school. The opulence of walking into the Saints, the elaborate dresses, the amount of insanely hot people, the *looks* they gave me and my friends as if they wanted to eat us. I didn't pay for a drink all night, so I was also drunk when Clarisse whispered in my ear about her VIP room where we could do more than dance.

I whispered, "Don't do it, Juniper," as Clarisse shoved down that young version of me—the one that still liked her name—straddled her on the chair, kissed her, felt her, ground against her, and then sunk fangs into her neck.

I clutched my neck and thumbed the two scar bumps. Rage flared through me, and the brand brightened to a molten white. My hands glowed red, the veins like black cracks.

I howled as I barreled through the illusion, slashing through the ghosts that sizzled against the brand.

I crashed right through a wall of the Haunted House, the edges of the plywood and plaster smoking and dripping sparks. Colton would ream me out over that, which seemed absurd to even think about considering the circumstances. I kept running through a fancy kitchen-turned-cannibal butcher shop and juggernauted into the next wall.

The next room should have been a decadent but rotting ballroom full of monster courtesans that shrieked and howled if the passersby didn't follow the unmarked maze. Instead, the piercing desert sun vanished from the walls.

The Adaven ghost town surrounded me. A hot wind gusted my hair over my face, and it stuck to my sweaty skin. My eyes ached as they readjusted, and I shielded my face in my shoulder for a second too long.

Mike gut-punched me hard enough that I took a knee. Blood bubbled onto my tongue as I tried to suck in air, only to hiccup it back out.

He'd lost the pouty James Dean face for his former quarterback turned 1950s CEO.

I looked up, squinting against the sun. Fuck, were we even in the Saints?

"Yes and no," he said. "We are gods. In our domain, we are time and place."

I struggled into a crouch. Blood and bile filled my mouth, and I spat on his shoes. "You must suck, then, since you didn't kill me weeks ago."

He ran his fingers over my hair, and I shivered, my lips curling. "I want you by my side, so I decided to wear you down. I can *always* extinguish you. I've chosen not to."

I scanned the horizon. I should have followed the plan and forgotten about rescuing the others. Colton would have told me to forget about them. Now, he couldn't help me, and who knew if my plan would work. It might, since I was still on Nevada soil, but the Saints was my home turf, not this ghost town.

Mike dusted off his hands. "Since you haven't tried to bite my throat like that unpleasant boss of yours, let's approach this partnership like civilized beings."

I straightened, slowly, carefully adjusting my grip on the brand. If Leia and the others couldn't help me, then odds were, I was a goner destined to be locked in some psychic box designed by Mike.

I edged nearer, slipping my feet into a stronger stance and braced myself in the desert grit. Still, I had to try. What else was there? "What do you want?"

He spread his arms. "To train you, teach you, love you—and

when you fully understand your godhood, we will rule our terrain."

I raised the brand, resting it in my other palm, pretending to examine it as if considering. I let my sixth sense sink through my boots into the Nevada soil. *Please, Leia, hear me.* I couldn't let him keep jerking me around. It was now or never—now or die.

I locked onto his gaze. "Gods do not share power."

He grinned. "Good, you're learning. You're right. We will have to nuke some new territory for you—"

I gripped the brand in the middle, pointing the molten head at Mike while the spiked handle speared against my gut. I lunged toward him, hugging my dad for what I hoped would be the only time, and the brand connected us. Pierced us together.

"What are—you can't!"

He tried to shove me away, but ghostly hands pressed into my back, and I held him tighter.

"You know, Dad." I visualized mutating cells absorbing the healthy ones. "You're missing the point." I imagined the bomb flash turning all to whiteness. "There just isn't room in this world for both of us." I pictured the mushroom cloud absorbing the ghost town of Adaven.

I pressed Mike against me, joined by the brand, until all I held was myself.

30

I collapsed on my side in a dark, haunted house. The brand still stuck through my gut, but the other side had burned clean, the jackalope head ghostly bright and wavering with heat.

I pulled it out before I considered if it was the key in some sort of lock or if Mike might explode my chest cavity. He didn't.

Ripping that brand free, I screamed loud enough to rattle any leftover zombies. I tossed it aside, and it clattered like any normal piece of metal.

My head rang as if I had witnessed a bomb go off, and my eyes burned. I felt for my bloody wound, but already, the pain faded faster than ever before. A round scar of wrinkled skin swelled over my gut. Another patch marked my lower back. just like the radiation scars I'd seen on the zombies.

Holy shit, it worked.

I sat upright, my legs splayed in front of me. The Haunted House felt...quiet. The whole of the Saints did, actually. I pressed a palm to the floor and closed my eyes.

Desert brightness flashed shapes behind my eyelids as if I were back in Adaven. Wood creaked.

I flinched and scrambled to my feet, but Mike didn't reappear.

I flipped the brand into my hand. It had landed in a dark spot on the floor, some sort of stain. A slash blackened the ground behind me as if my shadow had been burned out. I shivered.

The Haunted House had no more surprises. It slept, dormant, with the same sense of ease that pressed against my feet, brushed my shoulders as if the Saints were thanking me. I didn't want to think what I'd sacrificed for that thanks.

The safe room door was hidden in a coffin. A scramble of zombie parts littered the front, but nothing remained animated. I kicked the pulpy mess aside, swallowing back bile, and yelled for Colton to open up.

Floodlights flicked on, and I shaded my eyes. "I think it's all right!"

The door half-opened, and Colton blocked the entrance. "You think? I've got a dozen people in here. I need better than..." He squinted, then jutted his chin at me. "Back up against the wall."

I took shaky steps backward until I slouched against the wall. Colton cracked the door wider, and the last of the Saints' employees hurried out, including Nash. When he saw me, he limped forward, gripping his bandaged thigh.

"Gin!"

I couldn't help smiling, but Colton snarled at him. "Don't take another step. Get the others out of here!"

Nash turned on Colton as if he thought about punching him. He glanced back at me, then thought better of whatever had flared up, slid his shoulder under another patron's arm, and headed toward the exit. I looked away. If Colton thought I was that dangerous, maybe I was.

Once we were alone, Colton stomped forward. "What did you do?"

"Uh, I'm not sure."

He looked me up and down. "You shook hands with the devil."

I felt fragile, not because I felt sick or out of control, but like a cracked bomb casing—what if whatever I'd let inside went off? "I think I might have done more than that."

He glanced around the room. "Where's Mike?"

I lifted my shirt and showed the two scars. "It was either him or me. I think I won."

"For now."

Hot, sludgy anger burned up my throat. "I saved your fucking house—can't you at least say thank you? After you betrayed me, like, four times, I still took the bullet for you!" Whitehot anger fuzzed the edges of my sight.

"Not for me. For this place, for them." He motioned after the employees. I'd known each face, had sweat beside them, and gotten drunk afterward. We had complained about scheduling or customers together—gossiped about who Colton had taken out on his arm or the latest guy working the tables whom Franklin had flirted with. Most of the employees hadn't looked at me as they'd hurried past. If Colton kept me at arm's length, that meant a danger they couldn't even dream of facing.

Colton gripped my shoulder. "I just need to be sure, Gin."

I shrugged away his hand. "Maybe I need to be sure of you, Colton."

He sighed. "I have some explaining to do, you're right. First, I want to know my people are safe."

I raised my hands. "Fine, what do you want out of me? First

time I puked in the Saints bathroom? The first fey I had to kick out because he was magicking drinks? First time—"

He grasped my hands. "I can't drink your blood, but I know what it tastes like."

"What?" My voice broke. "You don't think a god couldn't—couldn't copy my genetic code or just make me taste the same?"

"No, I do not."

I squeezed his hands. "It's me, Colton. Can't you trust me with this?"

"Too many are relying on us. I need to be sure before I let you go."

Anger flashed hot again. "As if something dead like you could stop me." Except I would never say that to Colton. I took a sharp breath, a hand coming to my mouth.

He bared his fangs as if to say *see?*

I turned my face, exposing my neck. He stepped closer, one arm sliding around my back.

His cold exhale prickled my skin. "This isn't over—I need to know I can trust you during whatever comes next."

Except I couldn't find an answer as easily—how could I trust him after his mistakes had led to me taking on a god?

His fangs slit my neck, and I grimaced, even though the pain hurt less than the idea of him drinking from me, the one thing I believed I'd never have to allow again.

He raised his head, hiding his mouth with his hand. He spat behind him and wiped his lips with a handkerchief. "You imprisoned him inside you."

I rubbed my neck, the bite marks already fading as my god power healed me. "They're always dumping nuclear waste here. Might as well take in a little more."

He stared at me for too long. One of the good things about having Colton for a boss was he always bowed to a sob story. Need a raise because of a sick kid? Done. Need extended leave to take care of your opioid-addicted brother in West Virginia? Sure. He had that look on his face now—empathetic. He'd made tough choices, and maybe the worst of those were flitting through his thoughts. The big difference between this and a mom asking for a raise? He'd *caused* some of this shit. He wanted a demigod or whatever the hell I was linked to the Saints.

I stepped back. "Don't look at me like that. I'm more powerful now—that's what you wanted."

"I wanted you safe and—"

"And benefiting your casino."

"I've given you a home," he hissed. "What do you think Mike would have given you?"

I shook my head. "Nothing, but I still needed you to give me the truth, a choice."

I left Colton in the ruins of his haunted house.

31

The first big snow rebounded the Saints with the Tahoe spillover. Evelyn's people still ran the place, keeping Colton on house arrest. She didn't need to assign watchers to me—between the fey, the local covens, and Clarisse, I doubt I walked anywhere without a few pairs of eyes on me.

I didn't blame them. Mike still lived inside me. Geiger counters beeped in my presence. A few zombies lingered around the dumpsters, becoming part of Reno's Darkside fauna.

I pretended I still worked at the Saints. I had nowhere else to go. The vampire council planned an emergency session a few weeks after everything quieted, and, once again, I was the major topic of discussion. One mystery solved, but now a more dangerous game had begun.

By relaying messages through Franklin, Colton asked me to come talk to him. I was a few drinks in the fourth time Franklin asked. We sat at the bar on the casino floor. The jangle of false wins played over the hidden speakers while tourists slurred through their drinks.

"Why?" I asked. "I can't trust him."

Franklin sipped a michelada. "He wants to rebuild that trust, I believe."

"No, he wants the power of a nuclear bomb at his disposal."

"Is that how you see yourself, Juniper?"

I slurped the dregs of my G&T and motioned for another. "Yep."

"Then you do yourself a disservice."

"I appreciate the grandfatherly touch, but I literally have a god inside me fucking with my brain. Best case scenario, I help some folks before I go nuclear."

Franklin smoothed his mustache. "That's a low bar for a god."

I flicked aside the straw and gulped my fifth drink—I only had the energy for my most familiar coping strategy. "I'm not a god, just the child of one."

Franklin finished his drink. "Fine, if you only intend to mope, then I'll tell Colton better luck next time."

"I'm not moping."

"You're drinking in a casino bar."

"I work here."

He quirked an eyebrow.

I rolled my eyes. "Okay, it could look like moping, but I did just survive a pretty awful few weeks."

He inclined his head. "Then go have some fun. Or start moving forward. You will have to talk to Colton eventually."

"Is—is he being genuine? This isn't just another lie?"

Franklin shrugged a shoulder. "You will have to see for yourself. I will say that Colton was—is—fond of you. An 1800s-era vampire and a half-god twenty-two-year-old are an imperfect match, though. There's bound to be some friction." He patted my shoulder, then wandered into the land of slots, greeting the old timers and joking with the waitstaff.

I ordered a straight shot of gin and then headed for the elevators. Franklin was right—I'd have to confront him eventually. Might as well do it with some privacy rather than in front of the vampire council.

~

"Come in, Gin."

I hadn't even knocked yet. This guy and his freakin' vampire senses. I took a deep breath and pushed open the door.

Colton sat near the entrance, an overstuffed chair pulled up to the window. A bottle of blood-twisted wine set on a side table.

For once, he'd stripped off his typical cowboy gear. He only wore a black t-shirt over loose pajama pants, his hat left hanging by the door.

I crossed my arms and leaned against the doorframe. "Say whatever you need to so I can go back to the bar."

He motioned to his personal bar by a wall of windows. "Help yourself."

"Not a fan of the company."

He smiled, baring his fangs. The blood in the wine had stained them. "Won't give me a chance?"

"You had two years of chances to tell me everything instead of lying."

He sighed and topped off his glass. "That I did."

As the silence unspooled, I kept glancing at the minibar. Finally, I stalked over, snatched the bottle of Bulleit whiskey, poured myself a few fingers, and drew a chair up.

"You better make this good."

He knocked the stem of his wine glass against my tumbler. "It's rather boring, like most power grabs. For keeping an eye on you, Mike would use his power to help me take over

Evelyn's casinos in Vegas. You were never supposed to work for me. You were meant to graduate college, get a good job with me pulling the strings, rise in the ranks, and when you'd achieved enough corporate power, Mike would reveal himself and what you are."

Colton gulped the wine, then looked out the window.

"But?"

"But you came to my silly Halloween party."

"Doesn't seem like much of a wrench in the plan."

"From where you're sitting, maybe. But the council wanted to classify you as a weapon and destroy you or jail you. Only by chaining you to the Saints did I satisfy them—for a time. Mike's plans of leveraging you in a powerful position were gone. So, I arranged for the barrel of waste holding his remains to be on the first truck to Yucca Mountain."

I snorted. "That was a dick move toward the Western Shoshone Nation."

"I hoped the sacred of another culture might keep him sedated, or better yet, destroy him. Bad idea, turns out."

I took a slug of whiskey, and it burned all the way down. "So, Mike gets out, isn't happy."

"And comes for you. It should have been an easy exchange, but well, I'd grown rather fond of you."

I rolled my eyes. "Here we go."

"In all seriousness. I couldn't think of you as food—"

"Wow, thanks."

He raised a hand. "You were not a temptation like other humans. I knew you weren't loyal only as a desire to be turned. I sensed the power inside you much more clearly than you did, and I wanted to mold it. Plus, a demigod would solidify my power in the region. Something I could shape however I desired. I could still have Evelyn's casinos with you at my side."

I sloshed out more whiskey into my glass as my hands

heated, which now happened whenever I got angry. "Then you left me in the desert to die."

"Mike had no intention of killing you."

My jaw set. I wondered how hard I could throw the tumbler with my new god strength. "That makes it okay, then, that he hurt me?"

"I realized my mistake once I escaped the desert."

"Because you wanted to keep me around or because that's a shitty way to treat someone?"

He ran his tongue along his teeth. "When you signed on, do you remember one of the first things I said to you?"

I sipped the whiskey. At least whatever lived inside me could still get drunk. "I don't remember much other than your teeth in my wrist." Shit, I hadn't meant to slur it like some sort of come-on. By the way Colton smirked, his tongue worrying a fang, he'd keep that one for later.

"Do not apply your human morality to me. You do not judge me."

"It was my life, Colton."

"And Mike wasn't going to take it. You are immortal—for the most part. You have time to heal."

As if taking time to heal made the violation okay in the first place. Maybe Colton was willing to risk his body and soul, but I wasn't. I didn't want an immortality of scars and nightmares.

We sipped in blurry silence, both looking out the window. The Saints' orange lights flickered over the carpet.

"What happens to you?" I asked.

He prowled to the bar and chose another bottle of wine. "That depends. Your godhood gives you autonomy, at least where the vampires are concerned. That being said, you are a part of the city. If you say you want me to remain in charge of the Saints' holdings, supervised by your girlfriend, the council would be inclined to listen."

I smirked at the thought of the wardship being flipped. "Or I could ask that you be thrown in jail and kept alive on pig blood." Except revenge was my father's thing, carrying the bigger stick. If I ever started acting that way, I'd need to have safeguards. I didn't need Colton in charge of me anymore, but I didn't want him chained up, either.

He refilled his wine glass. "Now, now. You wouldn't want to make an enemy of me."

I set aside my whiskey and leaned forward with my arms propped on my knees. "All right, what do I get?"

"You would retain your position at the Saints—"

"Not good enough."

He glared. "And my full resources at your disposal to exorcise Mike—plus a safety net for when he attempts to possess you. We both know he will."

I winced and stared at the carpet. The booze had been helping me avoid thinking about what that day might be like. Would I rather have Colton at my side or the Vegas vampires? Maybe that wasn't my only choice, but at least Colton knew me and my father. That had to count for something. "This all sounds like the bare minimum just to fix your terrible decision-making."

His lip twitched. "Who else will take you in if not me?"

I settled back in the chair. "The coven, the fey, Evelyn's people. I have options. I'm not a scared kid anymore."

He steepled his fingers. "Then make your choice."

The thing was, I wasn't sure what I wanted other than the lingering desire for Colton to prove that I could trust him again, but no promise could guarantee he wouldn't cross me. I wanted to stay at the Saints, not necessarily for Colton, jerk that he was, but because it had become home in the past two years. With the whiskey making me honest, I wanted to—was ready to —be something more than human. I owed favors to Leia and

Winston, and I wanted to be there when they needed me. I wanted to help Bobbi and Kia come into their own at the Saints. I wanted Franklin to be able to retire someday and take his place. I wanted them to trust me like they trusted Colton.

I rubbed my hands on my thighs and stood. "All right. But this"—I motioned between the two of us—"has to change. I am not the girl you get to yell at and order around. I get it. I'm not your equal in your world, but you're not mine where I stand either. I am not your underling, even if you become king of all vampires."

He rubbed his chin. "I rather liked it when you got all red-faced."

Heat crawled up my neck. "Yes or no?"

"I'm out of choices for now."

I held out my hand, but Colton chuckled.

"Vampires seal the deal by trading blood, but since I can't drink yours, I can think of some other fluids we could swap."

I stared into his dark eyes. Slowly, I took his wine glass, sipped it, and forced down the coppery blood-twisted liquid.

He sighed, nodded, and knocked back my whiskey.

I turned and tried to stalk out of the room, but I'd drank too much to walk straight. I slammed the door and leaned against it. My skin tingled, and if I closed my eyes, the world tilted beneath me. It felt like we got somewhere for once. He seemed honest, at least for a vampire talking to a new demigod, and I knew I wouldn't let him control me like that again.

I gritted my teeth and stumbled to my room.

<h1 style="text-align:center">32</h1>

I probably shouldn't have drunk so much the night before the council meeting, but either because of my godhood or my age, I still didn't get hangovers. I even worked out and had a healthy breakfast. Instead of my signature black jeans and band shirt, I put on slacks, a button-down shirt—the only one I owned that wasn't a ripped flannel—and a cardigan. I would have felt more godlike in my leather jacket, but these vampires would only remember me as the scared kid Colton tossed out the window. If I was going to navigate this mess on my terms, they had to see me as something more.

Just shy of midnight, I walked into the Nightmare. I looked out of place in my slapdash equivalent of business attire, but even if things went right, I had no intention of partying. And by going right, I meant not getting thrown out a window or chased across the dance floor again.

I thought I glimpsed Clarisse beneath the strobes, but the crowd swallowed her. I sighed and made the jump onto the catwalk. I could have taken the back stairs, but exercising my power reminded me that I was, in fact, more than human.

I stepped into the chamber. The masked vampires turned toward me. All the chairs were filled except Evelyn's and Colton's.

I took Colton's chair. I felt all too young and too ordinary in my clothes. The others wore fancy suits or party dresses suitable for the club afterward. My leather would have helped me fit in better than this getup. Fucked up again, Gin.

The door opened. Evelyn entered, followed by Clarisse and two aids flanking Colton.

He flashed his fangs at me, either as a greeting or a threat. I wasn't sure. I kept his seat.

They left him beside me, the two vampire attendants standing on either side of the door while Evelyn took her seat. Clarisse took up her position behind her mother. Like last time, she wore a black dress that looked more like a few scraps of cloth magically held together. Her bra laced over the top. It looked like the same one from a few weeks ago when she'd surprised me in my room.

Colton cocked his hip against the table, half-sitting on the corner.

Evelyn opened the meeting—in Vampiric. It sounded as unintelligible as ever. Heat flashed up my neck. My palms sweat. I glanced at Colton. He tipped his head toward me and half-closed his eyes.

Damn, I remembered that dreamy look. But with all of them speaking Vampiric, I might not be able to get through a council session without him helping by dreamwalking into my head. Surprisingly, he hadn't used that for leverage last night. Maybe he wanted a trick up his sleeve. I still needed him, whether I wanted to or not.

Wait, I was part god, wasn't I?

I stared at Evelyn's mouth, then at the vampire who

responded. I stretched out whatever power burned beneath my skin.

Snatches of English swirled beneath the Vampiric echoes. *Too dangerous . . . the girl . . . untried.*

Under the table, Colton's foot hooked around my leg.

With his help, the voices became crisp. I glared at him, and his left shoulder twitched as if to say *it is what it is.*

Colton's translation created a lag of about a second and overlaid the other voices. Currently, they argued his fate.

A few voices wanted him dead—drained of blood and left in the sunlight. The majority thought he should be punished, but not so severely. To work with a god to advance one's situation was not that uncommon. The punishments ranged from apprenticing to another vampire to community service—whatever that meant for vampires. It also extended to suggestions of selling the Saints.

After twenty minutes, Evelyn turned her chair toward me, switching to English. "What does the local deity wish?"

I straightened my posture. I'd scratched out a few answers to these types of questions just in case I was actually taken seriously. "Colton knows the Saints better than any newcomer. The Saints is part of Reno, and so is Colton. I request he maintain partial ownership while strictly observed."

A vampire in a mask featuring the curling horns of a ram dipped his head as if the horns were real. He'd called for Colton's blood. "Let me guess, you would oversee? That is merely the end of his plan. He holds all the cards."

"It should be another vampire," I said. "For their troubles, I'll pay them out of my shares."

Colton stiffened, but I didn't glance up at him.

"Then it should be Evelyn," said the horned vampire.

My gaze snapped past Evelyn to Clarisse, who just stared

at the wall. I'd hoped it would be Evelyn, but this sudden pivot by the leader of vampires wanting Colton dead didn't sit right.

I glanced between Evelyn and the horned vampire. I was missing something, but Colton didn't seem able to help. He only stared down the vampires that had called for his death.

Two vampires seemed to shrink under his gaze and focused on the table. Only the horned vampire met his eyes from behind the mask.

"I call the vote," Evelyn said. "My coven will observe the workings of the Saints for a trial period in partnership with the local deity Gin. After a hundred years, his actions will be reassessed."

"Hold up," I said. "A hundred years? I was thinking more like a year."

The horned vampire rapped his knuckles on the table. "Aye." He swiveled his chair toward me. "A hundred years is the minimum sentencing for an immortal."

The other vampires knocked on the table, except for one who flattened his palm. He'd wanted Colton dead, so I assumed any comments now would be more of the same.

The vampire took off his mask. I expected an older, grizzled face. In action, Colton seemed the youngest of the group. Either this guy had aged better, or he'd been turned straight out of high school. He looked like the nature type with a wiry beard and pale skin tanned to toughness.

"You have my vote if the High Sierra coven may also observe." He dipped his head to me. "That is, at the approval of Gin."

A ticker tape of expletives passed through my head. I opened my mouth, but Colton slapped his hand flat on the table.

"You are here out of pity. Don't try—"

"Silence!" Evelyn half-rose from her seat. "You've lost your spot at the table, Colton, while Lark has earned his place."

I knocked on the table. "I agree to—Lark's—proposal."

The anger roiling off Colton burned through my head like a migraine. I winced. Evelyn also glared but agreed with my vote. I'd disrupted something happening over my head. Good. Even if I didn't have much of a clue, I could assert my presence with a little chaos. Hopefully, it wouldn't bite me in the ass as badly as this hundred-year bullshit.

Lark fitted his mask over to the side, a simple beaked design matching his name. He kept his eyes on me during the remainder of the meeting. Colton also bored holes into the side of my head. I glanced at neither, keeping my focus on whoever spoke even though Colton had cut off his dreamwalking and translation ability. We'd have to have a talk about that.

I waited by the door as the vampires filtered out, passing Evelyn as she played host. Lark ignored Evelyn and half-bowed to me.

"I will see you soon."

He sauntered out, then swung off the catwalk, dropping onto the dancefloor below.

Colton gripped my bicep hard enough to bruise. "What was that?"

I ripped away my arm. "To ensure I wasn't kept out of the loop."

Only Evelyn and Clarisse remained in the room. Evelyn seemed to shrink and leaned against Clarisse. "I require fresh blood."

Colton held the door for them. "Of course, Eve. Plenty have signed tonight's waiver."

Before I could pass the threshold, his arm shot out and blocked the doorway. He hissed. "Next time, you follow my lead."

I ducked away and stomped after Clarisse, my boots making the catwalk clang. "You forget, Colton. I am not your underling."

"Old habits die hard."

I glared at him, then jumped the catwalk. The landing ached in my bones, but as I straightened to appraising looks from the clubbers, it reminded me that I wasn't human, even if I looked like an undergraduate English major tonight.

I crossed to the bar and hunched on a barstool. I hoped to finish off the anger with a drink, but I still wanted to punch a hole in the wall. Well, it might have been embarrassment more than anger. If the council saw me as anything other than a road-side attraction to snicker at, it would take longer than Colton's hundred-year release. I'd have to earn it, and apparently, swallowing a god wasn't enough.

I swung around and faced the dancefloor. For the first time, I wouldn't have minded Clarisse sneaking an arm around my shoulders, leading me into the crowd. I'd help put her and Evelyn in charge a little longer—time to see if a matriarchy was any better.

But Clarisse had duties and appearances to keep up. And I should look respectable as the local deity, though the optics on that were total shit. Some white girl who used to live outside Vegas did not need to be Reno's newest attraction. Didn't matter how much I screamed to the stars that I did not want to be a magical person of the night—here I was.

Yet, somehow, I still didn't fit in with the vampires. I counted half the council ready to sink their fangs into "consenting" people who'd signed a form while sober and now were nowhere near it.

Scanning the crowd gave me recon on which council members liked what—the horned vampire dug women who looked like they were twelve, while Lark preferred the hipsters who came here to make fun of everyone else and grind on the college girls. When I caught sight of Colton necking with a hot snowboarder bro, I sighed. It didn't matter—but it still sucked.

The behavior seemed totally childish to me, but the council members practiced it with such abandon that maybe it was a type of rite. Like the fetishes the uber-rich developed.

Or maybe extreme old age regressed them to horny teenagers.

Across the bar, something glittered in the dim light. I squinted at the shadow until my dark vision kicked in. Kia's glittery crutches gifted to her on Halloween Eve leaned against the bar. Hell no, I'd made sure she, Bobbi, and Nash were scheduled to work tonight—far away from the club—in order to make sure they didn't end up here after the council meeting.

I hurried over and spun around, searching the edges of the crowd. She'd re-injured her leg during the fight, so she couldn't have gotten far.

Oh god, Kia and Bobbi were talking with Lark. The three of them leaned close as the music made talking almost impossible. Lark had a hand on Bobbi's shoulder, and Kia steadied herself against Lark's arm.

I hurried over and stepped between Kia and Bobbi, toe-to-toe with Lark. "What are you doing?"

He kept his hands on both of them. Was he manipulating them? It couldn't be coincidence. "Gin!" He dipped his head. "I hoped to become acquainted with your followers." Somehow, his voice carried over the bass.

Anger within me whispered to shove him back, trip him into the crowd. Stomp on his hands that dared to touch my—my friends.

I squeezed my eyes shut for a second. "They're not my followers! They're my friends!"

Bobbi crossed their arms. "Gin, chill. We can be both." A

wide, unbuttoned collar emphasized their scar. Even in the club light, the scar tissue glinted waxy over their neck. Somehow, it had already healed and turned pinkish. They should be hiding it, not showing it off. Why would they want to remember that day, let alone make it stand out? I just wanted to forget that I'd hurt them, even if I had to.

Kia leaned against me. She took my hand to brace herself. "Lark says he's going to be helping out here. He wanted to get to know the employees."

"Not you." I glared at Lark, and he took a step back. "You shouldn't be here."

Kia squeezed my hand. "Listen to me. You're one of my best friends because of the Saints. Our friendship is part of the Saints, and now we have something deeper." She touched her scar. She'd emphasized hers with some sort of glittery foundation that made the scar tissue shimmer—a twitching jackalope's head in profile, the horns rising perfectly between the dip of her collarbones, almost like the scar belonged there.

Bobbi shoulder bumped me. "You aren't listening. We *want* to help you. You give us all this shit about protecting us—but you need help, too. And we can do that."

Lark still stood there as if he were part of the group. His head tilted slightly, like a bird waiting for the worms to rise.

I nodded at him. "I'll see you around, Lark."

He smiled and raised his hands slightly. "Of course. Goodbye, Gin." He slipped into the crowd quick as a bird in the woods.

Kia pulled me toward the bar. With each step, she leaned on me. "I liked him. Is it true he's part of the Saints, now?"

"You like any vampire with a beard."

She sunk onto a bar stool, massaging her upper thigh. "Okay, true, but he's got good vibes."

I winced. "I think that was his vampire magic working on you."

Bobbi groaned. "Ugh, we got to get better at avoiding that." They nudged me. "Can't be giving away your secrets."

I gripped the bar hard enough that my fingernails dug into the wood. "You both should be avoiding me like the fucking plague. You should forget you ever knew me."

The bartender, Cody, brought us three shots of gin and winked at me. Great. I would have preferred tequila, but now I was a god named Gin.

Bobbi huffed. "We've talked about this. You're being dramatic." They downed their shot and grimaced. "I wish I liked gin more."

I pushed aside my shot, then knocked it back so Cody didn't feel bad. He'd only worked at the Saints three weeks, totally clueless, but had his introduction to the dark when he had to run away from zombies and hide in an emergency bunker like so many others. His trauma was on me, too, even if I didn't have to scar him. "Please, I mean it." My voice grew husky. "I don't want to hurt you again."

Kia slipped an arm around my waist. "We want to be here, Gin."

"Look," Bobbi said, "you're going to need advisors or aids or something. Just consider us volunteers."

"This isn't a game, Bobbi."

They frowned. "Yeah, I fucking know." Their fingers brushed the brand. "We watched you take care of those zombies by the vault. You didn't see yourself. You looked like— like a real warrior."

I twisted in my seat to face the crowd. The crowd parted, moved by chance or some shift in the music, and a figure in all white flashed across the floor. From the back, he slouched like James Dean. Had the same messy hair. Fear pulsed fast, and my adrenaline spiked. I squeezed my eyes shut as terror burned through me. When I looked again, the crowd had swamped together, and he was gone.

I shoved off of my stool. "I have to go." What if he was threatening them again, somehow making me see shit? Kia snatched at my jacket, but I swung away. I shouldered outside.

The smokers glanced as I bent over, heaving. Bile coated my throat. I swallowed over and over, still with my hands pressed hard against knees. A sludge-y taste coated my tongue, like that day in the desert. Plenty of hipsters mimicked that retro look. I couldn't freak out over every lookalike.

"Gin?" Clarisse's voice pitched high—concern or surprise, I wasn't sure.

I straightened. God, couldn't everyone just leave me alone? "I'm fine." So much for running off unseen and processing in a healthier way than flirting with my frienemy.

She touched my shoulder and slid her hand down. "I thought you would come onto the floor. That's what the council does." Her hand dipped deeper, fitting into the hollow of my lower back.

Just another horny teenager.

I turned on her. "How old are you?"

So close, in the golden glow of the streetlights, a smokiness clung to her like the skimp of a black dress. She reminded me so much of the freshmen girls parading from the dorms my stomach churned again. I spit.

She frowned. "Why?"

"It's just—what is this? You do business, then go fuck some kids? Just like what happened to me."

"They sign—"

I stepped into her. "They don't know what they're signing! Vampires aren't real!"

She glanced at the smokers and folks standing around for fresh air.

I laughed. "This is Reno. Nobody's gonna notice."

She raised her hand as if to cup my face, but I gripped her wrist. She huffed but didn't pull away. "What's got you pissed off?"

Because I was afraid she or someone else would do it to me again. Clarisse had started it, then Colton just took advantage of me, then my real dad had wanted to possess me, and now he kinda had. I just needed a moment to figure it all out.

"What do you want from me? Must be something. You could screw the hottest person in the club tonight, so I know I'm not just an easy fuck."

She tried to cup my face again, but I stepped back. "Every time Evelyn mentioned killing you or trying to chain you up, I whispered in her ear you should be free. Think I would risk myself like that if I didn't like you?"

I groaned. Something about the word *whisper*, the image of Clarisse bent over Evelyn's shoulder, clicked the pieces into place. "Of course. Evelyn. She's starting to get old, really old, isn't she? If I fell for you—if I stood by your side—then you'd be her successor. Nobody could stop you."

Clarisse worried a fang with her tongue.

I brushed past her. Score, even though I wished I hadn't. Is that all the vampires saw me as, some battery waiting to be used up?

"Gin!"

Even my godhood hearing wasn't good enough to hear a vampire coming. She caught me by the back of my jacket and jerked me around, slamming me into the wall. She dug a heel into the top of my foot, bruising me through my boot. Shit, what were her stilettos made of, steel?

"Listen, Gin." She spit my name like a bad shot. "This isn't just about you. Stop thinking like a selfish human—"

"At least I don't fuck like one."

She leaned in, bearing her fangs.

I grinned. "Bite me."

She whispered, her lips brushing my ear. "I'll take that as consent." She sunk a fang through the shell of my ear.

I yelped and shoved her back. She stumbled off the curb, laughing. Blood darkened her lipstick. She spit between my boots.

"If you're going to act like a bitch, I'll treat you like one." She wiped her lips with her thumb, then sauntered toward the club.

I pressed the meat of my palm against my throbbing ear. "Shit." I wondered if this embarrassment hot in my face was how dogs felt after a human bit them. Which made Clarisse the master and me the pet.

When I found Leia deep in the library stacks later that night, she took one look at me and pulled out a flask.

"I thought the alcoholic accessories were my thing." I took a swig. Good whiskey burned my throat.

"Well, fighting off a god has made it hard to sleep."

I wet my fingers and rubbed the ragged fang hole in my ear. Leia raised an eyebrow.

"You going to tell me or nah?"

"Clarisse."

Leia smirked. "Didn't know you screwed like that."

"This was the punishment for refusing to screw." I left out the part about guessing her master plan. Leia didn't need anything else on her plate when it came to me.

"Ah."

I sunk to the floor and leaned my head against a shelf. A quiet mustiness surrounded me. I sighed. "I still don't know what I'm doing. At least they don't look at me like a cookie they've been forbidden to eat."

Leia trailed her fingers along book spines, then pulled out a ragged hardcover. "Council meeting not go well?"

"I don't know. That's the problem."

"Ah."

"Stop saying that."

She paged through the book, then returned it. "That's your world, not mine. My coven is cool with the vampires. We leave each other alone, so I don't have anything else to say other than 'ah.'"

I hugged my knees. "Why did you help me, then?"

"Because Reno might have blown up."

That was Leia for you. Pure practicality. Not because we were friends again but because it would impact her and her family. The same kind of shit she always did back in school, letting me wander off to a vampire party because there were consequences for telling me what she was. Maybe the breakup had been two ways, and I just misremembered it as my fault.

I rocked to my feet. "Yeah, I didn't want that to happen, either." I split from the shelves.

"Gin. C'mon, don't be that way."

Her hand brushed my shoulder. I whipped around and stomped my foot.

The floor cratered.

We both yelled *shit* and stumbled backward as the floor crumbled through insulation and steel, opening into the next ceiling.

Bookshelves teetered forward and tilted until they formed a triangle. Books spilled onto Leia.

I lunged forward as she yelled a word in another language. The books kept spilling, but they formed a dome over her. Once the shelves emptied, she straightened, and the books sloughed off.

She leaned forward and looked down the hole. "Gin, you

can't go this way. You can't drink your way through this. You need help."

The emergency lights blinked, and a siren wailed. It stirred a memory older than me of fake towns waiting for an explosion.

I shook my head. "Is that all I am to you? A bomb?"

"If you keep acting this way." Her eyes met mine. "Maybe Reno isn't as safe as I thought."

The words slapped me hard enough that I teared up. "I-I'm sorry."

I ran for the back stairs.

Stupid, stupid! Even now, after everything, I still acted like the drunk girl who had smashed up our dorm room sophomore year. I had a god in my head, was surrounded by vampires, and had Clarisse whispering in my ear. I couldn't count on Leia. Winston would be there, but his life was largely rooted with the humans of Reno through his work with the unhoused, Food not Bombs, and DIY venues. He'd make time for me, like when he'd helped me get the drinking under control, but he couldn't be an advisor. There was always Franklin, but he was Colton's right-hand man first and foremost.

I hurried through campus, the sidewalks empty except for the occasional grounds person. Walking down sloping Virginia Street, the city opened. The casinos played their false sunrise and drew me to their lights like the summer moths.

My phone buzzed, and I sighed. My shoulders slumped as instinct already said it was Colton. I tapped open his message.

A photo showed the brightening sky with the city spread below. His hand held two beers in the frame.

A second text appeared. *Join me? If you like.*

Not a direct order—that was new.

I took my time, but the Saints drew me like a magnet, as always. Maybe that was what it meant to find home—you always come back around like the moon.

He sat on two Adirondack chairs pulled to the roof's edge. A six-pack of Icky IPA set between the chairs.

He reached a bottle back as I came around. I took it but didn't sip. I hunched on the seat's edge while he lounged, his long legs stretched and crossed at the ankles. His cowboy hat was pushed forward against the dawn's first streaks. The Saints flickered orange and purple, a lurid mixture with the Eldorado's singular green next door, all smeared together with the coming sunrise.

Colton wore his traditional black and silver, once again the cowboy in charge of his casino. "You might have saved my afterlife, Gin."

I shrugged a shoulder. "I'd be out of a job if I didn't."

He chuckled. "One way to see it."

I side-eyed him. "It wasn't out of fuzzy feelings; I can tell you that."

He drained his beer and sighed. "Let's be honest. We never had the fuzzy feelings."

I set the cold beer bottle on the ground and wiped my sweaty hands on my jeans. He hadn't, of course, but I'd crushed hard up until he abandoned me in Rachel. I wasn't about to contradict him, though.

"So what now? Or was this an actual thank you with no strings attached?"

He swept off his hat and pressed it to his chest. "I'm hurt, Gin."

I dug my fingernails into my thigh. "If we're going to be actual allies, then I'd appreciate it if you played straight with me."

He tipped his head back and laughed. "You got a lot to

learn before we call ourselves partners on more than just paper."

I wanted to make another hole in the floor and fall through it. Taking my open beer in hand, I snatched two more from the pack. "Okay, then, thank you, and goodnight. I hope the sunrise burns out your eyeballs."

I hurried toward the stairs, but for the second time that night, a vampire stole up behind me and swung me around. I needed to figure out a good defense. Something that was nonchalant but still cool and got the point across.

He sniffed, then frowned. "Who bit you?"

"That's my business."

He grinned. "I thought we were partners."

"I'd really like to go to bed, all right?"

He cupped my face in both his hands. I stiffened as his eyes searched mine.

He sighed the words, "It's still you in there."

"Um, yeah?"

He lowered his hands, and I stepped back. "Keep it that way."

I nodded. He sauntered to the chairs, his hands stuffed into his back pockets.

When it all started, when he'd bit into my wrist on Halloween night, trying to taste why my blood wasn't human, I wouldn't have imagined he'd become part of my home. Or that the vampire who terrified me would send a shiver down my spine for other reasons. I couldn't have guessed that the fanged cowboy would care for me in his own way, and I'd need time to decide if I wanted that type of care in my life.

But for now, it was Colton and me, just like that night years ago, trying to figure each other out.

Acknowledgments

Thank you to Parliament House Press and my editor Malorie Nilson for believing in Gin and making this novel better in every way! Thanks to Alexandra Buchanan for all the help throughout the publishing process.

Thank you to David Anthony Durham for his feedback on the early chapters of this novel and to his fiction workshop at University of Nevada, Reno in the fall of 2019—you all gave me the courage to keep working on this project. A special thanks to Naseem Jamnia, December Cuccaro, Leanne Howard, and Andy Butter for all the support over the years in Reno and for your feedback on this novel.

Thank you to Cameron Gibson, a true friend. Your words of encouragement and celebration have meant so much over the years.

Thank you to my husband, Andrew Dincher, for always encouraging me, championing me, and giving me the time to write.

And finally, thank you to my family, who read my first stories almost two decades ago.

About the Author

Phoebe Wagner is a writer, editor, and academic working at the intersection of climate change and speculative fiction. She is the editor for three solarpunk anthologies, including *Sunvault: Stories of Solarpunk and Eco-Speculation*. Her short fiction has been published in *PANK*, *Diabolical Plots*, and *AURELIA LEO*—among other places. She blogs about speculative literature at the Hugo-winning *Nerds of a Feather, Flock Together*.

PHOEBE-WAGNER.COM

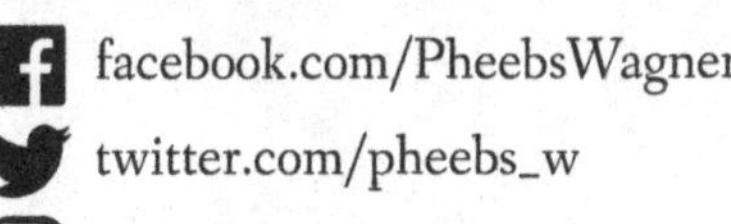

facebook.com/PheebsWagner

twitter.com/pheebs_w

instagram.com/pheebzw